I0612427

QUICK BRIGHT THINGS

LILY McCARTHY

QUICK BRIGHT THINGS

LILY McCARTHY

Published in Canada by Engen Books, St. John's, NL.

Library and Archives Canada Cataloguing in Publication

Title: Quick bright things / Lily McCarthy.
Names: McCarthy, Lily, author.
Identifiers: Canadiana 20210365625 | ISBN 9781774780695 (hardcover)
Subjects: LCGFT: Novels.
Classification: LCC PS8625.C379 Q53 2021 | DDC C813/.6—dc23

Copyright © 2021 Lily McCarthy

NO PART OF THIS BOOK MAY BE REPRODUCED OR TRANSMITTED IN ANY FORM OR BY ANY MEANS, ELECTRONIC OR MECHANICAL, INCLUDING PHOTOCOPYING AND RECORDING, OR BY ANY INFORMATION STORAGE OR RETRIEVAL SYSTEM WITHOUT WRITTEN PERMISSION FROM THE AUTHOR, EXCEPT FOR BRIEF PASSAGES QUOTED IN A REVIEW.

This book is a work of fiction. Names, characters, places and incidents are products of the author's imagination or are used fictitiously. Any resemblance to actual events or locales or persons living or dead is entirely coincidental.

Distributed by:
Engen Books
www.engenbooks.com
submissions@engenbooks.com

First mass market paperback printing: November 2021

Cover Design: Graham Blair Designs

To Jeff Crant,
my biggest fan.

CHAPTER ONE

Piper quite liked the rain. There was a certain euphoria that came along with the smell of mud and the feeling of ice cold water droplets hitting your skin. She especially liked the sound of it. Whether it was hitting the roof, the sidewalk, the car, her umbrella; she loved it all. It was like real life magic, which was an idea she obsessed over for countless years. *If only I was a wizard*, she'd think, *Then, I could make it pour rain every day.*

Sundays, in her opinion, were the best rainy-days. Sundays were meant to be comfortable, slightly inconvenient, and devoid of obligations. Unless you attended church, which Piper never did. Even when she was little and her grandparents fought with her parents over it, they still managed to avoid it completely. She spent Sundays the way they were meant to be spent: alone in her room, surrounded by scented candles, with a good book. And what better book was there than *The Outsiders* by S.E. Hinton. It was Piper's favourite, and her go-to when the conditions were just right.

Sundays went best when you turned your phone off. She liked to read without distractions. She could get distracted very easily and when she did, it was hard to refocus. She powered her phone off early in the day and left it alone after that. It didn't matter much whether it was on or not, anyway. Only one person texted her semi-regularly.

Her bedroom was a cozy place to temporarily isolate. She had a double bed with an oak frame pushed up against the back wall and a big window looking out on her backyard. She had a small wooden desk, littered with books, homework and long-outdated makeup. She had a short—yet wide—bookshelf beside her bed with two shelves. Each shelf held two neat rows of novels, one row placed in front of the other. On top, she had leftover mugs or teacups and her spare glasses (that she never wore, since they had translucent turquoise frames—That was the last time she let her dad pick out frames for her). Her room wasn't anything fancy, but it was hers, and that was all that mattered. It was just her and her father living there, and while they weren't rich by any means, she never wanted for anything she couldn't have. They could afford to indulge in things they didn't need, like fancy hardcovers instead of paperbacks, and hefty weighted blankets. Sure, they weren't extraordinary. But they were satisfied and happy.

They lived in the final house on their street, meaning their closest neighbours were still blocked by a row of trees. Privacy was important to her father when they picked the place. He hated having nosy neighbours. Thankfully, they were very much alone where they were.

For some odd, unexplainable reason, Piper had the urge to check her phone. She realized it was a dumb urge before she even had it. She'd read enough articles on the addictiveness of social media to know she should just delete every page she had and release herself from the torment. But she wasn't that dedicated to the cause quite yet.

She bookmarked *The Outsiders*, though it hurt her to do it. She was coming up on one of her favourite parts: Johnny was about to bleach Ponyboy's hair. She picked up her phone and held the power button until the screen came to life. Immediately, she was bombarded with notifications. No messages, of course. But updates on who posted or added to their story or shared a status. Each of them were the same; snapshots of a weekend they'd never remember, or a so-called "night we'll never forget." She pitied their hangovers.

She only wanted to check for a moment, but she ended up scrolling endlessly, seeing the same posts essentially copy and pasted, just with different faces; "Weekend with my girls!" "Saturdays are for the boys!" "Date night!" "I was so wasted!" It was like they all synced up the minute Friday hit. Every teenager she knew was either partying with friends or out on a date, while she was home, sleeping in until noon and staring out the window. She could go out. She was effectively invisible at her school, so no one would think it was weird if she appeared at a party. She just never had the urge to.

A wave of FOMO came over her. She had a very familiar question buzzing around her head. One she asked herself a million Sundays before and never quite found the answer to.

Was she missing out on something?

CHAPTER TWO

To her dismay, it wasn't raining on that Monday. In fact, it was clear and bright and beautiful. It was even warm. She wasn't overly fond of warm weather. She wasn't a fan of the fashion that came along with it, but she did like sitting in the passenger seat of her best friend's convertible with the top down. So, that was a plus.

Despite the warm weather, she pulled a brown, knitted sweater over her head along with a pair of black jeans. Piper woke up especially early that morning and was going to pick up where she left off reading yesterday, but got distracted while gazing out the window and wishing it would pour. Daydreaming was always her guilty pleasure.

It didn't really matter what time she woke up, anyway. Her best friend, Hally, was always late. The girl had a talent for showing up at least five minutes after she was supposed to. Perhaps she only did it because she knew she could get away with it.

Piper grabbed her backpack and (mostly) finished homework before leaving her room. She bounded down the stairs, her footfalls a rhythmic "*thump-thump, thump-thump*" like the beat of a healthy heart.

Her dad was sitting at the dining table, dressed for

work, reading the paper. He had a cereal bowl that had approximately ten percent of the cereal and milk remaining. Piper thought that was a rather pathetic amount to leave behind. *What, you couldn't stomach two more spoonfulls?* She thought.

"Good morning," he greeted. He made a show of savouring the final words of a paragraph before laying the paper down on the table. Piper glanced at the page he was on and smiled when she saw. He wasn't reading anything. He was doing a crossword.

"Good morning," she replied. She took the seat beside his and looked disapprovingly at his bowl. "What's wrong with the cereal?"

He pushed the dish away from himself like a child. "It's soggy."

She scrunched her nose at the mushy, rejected cereal. "Gross. You should've eaten faster."

"I was engaged in a riveting article," he declared. She snorted and nodded to the paper smugly.

"Yeah, sure. Number four is Morocco." She got up from her chair and got a banana from the cupboard, leaning against the counter as she peeled it. He grabbed the paper and pulled a pen out of his shirt pocket.

"How did I miss that?" He muttered to himself as he scribbled in the answer.

Satisfied with his work, he folded the paper up and plopped it on the table once again. He picked up his bowl and threw the sad remnants of his breakfast in the garbage.

"Is Hally on her way yet?" He asked as he took the bowl and placed it in the sink. Piper took a bite of her banana and held it in her cheek as she replied.

"I doubt it."

"That seems about right," he chuckled. "Tell her to hurry up. Education is of the utmost importance!" He declared, deepening his voice and using a pitiful British accent. Piper swallowed her bite and giggled at her dad. He made Mondays much more bearable.

She couldn't help but play along. She straightened her posture and furrowed her brow, trying to match his impression as she said, "Yes, Father! I shall absorb all the knowledge I can!"

"Marvelous, Daughter! Are you excited for another week at school?"

Breaking character, she slumped her shoulders. She let out a loud, overly dramatic groan in response.

"Well said." He gave her a kiss on the forehead and a pat on the shoulder, (the most fatherly goodbye there was) and started toward the door. "Have a good day," he said in his normal voice as he left the kitchen. "Get smart, overthrow the government. Do something productive."

Piper gave him a salute. "Will do."

He left for work, keys and bag in hand. She listened as his car pulled away from the house and off down the street. There wasn't a sound left in the house.

Once she was done her banana, she threw the peel away. She went to the bathroom and brushed her teeth and checked her appearance in the mirror. While she was making a valiant effort to tame her cow lick, her phone buzzed in her pocket. She checked it to see a text from Hally.

"Hey, I'm running late. Don't kill me. I'm almost there."

She sighed and texted back:

"You better not be texting and driving."

A moment later, she received:

"You think I can text this good while driving? No way. Voice to text, baby!"

Satisfied, she put her phone away and wandered out of the bathroom. When she was halfway down the stairs, she heard Hally honking the horn outside. She pulled on her shoes, grabbed her backpack and left the house.

Hally's car was blaring music, but it wasn't even the type of music that was meant to be listened to loudly. It was a soft vaporwave song. It sounded like something that would be played in an extremely cool elevator. Piper thought, *Is that an oxymoron?*

Piper got in the car and threw her bag into the back seat. The leather seat was hot, charged by the sunlight all morning. She was glad she hadn't worn shorts. Her thighs would have stuck to the leather like eggs on a pan. When she settled in, she reached over and turned the music down significantly.

"Just because you have weird music taste doesn't mean all my neighbours need to hear it," she said. She buckled her seatbelt and settled in, laying her arm on the door (which was also roasting hot, but it was worth the sacrifice, since she loved the feeling of air rushing over her arms as they drove.)

"Vaporwave isn't that weird. It's calming," Hally rebutted. She pulled away from Piper's house effortlessly (she had plenty of practice) and started toward the school. "You just don't like it because you have no chill."

Piper shrugged. "You got me there."

Hally chuckled and their conversation ended there. Hally tapped the steering wheel with her manicured nails idly as she drove.

Once they were moving, Piper turned her attention to the radio again. She skipped through songs, looking for one she recognized out of Hally's playlist. It was a fruit-less venture. She loved Hally, but her music taste was her tragic flaw. Her playlists were mostly made up of party music, and not the fun early 2000's type. It was purely top 40's party mixes with some vaporwave sprinkled in for flavour. Piper couldn't think of a worse cocktail of sounds.

"My weekend blew chunks," Hally announced.

Piper was still fiddling with the stereo when she idly asked, "Literally for figuratively?"

"Of course figuratively, asshole." Hally sighed and Piper got the feeling that this wasn't a funny topic. She settled on turning the music off completely and leaned back in her seat, looking at the other girl.

"Go on."

Hally huffed dramatically. "I had a date with Randy and he—"

"Who's that again?" Piper interrupted. Hally rolled her eyes.

"You know Randy, we've been in school with him since the eighth grade."

"I don't remember a guy named Randy being in our Grade 8 class."

"You have to remember him. He *had* a mullet for three years."

"You dated a guy with a mullet?"

"No. He had a mullet for three years. Past tense. Can I go on now?"

"Right, sorry."

Hally gripped the steering wheel. "Anyway, the date was supposed to be seven o'clock. I said I'd meet him there—his car is gross, it always reeks like pot—and I got to the restaurant a couple minutes early. I got a table and waited for, like, twenty minutes."

"Yikes."

"Yeah. He finally texted me at half past seven saying he wasn't going to make it. The bastard stood me up when *he* was the one who asked *me* out."

"What a dick. I'm sorry, Hals."

Hally waved her hand nonchalantly. "It's not a huge deal. I mean, I hardly wanted to go out with him anyway. I just wanted a night out. But still."

"Yeah, still," Piper muttered. It was a lame response, sure. But this wasn't her expertise and she learned it was better to just let Hally talk and agree rather than attempt to give advice. All Hally needed was to talk about it.

"It's just such a dick move," she went on, hitting the steering wheel once in frustration. "It was fucking humiliating, sitting by myself."

"You should have called me," Piper said. "I could have pretended to be your date."

"No way," Hally replied. "That's a rumor I don't need following me."

Piper glanced over at Hally hesitantly, but didn't say anything else.

Piper was very used to dating stories from Hally. Everyone loved her, so it wasn't surprising that she had a date lined up almost every weekend. The bad part was that there weren't a lot of good guys around, so usually the dates were one time things. Hally didn't mind too much. She said they made for good stories.

Hally was the resident "*it girl*," for lack of a better term. Piper paled in comparison to her. Especially since Hally radiated confidence and power. She had long blonde hair that lay in loose ringlets around her shoulders. She had plump lips and high cheekbones. When she smiled, she could bend anyone to her will.

Piper was smaller than her, in all meanings of the word. Piper was shorter, but only by an inch or two. She was also scrawnier, which made her long limbs look awkward, like they were made of yarn. Piper's hair was auburn and cropped above her shoulders, and her cheeks were sprinkled with freckles. Unlike Piper, Hally never let anyone get to her. No matter what they said. She'd been teased in the past for various reasons, like her size, her bold outfits or her father spoiling her. But none of it sunk in. She was always a force to be reckoned with. Nothing anybody did or said would change that.

"The guys around here are so shit," Hally went on. "I mean, next level shit. I can't wait to get the fuck out of this town."

Piper nodded in agreement. "Tell me about it."

When they arrived at school, they were surprisingly on time. However, Hally couldn't find her math book, so they spent ten minutes taking everything out of her backpack in the back seat to find it, and then struggled trying to fit it all back inside.

Nevertheless, Hally walked into the building like she owned the place, which was par for the course. No matter where she was, she radiated the same confidence. Piper really admired that about Hally. It was rare you found someone so beautiful who was aware of their beauty. Piper always looked up to Hally. She was an only child, so Hally was the closest she had to a sister. Like a sister, Hally took her under her wing. She sprinkled notes of wisdom into her stories and tried to push Piper out of her comfort zone. Piper wasn't sure what she offered Hally in return.

They parted ways for the first period. Hally had psychology and Piper had English. Piper wanted to take psychology but she had the psychology teacher the year before for biology and he was a real pain in the ass. He yelled all the time and he sent at least one girl to the office a day for dress code violations. Not to mention that he spoke really fast while he was explaining stuff and told anyone who couldn't keep up to drop his class. As interested in psychology as she was, she refused to suffer through another one of his classes.

Upon entering her class, she saw that her regular seat — the last desk in the front row, right beside the window — was empty and waiting for her. Joseph was already there, slouched in the seat beside hers.

"Hey," she greeted as she strolled up to her desk and sat down. He perked up when he saw her. The colour returned to his tan skin and he adjusted his posture.

"Hey!" He replied. She began digging through her bag for her books. They were studying *A Midsummer Night's Dream* which was appropriately named, since it was a major snooze-fest. The type-writing monkeys probably took a sedative before writing this one. She felt it hardly compared to *Macbeth*, but it was a hundred times more bearable than *Romeo And Juliet* so she couldn't complain too much.

"Did you have a good weekend?" Joseph asked. She laid her books on the desk and nodded.

"It was alright," she said. "Did you?"

He shrugged. "It was okay. I had to catch up on this stupid play. I still have no real clue what's going on in it and we have to write an essay on it next week. I swear, I am useless in this department."

Piper waved a dismissing hand at him. "Shakespeare isn't as hard as people think. His work is just intimidating so it seems like a daunting task to study it."

"Easy for you to say," he complained. "You love this stuff."

"Oh, contraire. I don't love Shakespeare. I'm aware of how influential his writing was, but influential and enjoyable don't go hand in hand." This didn't seem to comfort Joseph in any way, so she flipped open her notebook and held it out to him. "That's my notes on *Midsummer Night's Dream*. Maybe they'll help you."

He went to take them, but hesitated. That was something that always comforted her about Joseph; he was living proof that she wasn't the only one unsure.

"Don't you need them?" He asked, his brown eyes peering up at her like a guilty puppy. She couldn't see why. She offered.

"It's all up here," she said, tapping her temple with her index finger. "I only wrote them down so my ideas would be in order for the essay. Take them. Copy down the stuff you need or photocopy the whole thing, I don't care."

He inhaled and smiled, taking the notebook from her. "Thanks," he said. He began skimming its contents, his finger tracing the words as he read. When he got to one portion, he stopped and furrowed his brow. "Wait," he said, "I think you wrote this down wrong."

Piper raised a brow. Her notes were usually very thorough. Her mind was often scattered, so her notes had to be organized and detailed. And—obviously—100% accurate. She leaned forward to see what he was pointing to.

He read out loud, "*The overarching theme of* Midsummer Night's Dream *is love. More specifically, that love is foolish and reckless and changes who we are.*"

She sat back and nodded. "That's right."

He shook his head firmly, laying down the notebook and picking up the play as if it would agree with him. "I don't think so," he remarked. He flipped through the play idly, though it seemed he was looking for something. "I mean, I don't get a lot of what's happening in this play, but it's still a love story, isn't it?"

"Well, yes," she conceded. "But so is *Romeo and Julliet* and look how that turned out. The majority of Shakespeare's romances are also tragedies. What does that say about his perception of love?"

"This isn't about his perception. This is about this one play. Maybe it doesn't convey his belief and that's why almost every couple in his plays die horrifically, but this play in particular... it shines a light on the messy, stupid parts of love. You act like love is a bad thing."

Piper sighed. She glanced at her own copy of *Midsummer Night's Dream*. There was something tragic about it. It was a comedy, yes, but the funniest things were often the saddest. She supposed that was why comedians were so depressed. The love in that play seemed aimless to her, even when it was directed toward the right people. Love was careless. Fleeting. Ever-changing and enslaving. At least, that was what Shakespeare told her.

"Maybe it is," she muttered. He landed on a certain page and kept his finger there so he wouldn't lose it. Then, he met her eyes again. He looked conflicted and she could tell he was picking his words very carefully.

"I think you're wrong," he said. "Love changes us, but not for the worst. Sure, its ridiculous and stupid and drives people crazy, but it's also this uncontrollable, almost ineffable force. It's totally irrational but it's also beautiful and unconditional. All that *for better or for worse* crap. That's what this play is about."

She got lost somewhere in his words. For someone who didn't understand Shakespeare, he certainly had a handle on love. Or an incredibly injudicious view on what it was. She wouldn't know. She'd never been in love.

"Sorry," he mumbled. She suspected she took too long to reply. When she came back to earth to see him, he looked insecure. "Maybe that's a naive way to look at it."

"No," she said. "Maybe you're right. I mean, if love really is ineffable, as you say, none of us can truly comprehend it. For all I know, you're spot on."

He smiled sheepishly at her. He handed over his playbook, opened to a certain page, with one sentence underlined.

"This," he said, "Is true love."

She took the book and picked out the sentence. It was in the middle of Hermia's monologue in Scene I, Act I. It was the only thing underlined on the whole page.

"Love looks not with the eyes, but with the mind, and therefore is winged cupid painted blind."

CHAPTER THREE

When the final bell rang, Piper was more than ready to leave. She'd had plenty of learning for one day. She spent an hour listening to her math teacher talk about politics while a video on exponential functions played on the smartboard. That was second period, and the exact moment her monday became a Monday; mind-numbingly boring and borderline insufferable. It continued that way until three o'clock hit.

She couldn't find Hally at her locker, so she assumed she was waiting outside. Piper left the building through the front doors. She rolled up her sleeves when the warm air hit her and regretted wearing a sweater. It was much too warm.

She scanned the parking lot until her eyes landed on Hally. She was sat in the driver's seat of the car, twirling her hair between her fingers carelessly. Two boys were standing beside her car in their basketball uniforms. She didn't seem all that interested in them, but they were certainly interested in her. They were flexing and leaning against her car and smiling. She looked bored.

Hally met Piper's eyes and looked relieved. She turned to the boys and gave them an apologetic smile. She said something, but Piper couldn't hear her. Within seconds, she put the car in drive and the boys took a couple steps back.

Hally pulled up in front of Piper and huffed.

"Get in before those dick-wads come over."

Piper chuckled as she rounded the car and sat herself down in the passenger's seat. Hally checked her surroundings before taking to the road.

At the same time, Piper envied Hally and pitied her. Piper envied her beauty and confidence, something Piper could never master. But she definitely didn't envy all the attention Hally got. Hally never got a peaceful moment. Everyone loved her, and while it must have been flattering, Piper was well aware of how exhausting it was. Hally told her all the time, *"Some days, I wish I could disappear."*

That was one thing the girls had in common.

"Do you want to come over?" Hally asked, her eyes glued to the road. They didn't have music playing, which wasn't normal. Not that Piper minded. She liked the quiet.

"I don't know, I've got homework," she muttered in reply. Just after the reply left her mouth, her phone vibrated in her pocket. She took it out and turned it on to find a text from her Dad.

"Laura is bringing home dinner tonight. Any preference?"

Piper scrunched up her nose. She typed out a rapid reply as she spoke to Hally.

"Nevermind. Yeah, I'll come over."

They pulled up to Hally's place and she cut the ignition. Hally's house was much nicer than the majority of houses on her street (not to mention infinitely nicer than

Piper's), which wasn't surprising. Her dad wasn't literally swimming in cash, but he was pretty close to it. After all, he only had one child and no spouse, so he didn't have a lot of expenses and could use his money on more frivolous things. Hence the extravagant house and convertible. Plus he had a flexible, high paying job as a defense lawyer for a very prosperous firm in their area.

Hally didn't talk about her mother very much. Her father and mother weren't together. He was a single man, who had no interest in pursuing a partner, but wanted a child. So he chose to have a surrogate. He claimed to have scoured through tons of applications, but he settled on the woman with the best health and personal records. She was from France, she was incredibly beautiful, and her family line was devoid of genetic diseases or illnesses. He paid her enormously and covered any doctors fees, medications and even maternity clothing and accessories required. They became close friends over her pregnancy. After Hally was born, she picked up and moved back to France to be with her family, but she wrote to them regularly and sent gifts. Hally never felt that she missed out on having a mother. She never felt she needed one. Her father was all encompassing and she never longed for more. Her unwavering satisfaction was hard for Piper to relate to, since - no matter how good her life was - she always yearned for more.

They strolled in through the front door and Hally kicked off her shoes as she called out for her dad.

"Dad! We're home!"

Jack emerged from the hallway. Piper assumed he was in his office. He was lucky to be able to work from home most days, though he always dressed up for work no matter where it was. He was dressed in a white button up and a black tie. He had thin-framed glasses attached to a chain hanging around his neck. He smiled at them.

"Girls, how was school today?" he asked, as chipper as ever. He'd referred to Piper and Hally as "*Girls*" for as long as Piper could remember. He looked much older than he did when they were kids. His hair had grey streaks in the front and his eyes and cheeks had wrinkles from smiling. He had creases on his forehead from stress, and his posture considerably worsened. Piper hated looking back on how Jack looked a couple of years ago. It made her think about how her own father would look soon enough. Her dad was ten years younger than Jack, and much more active. Piper's father, Samuel, had hardly aged a day since Piper was born. Still, Piper was scared for the day that her father looked like an old man.

"Shit," Hally replied bluntly. She had no reason to filter her thoughts around anyone, especially him. "How was work?"

Jack shrugged. "Can't complain. I spent the majority of the day going over witness testimonies and trying to make sense of my clients handwriting, but it's certainly better than sitting in a room with those insufferable leeches I work with." He checked his watch. "I'm thinking of making pot roast for supper, but it'll take a while. If you're hungry now, I can whip something up?"

Hally looked at Piper for confirmation before shaking her head. "I think we're fine, thanks. Call us when supper is done."

"Will do," he replied. He disappeared into the kitchen. Hally grabbed Piper by the arm and tugged her upstairs. She released Piper when they were standing in her room before throwing herself down on her bed dramatically.

"Can I drop all of my classes and still graduate?" she

asked, staring at the ceiling. Piper smiled. She laid down beside her on the bed, their heads an inch apart as they both looked straight above.

"Definitely not," Piper answered.

"I fucking hate my classes."

"Why? You're passing all of them with straight A's, it's not like they're hard for you."

"I'm not worried about them being hard," Hally replied. "They're just mind numbingly boring. And I hate all my classmates and all my teachers and their classrooms and the font they type the worksheets in."

Piper laughed. "That's a lot of complaints. Could you be exaggerating this a little bit?"

Hally shrugged. "Maybe. But, you know what I mean. When you really hate something, everything about it bothers you."

"Yeah, I get it." Piper took a deep breath. It was hard to give Hally a pep talk about high school. There was no arguing that it was difficult and stressful. No one gave students enough credit. The social aspect alone was enough to drive someone insane. Not to mention academics. Even for someone as flawless as Hally, it took a toll.

Piper turned her head to look at her friend.

"Look on the brightside. We only have two years left until we're free. And besides," Piper linked her pinkie with Hally's, and Hally turned to look at her. "We've got each other."

CHAPTER FOUR

Every day in a high school week felt the same. Think *Groundhog Day* except instead of zany shenanigans, you watched paint drying on an endless loop. It was a very specific, dull purgatory full of people you don't know who know you, and people you know who have no clue you exist. Some days Piper felt like she was holding her breath for the entire duration.

To try and disrupt the monotony, Hally insisted on some coveted after school "girl time." Piper was tempted to resist. She had homework to do and she wanted to go to sleep as early as she could in an attempt to feel less spiteful about going to school in the first place. Regardless, she obliged. Afterall, she had a grand total of one friend. She had to keep her happy. Piper hoped the plans were something simple; a chick flick marathon, baking cookies, a sleepover, or any other at-home, stereotypical "bff" activity Pinterest endorses. But Hally wasn't a stay-at-home kind of girl, so she insisted they go perusing stores downtown.

They lived in a small community, so "the city" was just the area of their town that had businesses like cinemas, clothing stores, fancy restaurants, bars, etc. Unlike the portrayals of cities Piper saw in television shows, there was nothing glamorous about theirs. It was pretty in a "that-wad-of-gum-is-in-the-shape-of-a-heart" kind of way. The businesses were fine, but Piper couldn't imagine living there. The apartments were skinny and tall, with two doors (one below, for the basement apartment and one above for the upstairs.) They were so close together that neighbours couldn't open their windows at the same time without hitting each other. In the slim space between the buildings, they kept their trash bins, old mattresses, flat tires and other charming homes for rats. Piper liked the people that lived there, though. She didn't know how they survived the constant sounds of traffic and people. She couldn't imagine their walls were thick enough to block it all out. And yet, whenever she made her way through the street the apartments resided on, every person she met gave a smile and had no complaints.

The more she thought about it, the easier it was to understand. It wasn't necessarily a bad place to live. It was just different. Sometimes she got those things confused.

Once past the apartment buildings, the strip of businesses was easy to spot. Every store was bright and colourful, with flowers and banners and mannequins outside. The bars had chalkboard signs illustrating their karaoke and trivia nights. The cinema's sign was bright enough to light the whole block at night. They all tried to grab your attention and in the hubbub, they blended in completely.

They walked in sync down the sidewalk. They hadn't entered a single store and based on the fact that they passed three of Hally's favourites without her spending at least $100, it was safe to assume they weren't going to.

"Window shopping isn't as cool as it looks in the movies," Hally said. She was peering in through the window of a dress shop. The window display had indigo evening gowns, in three different styles. Since Piper hadn't the slightest clue what any of the three were actually called, she deemed them "long," "slightly shorter," and "dress code violation." That last one was programmed into her brain by the school board. It was a rather nice dress, even if her ex-biology teacher would send her home for wearing it.

"You could go in the store..?" She suggested, feeling a bizarre cocktail of boredom and amusement.

"My Dad said I have to stop spending money on clothes I'm not going to wear."

Piper squinted at her friend incredulously. "You could just wear the clothes you buy..?"

Hally rolled her eyes. "Do you have an answer to everything?"

Piper pretended to think about it for a moment before nodding smartly. Hally sighed.

"This is boring. Do you want to get a hot drink and go back to my place?"

Piper resisted the urge to do a happy jig.

"Sure."

Hally led the way, as she usually did. Head held high and oblivious to others in her path, as they stepped aside to let her through. Piper quickened her pace to keep up until they were side by side again.

"Do you have to be home for supper?" Hally asked.

"I don't think so," Piper replied, though she had no inclination either way. The topic of supper made some bitterness slip into her voice, which was very unnatural for her. *"Laura* is there," she said, drawing out her syllables and making a face that implied the name alone tasted rotten.

Hally glanced over at Piper, a knowing look on her face. "How long have she and your dad been together now?"

Piper tried to count back to when her dad first met Laura. It felt like forever ago, and yet, it seemed like just yesterday that she and her dad were alone. She wished she could go back to that.

"Three years, I think," she muttered. "Way too long, in my opinion."

Hally kept watching her. Piper knew her friend was waiting for her to go on, not that there was much to say. Surely, Hally had heard it all before. Countless times.

And yet, Piper said, "I just hate her. I don't know why she has to be around all the time. She talks to me like I'm her kid or something, but they're not even married. They hardly know each other."

"It's been three years," Hally reminded her, which earned her a glare.

"My parents were together for ten years," Piper rebutted, "And they were strangers the whole time. They still are."

Hally exhaled. "Not every relationship is like your parents."

Piper snorted humorlessly. "Thank god for that."

She gave Piper a pat on the shoulder, her way of comforting her. It wasn't exactly Hally's forte. The effort was appreciated, at least.

They were silent then, which Piper liked. Her blood wasn't exactly boiling, but it was simmering. Bubbling, for sure. It was a hot topic and one she wished was as easy to avoid as her biology teacher had been.

They reached the coffee shop and Piper was going to go inside but Hally stopped before the door.

"I'll go get our drinks," she said. "You get us a table. You want a hot chocolate, right?"

Piper nodded in response. She complied easily, letting Hally walk inside while she found a seat outdoors.

The shop was only small, and couldn't have more than four tables in the building. But they had a seating area outside. They built on a wide deck two summers ago, after their small town built on a subdivision that brought in plenty of new customers. The railing around it had yellow fairy lights, and the tables were wooden with glass table tops. Piper found one close to the shop window, so she could still effectively people-watch. That was the best part of coffee shops, after all.

She looked around. In the building, every table was full. One of them was occupied by three business men in suits, each holding a massive coffee cup, with papers crowding their area. They talked expressively between sips, jabbing fingers at spreadsheets like it had insulted them on a very personal level. The next table had a boy with short pink hair and circular glasses. He was typing on a laptop, his fingers moving quickly. He hit the keys harder than necessary and glanced around every so often as he did. He was working in a hurry, but he seemed to want others to watch him. He only slowed down to sip from his teacup or shake out his wrist. The one beside him was an older couple; a man and a woman who looked to be around sixty. The woman had mostly grey hair, with one section in the front dyed purple. The man had a t-shirt on that said *#1 Grandpa*. He stared at her, entranced as she spoke. They had a single slice of white cake between them and a fork each.

Piper found herself staring when she reached the final table, the one closest to the window. She didn't know why, but the last occupant caught her attention enough that she almost forgot where she was. It was a girl around her age. She had long black hair with purple ends. She was dressed in a black shirt with a band on it Piper didn't recognize, and a pair of purple plaid pants. She had on thick black boots and she was scrolling through her phone. Piper couldn't make out her eyes but she imagined they were a deep brown, since her hair was so dark. Something about the way this girl sat—with one leg crossed over the other horizontally, lounged back in her chair—made Piper think she was the careless type. The type of person to sit back and enjoy the heat of a house fire, or take hurtful words as heartfelt compliments and laugh. Something about the way this girl interacted with her environment—looking up from her phone every once and a while to smile at the people giving her judgemental stares, swirling her iced coffee around in its cup before she sipped it—made Piper think she was also very strong. And decisive. And positive. As if, when faced with a difficult decision, she'd make her choice with ease and relish in it, whether it was right or wrong. Piper loved coffee shops because they allowed her to see real people experiencing real life and imagine what it was like outside of her miniscule high school. But this time was different. She wasn't just making up a narrative for this girl. She was observing her in awe, the way someone from the city might look at a sky full of stars in an area with no light pollution; full of wonder and curiosity.

The moment ended before it had begun. She was awoken from her daze when Hally laid a mug in front of her and took a seat at their table.

"I love this place. Even on its busiest days, the service is so fast," Hally was saying. Piper was having trouble focusing. She felt like she just stared into the sun for too long. But from how Hally was talking, it must have been no time at all.

Piper stared at her drink. She never really believed in things like destiny before. She was much too logical for that (though some would call her cynical for it.) But she always loved the idea. She would think about it all the time, and read plenty of novels about soulmates and chance encounters, and being in *"the perfect place at the perfect time."* She still thought it was bullshit. And yet, every so often, she saw someone and thought they'd be her destiny.

Of course, she was never right, because that thought was ridiculous.

Hally snapped her fingers and Piper was pulled from her thoughts again.

"Piper," Hally said, looking mildly annoyed. Mostly though, her face was full of concern, which made Piper fix her deer-caught-in-headlights expression. "Is your drink too hot? I asked them to put cold milk in it so you could drink it."

"No, it's fine. Sorry, I just zoned out," Piper assured her. That didn't seem to ease Hally's mind so Piper picked up her mug to prove it. She took a sip without bothering to check how hot it was beforehand. The moment it touched her top lip, she winced and pulled the mug away, spilling a tenth of the liquid on her clothes. Her lip tingled from the burning sensation and she laid her tongue on the scalded part to try and soothe it. Hally suppressed a laugh and asked her if she was alright.

Piper glanced through the window again. Her eyes met the coffee shop girl's hazel ones (light hazel, like they had specks of gold in them. Piper had been way off) and she couldn't breathe for a second. The girl smiled at her. She picked up her iced coffee as a demonstration and pretended to blow on it. Piper managed to smile back, feeling suddenly like she had never looked worse in her life. She tucked her hair behind her ears and hoped she was presentable. The girl was still looking at her and raised her eyebrows as if to say *"It's your turn"*, so Piper picked up her mug and blew on it gently, watching the steam fly away. Then, she lifted it to her lips again and took a proper sip this time, without burning anything.

When Piper laid her mug down again, she noticed the girl wasn't looking at her anymore. She was scrolling through her phone again. Only this time, she had a smile on her face.

"What are you looking at?" Hally asked, craning her neck to try and catch sight of whatever caught Piper's attention.

Piper turned back to her, trying to shake her brain of its busy thoughts.

"Nothing..." She beamed. "Nothing. This hot chocolate is really good."

CHAPTER FIVE

At school the following day, Piper had English class again. They were supposed to be reading the next two scenes, but she already had; in the first twenty minutes of class, in fact. She read quickly and since she had a good grasp on Shakespearean language, she didn't have to look up words or annotate the play as she went. The rest of the class was still reading. It was dead silent. So quiet she was listening to her own breathing, making sure it never rose in such a way as to draw attention to herself. She wondered if she was the only one worried about that.

While everyone else was reading, she was staring out the window. That was why she sat where she did; windows were ideal for daydreaming.

The school's grounds weren't taken care of very well. The grass was long and yellow and full of ugly weeds. The shrubbery was too thick along the walkway, making it awkward to try and slip past it without branches scraping your clothing. There were cigarette butts strewn around the no smoking sign and various different wrappers, bags and cans left on the ground. On a sunny day, she would have much preferred to see butterflies and bumble bees flying around, flowers blowing in the wind, a field of green grass. But outside that window looked more like a dumping ground.

She had trouble keeping her eyes open. That was why she was looking at her litter-covered school yard. She couldn't get to sleep that night, even though she was dropping tired. Her mind was swimming. She even tried going for a walk to tire herself out. She went out in her pajamas and wandered around her dimly lit neighbourhood for a while, but she was still buzzing when she got back. She couldn't get her brain to shut up. You'd think she would be used to it by now, but it plagued her all the time. She was constantly restless. Never relaxed.

She rested her head on her hand. Her dad and Laura's anniversary was coming up next month. In October, their three years would turn into four. Piper didn't know how she felt about that. When she first met Laura, she was sure the relationship wouldn't last longer than a month. Now that so much time had passed, she didn't know what would come next. Four years was a lot of time to sink into one person. But still, Laura was a stranger. An outsider. She didn't belong with them. She could never move into their house. She could never be Piper's mother.

Piper resisted the urge to let out a sigh. *Of course Laura can't be my mother*, she thought bitterly. *My own mother can't be my mother*.

She felt this anger inside her. She resented feeling it, because she knew there was nothing she could do to change it. The way things played out would never be changed. Her parents could never mend their relationship. They hardly had one to begin with.

In all honesty, she didn't really want them together. Her dad wasn't happy when they were together. So what made him think Laura could make him happy?

What Joseph said about love replayed in her mind. She knew her father and Laura exchanged the occasional "I love you" the same way someone says "good morning" and "goodnight." It didn't feel like a declaration to her. It didn't feel like cupid's famous arrow. It felt so... mundane. So normal. Joseph talked about love like it was a science he dedicated years to studying and from his perspective, it seemed like magic. What Samuel and Laura had didn't look like magic but perhaps that was the point. Magic wasn't real.

The bell must have rung, but Piper didn't hear it. She was shaken from her thoughts when someone laid their hand on her shoulder. She jolted in surprise and looked up, meeting Joseph's eyes. He offered her a shy smile.

"Uh, it's lunch," he told her. He retracted his hand awkwardly and tucked it into his hoodie pocket. "Sorry, I didn't mean to scare you."

"Oh," Piper mumbled stupidly. She should have said something else, but words were lost on her. She packed up her things and stood up, slinging her backpack onto her back. Joseph waited patiently so they could walk out together.

There was a silence as they walked. Piper was looking straight, trying to focus more on a destination than on every thought that bounced off her skull. She hoped the quiet would give her a chance to reevaluate, but Joseph spoke up.

"Are you okay?" he asked. He glanced at her for a moment before looking down at his shoes again. "You seemed distracted."

Piper and Joseph weren't overly close. They never really hung out outside of school, if you don't count summer camp (which Piper didn't, because in her community, everyone in her school went to the same summer camp, except for the few who did sleepaway camps). However, they'd been in the same class since kindergarten. They had an unspoken agreement since then that if they were in the same class, they'd sit together. They talked almost every day. They interacted enough for him to be able to read her relatively easily. Then again, Piper didn't have a very good poker face to begin with.

Even though they both knew he was right, Piper shrugged and said, "It's no big deal."

He wasn't convinced. He glanced at her again but she didn't look back at him.

"Do you want to... talk about it?" he asked. He sounded more unsure of himself than before. While they did see each other often, talking about feelings was usually reserved to friends that properly knew you and didn't spend time with you in only one setting. Yet another unspoken agreement they came to. She met his eyes and gave him a smile.

"Thanks, but I'm okay," she answered. He accepted her reply this time, but he didn't leave her side. They continued to walk down the hall side by side. She felt him watching her, like an animal in an exhibit. She opened her mouth to say something, but he beat her to it.

"Your notes have been really helpful. I managed to catch up on the reading last night and I understood a lot of it."

"I'm glad."

"I think you're right about Shakespeare," he said. She paused and glanced at him. She'd been thinking about his words ever since he said them. She'd been mulling over them and debating with herself if love could exist at all, let alone exist the way he explained it. He seemed so sure when he spoke before. How could he change his mind now?

She swallowed. "Really?"

He nodded nonchalantly, as if he didn't just send her mind into a class A spiral. "Definitely," he confirmed. "His work isn't difficult, it's just intimidating."

The tension in her shoulders released. That was all he meant. He hadn't taken back his powerful declaration. All that thinking wasn't wasted.

"Oh, yeah."

"I think I get why I didn't get it," he went on, eyeing her as he did. She paused and waited for him to continue but then realized he wanted her to prompt him.

"Why's that?" she asked.

"I was scared of it," he admitted. "I was so scared of not understanding it that I didn't even try. I just decided I wouldn't understand it so I wouldn't be surprised when it didn't make sense."

She looked over at him, but he finally looked away. Her mind stilled then. Now it housed only what he'd just said, printed neatly in the centre of a black abyss. It was like a missing puzzle piece, only you have a hundred unfinished puzzles missing only one piece and you have no clue which one this piece belongs to and the idea of trying it in all the puzzles makes you want to throw all the puzzles in the garbage and never think of them again.

"How poetic," she joked in response. He chuckled and shrugged humbly.

"What can I say? I adore influential literature."

She laughed, her mood brightening just a little. She opened her mouth to respond when she heard her best friend's voice behind them.

"Piper! Piper!" Hally slowed down as she reached

them, a little out of breath from running. Piper was astounded at how fast Hally could run in heels without twisting an ankle. "There you are, I was looking for you. I thought you had math?"

"No, I had English," Piper replied.

"Fuck, I guess I got your schedule mixed up…" She thought to herself for a moment, trying to work out which days Piper had what classes, but she shook her head to get back on task. "Oh, nevermind. I need you."

Piper glanced at Joseph hesitantly. Hally was her best friend, so she had an obligation to go with her whenever she was needed. Still, she felt bad leaving him when they were mid-conversation.

He waved her off, a polite (slightly disappointed) smile on his face. "Go ahead," he said. "I'll see you later."

She smiled back before letting Hally tug her away down the hall.

"What do you need?" Piper asked, struggling to keep up.

"You're not busy this weekend, are you?"

"No, why?"

"We have a date."

Piper's chest felt tight. "We?"

"Yes, we!" Hally came to a stop at her locker. She released Piper's arm—which she grabbed to ensure Piper kept up—and fiddled with her lock. "This guy asked me out on a date and—"

"What happened to '*The guys around here are so shit*?'"

"He's so nice, Piper. He's such a good listener. And he's so handsome. He looks like a prince. He hardly talks, but if you ask me, that's a good thing. The things some guys I've dated have said—ugh. Remind me to tell you about Henry O'Neill. He was a real winner. We went to see a movie together and he talked about his ex the whole time. I don't remember a minute of *Game Night* but then again, it didn't get great reviews anyway."

"Back on topic. The date?"

"Right! It's just... Well, he has this friend. The two of them are practically attached at the hip. I mean, they don't go anywhere without each other. It's as cute as it is annoying but he wanted me to bring someone along for his buddy."

Piper huffed. She crossed her arms stubbornly and leaned against the locker, looking at Hally side-on. She didn't say a word, giving Hally a moment to tell her why in hell she should agree to this. Hally opened the door to her locker and collected her things for her final class of the day.

"We're just going to hang out at one of their houses for a couple hours," she said. "If you get sick of it, I'll drive you home. No sweat. Cool?"

Piper continued to stare at her, waiting for a better reason. While Piper had accompanied Hally to parties before, and helped Hally get ready for dates, she was never asked to attend a date. Why would she be? She wasn't interested in anybody at their school, and surely Hally could get a date on her own.

"Piper." Hally shut her locker and turned to face her, eyebrows cocked. "Come on. It's not like I'm asking you to marry him. One evening, that's all. Besides, he's not too hard on the eyes. You might even like him. You never go out on dates and it's not because guys don't like you. Your comfort zone is miniscule. This is an easy, safe environment to expand it."

Piper wished she could contest that, but she really couldn't. She had a hard time branching out and doing different things. Hally and her were very different and though Hally had more extravagant ideas for a good time, she never pushed Piper past her limits. She had no reason to distrust her. Besides, she loved Hally. Hally had done a lot for her in their many years of friendship, so Piper could sacrifice one night for her. That was the least she could do.

"Fine," Piper caved. "But if it sucks, I'm leaving."

Hally grinned ear to ear and hugged Piper tightly.

"Thank you! You won't regret it!"

CHAPTER SIX

Piper regretted it.

They were sitting in one of the boys' basement, faint music playing from a Bluetooth speaker. It was an insanely nice house. Not as tidy or organized as Hally's, but it was equally (if not more) extravagant. The owners of this house were much more obvious about their wealth, with professional family photos hung everywhere, random jewelled knick knacks and two flatscreens in one room. It was a little excessive, like they were making an effort to prove they had money. The basement had two full-size leather couches that had consoles in the middle for drinks. The carpet was red, fluffy and lavish and they had at least five different gaming consoles hooked up to either television, with every accessory you could connect to them strewn around it. It was a modern style house, so the windows were massive. Piper hated that. It felt invasive to have windows big enough that passerbys could see you in your natural habitat. It was like they were on display.

They'd planned to play some card games, but that was abandoned early on. For the couple minutes that they did play, it was awkwardly quiet. They turned on music to try and improve the situation, but it was still awkward —

the awkwardness just had a soundtrack. One by one, they gave up on the game and sat quietly, waiting for… something. Piper didn't know what everyone else was waiting for, but she was waiting to go home.

The boy Hally was with was named Drew. He was a foot taller than his friend, and certainly broader. He had gentle green eyes and his hair was cut close. Hally was right about him; he was princely handsome. He looked equally as strong and angular as he did friendly. Though he was big and made of pure muscle, he wasn't opposing. He had a soft air about him.

He didn't talk very much. In fact, Piper wasn't sure she heard two words come out of his mouth all evening. Then again, he and Hally had been locked at the lips for the majority of the night. That was certainly annoying for Piper, who wanted to go home an hour ago but felt too uncomfortable to break up their makeout.

Piper's date was Brent. He was smaller, more lean than broad in muscle. He was also more clean and put together. His hair was slicked back, and he had some of the whitest teeth Piper had ever seen. He was more boyishly handsome, with round eyes and pursed lips and slightly pink cheeks. He kept twiddling his thumbs and glancing at Drew like he needed help. Piper pitied the guy. Clearly he didn't enjoy the match up.

The house was obviously his. Something about his mannerisms dripped money. Plus, he was prominently featured in all those aforementioned family portraits.

Piper looked up at the clock again. Her curfew was slowly approaching. She was grateful for it. She couldn't wait to go home. It would be some time yet. She was counting the minutes to keep herself occupied.

"Do you have to go home?" Brent asked.

Piper was startled when Brent spoke, especially since he somehow read her mind. She expected him to stay quiet and awkward all night. That was her plan, anyhow. In response to him, she shook her head.

"Not yet, why?"

He nodded his head toward the clock. "You keep checking the time," he replied. She looked down at her hands in her lap. She didn't realize he was watching her. She felt bad. She didn't want him thinking she was having a bad time, even if she was.

"I have a curfew," she told him honestly. He ran a hand through his hair, but it had enough product in it that it hardly moved.

"Oh." He shifted in his seat. He wasn't relaxed, but neither was she. She was way out of her element. Hally was right about her comfort zone before, but Piper decided she didn't want to expand it. She wished she'd come to that realization before she got there.

He asked, "What time do you have to leave?"

"Eleven," she replied.

He glanced at the clock himself and, to her surprise, he sank in his seat like a deflated balloon.

"Thirty minutes," he declared, a sorrowful look on his face. "To think I wasted the whole night in silence."

She scanned his face curiously. "Not total silence," she muttered. "Johnny Cash has been playing for at least forty five minutes."

He chuckled heartily. While she appreciated what a good audience he was, she didn't find her own comment overtly funny.

"Do you want me to change the music?" he asked her with a grin. She shook her head.

"No," she said. "I like it."

"Good. I do, too." He rolled his shoulders. She could see him adjusting—sitting taller, turning to face her more, laying his arm on the back of the couch. He was settling in, becoming more comfortable and confident. She was grateful for that. Him being tense all night only made her feel weirder. "What else do you like?"

She smiled dumbly. It was quite a vague question. "What do you mean?"

"What do you do for fun? What kinds of stuff are you interested in? Where would you rather be than this horribly awkward double date?"

This time, she laughed. She hid her smile behind her hand and tucked some of her hair away from her face. Now that she was aware of him watching her, she was overly conscious of how she looked. She didn't want to look beautiful or elegant or effortless. She just wanted to look different, so maybe he'd stop staring.

"Um, I like reading, I guess," she answered. "If I weren't here, I would probably be rereading my favourite book or asleep at, like, nine o'clock." It was a rather lame answer, but she preferred to be lame than dishonest.

"A real party animal, huh?" He was smiling at her like nobody ever had before. It gave her a weird feeling. Not quite butterflies. More like... wasps. "What's your favourite book?"

"*The Outsiders* by S.E. Hinton."

He thought for a moment, staring off like he was going through every novel he had ever read. She doubted that list was very long.

"That's a movie, isn't it?"

She huffed out a quiet laugh, but stopped herself short. She didn't want him to feel bad for not reading it. There weren't many things more annoying than someone who shames you for not knowing a certain book or film. "There was a movie adaptation of the book, yes," she said. "But the novel is always better than the movie. You should read it."

"But I already know the story from the movie..?" He said it as if it was unheard of to ever read a novel after watching the movie.

"Ninety minutes is not enough time to fully understand the beauty of *The Outsiders*," she said, only semi-joking. "There's so much more to it than the movie shows. Just like everything in life, it's the little details that push it over the top. There are these moments in the book—that obviously can't be converted into film—where it's just you and Ponyboy and it's like he's talking right to you. It's beautiful and tragic. It's a story about unity and loyalty and love. When you're holding the novel, it's like you can feel the story pouring out of it. It's the most incredible feeling."

She was rambling, and she only noticed when she finished talking. Her mouth was moving a mile a minute without consulting her brain first. Brent was still watching her, his eyes focused on her face with a small grin. She flushed and looked away.

"Sorry," she mumbled.

"Don't be," he said quickly. "I like hearing you talk about it. Clearly it means a lot to you."

He was right. That book absorbed her for many years. She was on her third copy. The first, she had lent from her middle school and had to return it once she moved on to high school. The second, her mother had bought her for her birthday and sent it in the mail. There was no card, but she wrote a message on the inside. Some bullshit about new beginnings and the magic of herbal tea for alcoholics. That one, she burned in a fire after her mother quit rehab. She didn't want it around as a reminder. Her father bought her her current copy, two days later.

"It does," Piper agreed. "I can lend you my copy, so you can read it yourself."

"I'd like that."

His gaze was intense. She felt the need to look away from him, or perhaps put on sunglasses to protect herself.

"What about you?" she asked, hoping to take the focus away from her. "What do you do for fun?"

"I play football," he answered. "And video games." He paused, thinking for a moment, before shrugging. "I'm not that interesting."

"I'm sure that's not true. What else?"

He thought some more, staring up at the ceiling. Something seemed to occur to him, but he didn't look at her while he spoke. His eyes stayed fixed on the ceiling in thought.

"Me and Drew hang out a lot," he said. "Basically every day. We don't really do anything crazy, but it's always nice to spend time together. He's like my brother."

That warmed her heart. She never thought two stereotypical jocks like them would be so soft. It was comforting to know that the seemingly untouchable kids at her school were normal, under the letterman jackets and gold chains.

"That's sweet," she said. He looked back at her and nodded.

"Yeah," he said. "I think so. Me and Drew… we take care of each other. I'm not sure where I'd be without him. And of course, he'd be hopeless without me."

They both chuckled at that one. It was an icebreaker

they could have used within the first ten minutes of meeting. Maybe then the night wouldn't have sucked.

They stared at each other for a moment. She was still trying to figure him out. He wasn't what she expected. He was much nicer. Much less manly and didn't reek of testosterone like most of the guys at her school. And he was nervous to talk to her, for some reason. That didn't make much sense to her. Surely she wasn't intimidating. Not to a guy like him.

After a moment, he looked up at the clock and swore.

"Fuck," he muttered. "It's past your curfew."

Piper looked up at the clock. She couldn't believe time passed so quickly. It was 11:15. She stood up and checked her phone. She had a missed text from her Dad. She forgot that her phone was left on *do not disturb*.

She looked over at Hally, who was still… preoccupied, to say the least. Brent stood with her.

"I'll drive you," he offered. Piper smiled but shook her head.

"It's fine, I just have to get her attention… somehow."

Brent laughed, showing his pearly white teeth again. *How does he get them that white?* She thought. She expected a cartoonish sparkle to flash off his teeth. She imagined he couldn't drive on sunny days: he'd blind the oncoming cars.

"It's no problem, really." Before she could protest more, he grabbed a pair of keys off of the coffee table in front of Hally and Drew. He hollered, "Drew, I'm taking your truck, cool?"

Drew made no move to answer, so Brent just shrugged and shoved the keys in his pocket.

"Come on," he said to her. He opened the door to the stairway and gestured for her to go first. She did as she was told, giving him a gracious nod.

They left the house and climbed into Drew's pickup. It was a tall, army green truck, with rust around the tires and a step under each door so you could climb in. The truck smelled like spices, even though the air freshener on the mirror clearly said "*pine*." The cup holders had two paper coffee cups in them, one of which was still half full. The radio was very outdated, with a dial for the station and for volume and a tiny screen she could hardly read. It also had a place for an aux cord to be plugged in and an ashtray. Piper wondered just how old this truck was.

"Sorry, Drew doesn't live in this century," Brent said with a chuckle. "He hardly ever uses the aux, either. He loves the radio, even with all the talking and shitty advertisements."

"Very old school."

"Tell me about it. My grandpa has a more advanced vehicle."

Piper laughed. She buckled her seatbelt and laid her head back on the seat. For an old truck, it was very comfortable. The seat hugged her and the fabric was softer than your average couch.

Brent turned the key and the engine made a loud purr. The truck rumbled and shook her a little. She expected it to run roughly. It was ancient, afterall.

Brent pulled away from the house and onto the road.

"So, where am I headed?" he asked. She gave him her address, trying to explain the exact location the best she could, to which he replied, "I think I know where that is, but let's see where we end up."

She tapped her fingers on her lap idly. It was a clear night. Stars littered the sky above them. Even though a rainy day was much superior, a clear night was pretty impressive too. She could see the crescent moon from her window and she could barely make out Ursa Minor as well. They passed a scatter car, their bright headlights ruining the peace of the night. Piper was glad Brent didn't turn on the stereo. It was much too still and tranquil to be interrupted by an FM talk show.

"It's a nice night," Brent said. Piper turned to look at him. He had both hands on the steering wheel at a perfect ten-and-two. His back was stiff and straight and his eyes were dead-on the path ahead of him.

"Are you a nervous driver?" She asked.

He smiled sheepishly at her. "Is it that obvious?"

She shrugged. "The only time a teenager drives that carefully is when they're nervous. Or doing their driver's test."

"I don't drive a lot," he told her. "Usually, Drew drives, since we go basically everywhere together. I only got my license to get my parents off my back. Though, it does come in handy." He glanced over at her for a second before looking back at the road. Within that tiny second, however, she felt out in the open. Like everyone else was in black and white and they kept staring at her for being in colour. She couldn't say she liked the feeling. She sunk into her seat more to escape it.

"What about you?" He went on, oblivious. "Do you have your license?"

"No, not yet. I have my permit, but I'm not quite ready for my driving test yet."

"Why not?"

"I haven't practiced for it at all yet. Hally offered to teach me in her car but I can't picture myself in the driver's seat. It just doesn't feel right."

"I'm not sure I understand."

Piper gave him a polite smile. She could have explained that, to her, picturing something made it real. Or at least, made it seem more possible. If she couldn't picture something, it was unfathomable to her. Like trying to make up a colour that didn't exist.

But, that was simply too much to say. So instead she settled for, "That's alright."

He didn't seem bothered that she didn't go on. He'd already lost interest in the topic.

"Do you know anything about astrology?" he asked, out of the blue. She glanced at him and smiled incredulously.

"Uh... no?"

"Really?" he replied. "You seem like you'd be super into it. I took an astrology class last year—I hardly understood any of it—but I did remember a couple of the constellations. Well, that's a lie, I only remember Orion and the one that looks kind of like a ladle."

She paused, eyebrows knitted together in confusion. He was rambling on and she was lost. Then, it dawned on her and she tried to suppress a laugh.

"Wait," she said. "Do you mean astronomy?"

"Isn't astrology the same thing?"

She chuckled and shook her head. "No, astronomy is a branch of science that studies space. Astrology is like zodiac signs. I thought you were trying to ask me for my sign."

He let out a loud laugh. "Oh no, did I just sound like a total idiot?"

She smiled and shook her head. "No, you're fine. I was just thoroughly confused."

They pulled up in front of her house in no time. She was grateful for that. She was more than ready to call it a night. She unbuckled her seatbelt, ready to climb out, but stopped when he spoke.

"I had fun," he told her. She looked at him hesitantly. She wanted to say something equally as kind and genuine, but she couldn't think of a single word. Lucky for her, he went on. "Maybe we could do it again sometime. Except, maybe it could be just me and you."

Piper was somehow even more speechless than before. How was she supposed to respond to that? She didn't particularly want to go on this date, and while Brent turned out to be much nicer than she expected, a second one wasn't all that appealing to her.

She didn't have an answer for him, so she smiled and nodded politely.

"Thank you for driving me home," she said. He flashed her a grin.

"Anytime."

She climbed out of the truck and trotted up the walkway to the front door. She let herself in and shut the door without glancing behind her. She listened to the sound of the truck pulling away and getting quieter and quieter as it disappeared down the street.

She was prepared to climb in bed and sleep until monday.

CHAPTER SEVEN

Piper had never really had a crush. Out of all the lovely folks she'd laid eyes on in her life, none of them left an impression lasting enough for her to be romantically attracted to them. It wasn't for lack of worthy suitors. There were plenty of people she admired for their beauty. But beauty wasn't enough to entrance her. Her heart was looking for something more. She didn't know if there was more out there.

In middle school, when all the girls would sit together and talk about their crushes, Piper felt out of place. She would sit there and twiddle her thumbs the whole time while they fought over the handsomest guy, or vowed to marry the smartest. Occasionally, when asked, she would pick a random boy and throw his name out so they'd leave her alone. It always worked. They'd squeal and nod in agreement and it made her feel more included in the group, but she couldn't shake the feeling that she was missing out on something.

That's what Piper was thinking about in Hally's red convertible the following Monday. The top was down, music was playing, and Hally was raving about boys. Everything was as it was supposed to be.

Hally always had a crush. She'd always initiated the boy talks in middle school, and she still did. She liked talking things out. No matter what it was (good, bad, or downright weird), she preferred to lay it all out on the table. While her main way to channel that was by talking about guys, no topic was off the table. She talked herself (and Piper) out of a lot of rough times.

"I mean, he's just beautiful, isn't he?" Hally was saying. She was tapping her acrylic nails against the steering wheel, her eyes dreamy. She was as done up as she usually was. She had on red heels with ankle length white socks. She had a white long sleeve on under a red velvet dress with buttons going down the centre. She had cherry earrings dangling from her earlobes and crimson lipstick to match. Piper thought it was ironic that this elegant creature was calling someone else beautiful.

"He's like a prince. He's so handsome and I love his voice. He has such a nice way of talking. He hardly says a word, though. Not that I care, I just like looking at him." She went on and Piper listened to her rambling dutifully.

"It sounds like you really like him," Piper commented stupidly, as if that fact wasn't incredibly apparent as is. Hally rolled her eyes.

"How could I not? Come on, P. Indulge my boy talk for a couple more minutes. You'll survive it."

Piper sighed, but nodded. It was blatantly obvious to both of them that she wasn't any good at this kind of talk. Even with her years of practice, she never quite got the hang of it. It was hard for her to agree on the attractiveness of a guy she, herself, wasn't attracted to.

"So," Hally prompted, "What do you think of Brent?"

Piper shrugged. "He's cool."

"Cool?"

"Yeah. He's a cool guy."

Hally wasn't satisfied with that answer. She huffed dramatically and started again. "Do you like him?"

Piper wasn't sure how to answer that. She thought she liked him. She just wasn't sure that she liked him enough.

"Yeah," she answered anyway. "I like him."

"Good. Because he really seemed to like you."

Piper snorted. "I didn't think you were paying attention. You did have a dude stuck to your face the whole time."

Hally laughed and swatted at Piper's arm playfully with one hand, the other one clutching the wheel. They swerved ever so slightly and Hally pulled her hand back to keep the car steady.

"I'm your best friend. I notice everything!" she announced. They pulled up in the school parking lot and Hally parked far away from the entrance. She always did, since she was nervous someone would bump her car and scratch it. Once the car was stopped, she turned her body fully sideways to face Piper.

"He drove you home," she said suggestively, eyebrows wiggling like two dancing caterpillars.

Piper nodded. "Yeah. So?"

Hally waved her hand in a circular motion as a way of telling Piper to go on. "What happened?"

Piper chuckled. Hally was always so curious. Whenever something happened, she wanted every detail. But, there was nothing to tell this time around.

"Nothing," she admitted. "He drove me home and we talked a little."

"About what?"

"Driving."

Hally made a disappointed face. "Driving?"

"He's a nervous driver. Oh, and he took an astronomy class."

Hally huffed. She didn't bother hiding her disappointment. It wasn't the juicy answer she was hoping for. "Did you even have a good time?" she asked, exasperated.

Piper stared at her friend. Clearly, Hally felt some responsibility, whether Piper fell head over heels or wanted the guy dead. But she was somewhere in between. She didn't have much of an opinion on him, and the night was okay. Overall, she was pretty indifferent. She would have been fine staying home and going to bed early just the same. In fact, she was certain she would've liked that better.

But she didn't want Hally to feel bad. The date was her idea, afterall. So she said, "I had a fun time. He's a good guy."

Hally beamed ear to ear, her frustration and disappointment disappearing entirely. She playfully punched Piper in the arm, looking overly proud of herself.

"Well, you have a funny way of showing it," she teased. She was smirking and twirling her hair around her fingers. "Who knew I was such a good matchmaker?" she said.

Piper shook her head incredulously. *She certainly got over that quick.* "Whatever you say," she muttered. "Can we go in now? We'll be late for the first period. Again."

"Fine," Hally groaned, then jabbed a finger with a glittery nail at Piper. "But you better not be leaving anything out!" Her threats were playful and meaningless, that was easy to tell. Either way, Piper had told her everything there was to tell.

"I didn't leave anything out," she confirmed. "Promise."

Hally looked satisfied. She grabbed her bag and took the keys out of the ignition. With finality, she announced, "Good! Now let's go."

They both hopped out of the car and strolled into the school together, just like every morning.

The first few periods, Joseph chatted with Piper like any other day, but he must've known she was still preoccupied, because he wasn't angry that she wasn't really listening to him. Then again, Piper had never seen Joseph angry.

When they left the classroom, Joseph walked beside Piper for longer than he usually did. Normally, he'd part ways with her and go off to sit with his own friends at recess. This time, though, he stuck by her side.

Piper tried not to be rude, but she guessed that by the way she looked at him, he'd heard the unasked question.

He stumbled on his words as he said, "Uh, sorry, I just... my friend isn't here today, and I was hoping to hang out with you...? I don't know, I should have asked, you don't want—"

"It's fine," Piper replied, cutting him off. It wasn't that she didn't want him to sit with her, it was just odd that he wanted to. He never did before. "Come sit with me."

Joseph smiled widely and followed Piper to the cafeteria. She didn't feel very hungry, so instead of going to the canteen and buying food, she just sat down beside Hally.

"Hey," Hally greeted, not looking up from her cellphone. "Why's he here?" She nodded toward Joseph.

"This is Joseph. I think you guys have met before."

"Brent and Drew are sitting with us, too," Hally said,

sounding indifferent as if she hadn't heard Piper at all. "Is that okay?"

"Yeah, totally." But, Piper didn't really feel like talking to Brent. He was perfectly nice, but she just didn't want to pretend to pay attention. She didn't want to force a smile and a laugh and nod along to a conversation she only half knew the context of. If it was just her, Hally, and Joseph there'd be no forcing. She could sit there in trance the whole time and neither of them would say a word against it. They were two people who at least had a basic understanding of her. Brent and Drew were new. They didn't have their Piper Crash Course yet.

She felt bad that day. There was no other way to put it. The feeling came out of nowhere, catching her off guard like usual. It was a bad feeling without cause or reason, so for now, she just had to live in it.

Still, she didn't protest. Brent and Drew sat down at the table, and even though there was a whole other side of the table with only Joseph sitting at it, they sat next to Piper and Hally, in quite an uncomfortable closeness.

"Hey," Brent said, flashing a shiny grin at her. She smiled back, half-heartedly.

"Hi. I, uh, have that book I promised you." She pulled out her backpack and unzipped it, pulling out her copy of *The Outsiders* and handing it to him. She might have felt more remorse about lending it to someone else, but the day before she gave it to him, she finished rereading it. That way she wouldn't miss it too much. He took it and looked it over, flipping through the pages idly for a moment. His eyes didn't land on any sentence or word. It seemed more like he was estimating how long he'd have to spend reading it.

"Cool," he said. "Thanks."

"Just, don't bend the corners of the pages," she instructed. "Use a bookmark."

He nodded, chuckling quietly.

"What?" Piper asked. She didn't recall saying anything funny.

"You're adorable."

"Oh." Piper scanned his face for the source of this sudden compliment, but didn't find one. She wished he didn't say it. She nodded as a thank you, unsure of how to respond.

"So, can I see you again? Soon?" He asked. His voice was shy, with a hint of urgency. Piper shifted in her seat.

"You're looking at me right now."

He laughed again. She felt tired. "I meant, outside of school. A date. Can we go out on a date sometime soon?"

Piper smiled, but she didn't mean it. She figured she should want to see him again. He was a good looking guy. A nice guy. Plus he seemed to really like her. What was holding her back?

She was still unsure of herself.

She accepted his offer anyway.

CHAPTER EIGHT

Piper's chest felt tight. She was getting ready to go on her date with Brent and while she wasn't nervous about seeing him specifically, she was nervous about being on a date. Their double date wasn't a big deal, but this particular night, they'd be alone. She wasn't sure how she felt about that, but so far it wasn't a good feeling.

She avoided it the best she could. It was tempting to cancel altogether, but she made a promise to herself she'd at least try. Maybe something good would come out of it? Maybe the uneasiness and awkwardness were just signs that she liked him? Still she pushed the date back as far as she could without actually cancelling it. By the time it came around, it was late October, almost Halloween.

She had a hard time deciding what to wear. She didn't want to get dressed up—they were only going to a movie. Jeans and a t-shirt didn't seem appropriate either, though. Hally always looked perfect on her dates. She always knew what to wear. *Was there some kind of dress code?* Piper wondered. She'd pulled everything out of her closet in an effort to find something fitting for such an occasion. Her room was a disaster. She wished Hally would pick out her clothes for her. She was much better at it.

Piper gave up after an hour and decided that Hally should, in fact, pick out her clothes for her.

"What the fuck do I wear?" she asked urgently before Hally got the chance to say anything. She heard her friend laugh.

"You can't dress yourself?" Hally teased. Piper groaned and collapsed onto her bed.

"Not for a date," she complained. "Remind me why I said yes to this?"

"You like him?"

Nope, that's not it. "Right."

"What are you going to do tonight?" Hally asked. Piper closed her eyes. She considered cancelling. She could plug her nose and call him, cough a couple times to sell the facade that she was too ill to see him. It probably wouldn't work. She wasn't very good at lying and she took drama for a solid two months before switching to chemistry.

"We're going to see a movie," she said flatly.

Hally hummed. "You mean you're going to make out."

"No," Piper corrected, "I mean we're going to see a movie."

"We'll see about that."

Piper rolled her eyes, fully aware that Hally couldn't see her. She had no intentions of making out with Brent on their date. She'd go out with him, see the movie and he'd drive her home. End of story. Non-negotiable.

"Well, you'll be sitting down the whole time, so you can wear heels or something," Hally said, "As for the rest of the outfit, just wear something comfortable and cute."

"*Comfortable and cute* means nothing to me. Give me specifics."

"Fine. Do you have a skirt?"

Piper got up from her bed. She put her phone on speaker and laid it on her dresser. She rummaged through the few relatively untouched drawers. She went through girl scout uniforms, school spirit t-shirts, and halloween costumes, until she found a single skirt. The only problem was that it was a white pleated skirt that was at least three sizes too small. She remembered her dad buying it for her as a part of her Halloween costume when she was twelve. She was Draculaura from *Monster High*. It definitely wasn't her style now and even if it was, there was no way in hell she'd fit into it.

"I don't have a skirt," she said, dropping the skirt back into the drawer and picking her phone back up.

Hally sighed. "I swear, one of these days I'm going to buy you a whole new wardrobe and throw away everything you have now. Don't fret, baby girl. I'll be right over."

Piper exhaled, feeling a mixture of relief and dread. She hung up on Hally and made a valiant effort to clean her room while she waited.

In classic Hally fashion, she immediately showed up with a hot pink duffle bag. The only times she managed to not be late was when Piper needed her. She didn't knock. She let herself in and ran up the stairs, into Piper's room. She pushed the bag into Piper's arms and looked around the room in awe.

"Did a tornado hit?" she asked, hands on her hips. Piper huffed.

"It feels like it." She unzipped the bag and pulled out it's contents. It was a simple black skirt, a pair of argyle knee high socks, black heels and an earth-toned knitted sweater. Piper smiled.

"You're a lifesaver," she said.

"I know. Now, get dressed."

Piper did as she was told. She changed as quickly as she could. She realized she was cutting it close; he would be there any minute. When she was dressed, Hally gave her a little applause and some playful catcalling to ease her nerves. It didn't do much to help. She wasn't worried about looking bad. She was nervous about seeing him. Being alone.

She brushed her hair and braided the front section back, leaving the rest down. She went through every purse she had (which wasn't very many—She should have asked Hally to bring one of those, too) until she found one she didn't hate and slid on the heels. She couldn't really walk in them (she probably looked like Bambi on ice) but it was good enough. Just like Hally said, she'd be sitting the whole time anyways.

She heard a car pull up outside. The tightness in her chest felt constricting. She looked at Hally for guidance, but only got encouragement.

"Go get 'em!" she exclaimed. She gave Piper a thumbs up, as if that would do anything to help her. Piper gained some courage anyway (she had to make it out of nothing, like spinning straw into gold).

She whipped down the stairs and left the house, only pausing to shout to her dad that she was leaving.

The moment she left the house she came face to face with Brent. He was holding up a fist, just about to knock.

"Oh! Sorry," she said. She took a step back as she shut the door behind her to give him some room. He smiled and let his hand fall down to his side.

"No problem. You seem excited," he said with a laugh.

"Uh, yeah. What movie are we seeing?" she asked,

sliding past his statement so she didn't have to address it. She brushed past him toward his car, which was parked on the curb in front of her house. He followed after her.

"They're playing some old horror movies for Halloween," he told her, falling into step beside her, "So we have a few options. They're showing *The Shining, Psycho, The Texas Chainsaw Massacre* and *Jaws*."

They got to the car and he opened the passenger door for her. As she got in, she said, "*Jaws* is not scary."

"I was terrified of it as a kid." He closed the car door and she watched as he rounded the vehicle to the driver's side. He got in and turned to face her. "How do you not find it scary?"

"The special effects are so bad, it's almost laughable. I saw it with Hally when I was eleven and we just made fun of it the whole time."

He shook his head incredulously at her. He turned forward to face the road and turned the key in the ignition. The car roared to life and he drummed his fingers on the steering wheel with a thoughtful look.

"So *Jaws* is off the table," he said, "What about the others?"

Piper shrugged. She wasn't a huge fan of horror movies. Of those options, *Jaws* was the only one she knew. She usually didn't watch horror movies for Halloween. In her opinion, the best Halloween movies were vaguely spooky children's movies (bonus points if they're animated). To her, Halloween wasn't about being scared. It was about eating junk food, watching creepy stop motion films and enjoying the eerie yet cozy feeling the holiday had.

"You choose," she replied. "I have no preference."

"Do you want to see *The Shining*?"

"Sure."

"Cool."

Piper was unsurprised by the awkward silence that followed. She didn't know what to say. He was driving slowly and nervously, just as he did before. She was tempted to talk about Steven King, since the movie they were seeing was based on his novel, but she assumed that her weirdly encyclopedic knowledge about famous authors wouldn't interest him as much as it interested her.

She settled for wallowing in the silence. They spent the entire car ride wrapped in quiet.

CHAPTER NINE

When Piper returned to school the following week, the building was sprinkled with Halloween decorations. There were ghosts, pumpkins, bats and black cats. The walls and doorways were trimmed with spiderweb bunting and signs that said "Trick or treat!" and "BOO!" She smiled to herself as she took it all in. It was a surprising amount of work for a school that did the bare minimum when it came to academics. She was actually impressed. But it was the same type of "impressed" as when a four-year-old colours within the lines; it was better than she expected because her expectations were so low.

"How cheesy is this?" Hally complained.

"Pretty cheesy," Piper replied with a grin. She liked Halloween at school. Especially when the teachers dressed up. Oddly enough, it made them less scary to her.

The school sent out an email telling everyone to dress up. At first, Piper was just going to get a random mask from a nearby Halloween store and call that a costume, but Hally had the perfect two person costume for them. She called Piper the night before and demanded that they be Ursula and Ariel from *The Little Mermaid*. Piper was hesitant at first—she didn't like the idea of wearing a shell bra to school—but Hally assured her it would be simple and school appropriate. She ended up wearing a purple top and a pair of green jeans. Her hair wasn't as red as Ariel's and she still had to wear her glasses, but overall it wasn't a bad costume.

That is, until it was up against Hally's.

Hally had on a black body con dress that hugged her body gently. She had a pair of purple heels, a gold necklace and purple conch shell earrings. Her eyeshadow was blue and her lips were red. She even added the black mole below her bottom lip to make the costume as accurate as possible. She pinned her hair up loosely and while it wasn't white like Ursula's, it was still the perfect costume for her to steal the show in.

Piper noticed Joseph walking down the hall and broke away from Hally's side to catch up with him. He was in a white frilly shirt, brown faux leather vest, black pants and long brown boots. He had a tan holster around his waist and a black hat with a skull and crossbones on it. As she got nearer, she noticed smudged eyeliner around his eyes.

"Hey," she greeted. He looked up from staring at his shoes and smiled at her. "Great costume."

"Thanks," he said. "I wanted to be Captain Jack Sparrow but my hair is a tad too short so I had to settle for Generic Walmart Pirate."

She chuckled. "Well, I think it's great."

His smile widened. She almost swore he was blushing.

"Thank you. You look great, too. Ariel, right?"

"Bingo. Not my best costume, but better than plan A."

He nodded in understanding, his eyes trained on her.

She had a feeling he was trying to work something out but she didn't know what. She didn't get the chance to ask before he said something about it.

"I take it your date went well?" he prompted. She was slightly taken off guard. She'd mentioned her and Brent's movie date to Joseph the Friday before she went. Being school-exclusive friends, their main topic of discussion was weekend plans. And while she had no issue telling him, she didn't expect him to actually care.

"Why do you say that?"

"You just seem to be in a good mood, is all."

She shook her head firmly. "It has nothing to do with my date, trust me."

"You didn't have a good time?"

"It was kind of awkward," she admitted honestly. Even after their prolonged silence in the car, the night didn't get any better. Any time they tried to talk, either one of them didn't understand what the other was talking about or they had very differing opinions on the subject. Not to mention that every conversation ended in a tense silence. She still thought of him as a nice guy—he was a real gentleman on their date, she couldn't deny that—but he definitely wasn't the guy for her. She was just glad that the date was so obviously bad that there was no way he'd want to see her again.

"Oh, I'm sorry," Joseph said. He didn't look very sorry.

She shook her head. "Don't be. I didn't expect true love anyway."

He smiled sympathetically. Was she supposed to be upset that the date went bad? Hally probably would've been, but Piper didn't care all that much. She felt a little bad for Brent. Though, there was no doubt in her mind that he'd find someone else. Someone he had more in common with, hopefully.

"Are you going trick-or-treating?" Joseph asked. Piper stifled a laughed.

"No way. I'm way too old for that."

"You're only as old as you feel, Evans."

"Yeah? Well I feel seventy already, so I'll pass."

He chuckled. "What will you do instead?"

"Eat an entire bag of snack size chocolate bars, watch *Frankenweenie* and go to bed early."

"Careful, the cops might get called."

"What can I say? I'm a maverick." She was in an explicitly good mood that day for whatever reason. She didn't have an explanation. She didn't have a very good weekend and being in school wasn't on her top ten of favourite activities. Yet she still felt pretty good. It was a rare feeling, so she decided to savour it instead of question it. "I take it, since you're asking, that you are going?"

He nodded eagerly. "Of course! I'll be trick-or-treating until someone calls the police on the grown man begging for candy." The bell rang, signalling it was time for class. Luckily, they were together for the first period anyway, so they strolled in the direction of their class. "I mean come on! It's free food, first and foremost. But not only that. Walking the streets at night on Halloween is like being on a different planet. The only lights are coming from the houses because there aren't a lot of cars driving around— especially in those subdivisions where everyone just gets dropped off. And there's pumpkins and crunchy leaves and those giant blow up ghosts and skeletons on people's lawns. It's awesome."

She listened to him intently, totally amused by his adoration. "Wow, you really like Halloween."

"It's the best holiday."

She smiled and nodded. "I have to agree."

Her town was having it's Halloween festival. And just like every other year, Piper was indulging in the feeling of being excited. She didn't get excited for a lot of stuff, but the Halloween festival was always fun. It went on every year and there was always something new to see. They had snacks and games and costume contests. They brought in small, rickety rides and had actors from the community theatre play ghouls in the haunted house. She loved every moment of it. And even though her costume wasn't great, she still looked forward to showing it off.

The festival was crawling with small children when she first arrived but she knew that by dark, they'd all be gone trick-or-treating. That would be the best part of the night; all the lines would be short, stars would litter the sky and the moon would be front and centre to watch them play.

She went with Hally but ended up alone early on. She didn't blame her too much. Hally went to see Drew, but Brent was with him, so Piper didn't feel like tagging along. She thought it would be awkward after their date.

She wandered the festival alone, taking in the smell of cinnamon, fresh popcorn and exhaust from the few thrill rides. Not the most pleasant mixture, but it was enough to spark some nostalgia in her.

The festival had hay bales lining the walkway. There were booths scattered around that had everything from food, to games, to fortune telling. None of them particularly caught her eye. For the time being, she was merely an observer. There was something at the festival for everyone, she just didn't find her thing yet. Last year she spent an embarrassing amount of time (and money) at the fortune teller's booth. The worst part was, she knew she was being scammed the whole time. She just liked living in that fantasy, if only for a little while. It was nice to pretend clairvoyance was real, and everything this woman told her was true. Of course, none of the predictions came true. She did not "come into a large sum of money" nor "meet a very important stranger."

This time, she avoided the fortune teller's booth like the plague.

Instead, she wandered over to the haunted house. It wasn't actually a house. It was a large black tent with fake spider webs hanging off of it. There was a man dressed like the headless horseman posted outside the door. You could see the smoke from the fog machine leaking out from under the curtain and hear hollers from inside the tent. The line was relatively long and it only grew behind her. She had high expectations, considering the crowd that was building outside of it.

"Jesus, this line tripled in ten minutes."

Piper turned her head when she heard the voice. She didn't recognize it and wasn't sure if they were speaking to her. When she laid eyes on its owner, she almost lost her breath.

The girl had black and purple hair, hazel eyes, a cheeky smile. Piper recognized her; the girl from the coffee shop. She hardly had an interaction with her that day—eye contact wasn't exactly an interaction—and yet the girl's face was familiar. Like someone she'd known a long time.

Piper opened her mouth to speak but she saw a realization spread across the girl's face that made her close it again.

"Wait a second, I recognize you," she said, her grin

widening. "Hot Chocolate Girl! How's your lip?"

Piper turned beet red. What a humiliating thing to be recognized for. She didn't even know how to respond to that. How was she supposed to respond? *"It's okay, the blister went away pretty quick."* She definitely couldn't say that.

Again, the girl went on before Piper spoke up. Piper was endlessly grateful.

"Sorry, that's a weird question," she chuckled and Piper found herself smiling at her. The girl had this contagious, friendly grin that was impossible to not reciprocate. "I like your costume."

Piper looked down at her costume as if she didn't know what she was wearing. She blinked and collected herself enough to reply.

"Thanks," she replied.

"Have you done this haunted house before?"

"Sort of," Piper answered. The line moved, so the two of them took a step forward in sync. "I mean, I've done the haunted house a couple times. But it changes every year. It's never the same two years in a row."

"Awesome," she said, glancing toward the tent. "I've never done it before. This is actually my first time at the festival."

Piper raised a brow. Everyone in town went to the festival. "Did you just move here?"

"Not really," the girl replied. "I lived one town over for most of my life, so I'm familiar with everything around here. I just don't like Halloween very much."

Piper tried to act like that wasn't a horribly offensive thing to hear. She asked, "Oh? Why not?"

The girl shrugged as the line moved again. "It was never my favourite holiday. We didn't celebrate it much at my house when I was a kid."

"Oh," Piper muttered. She couldn't imagine not celebrating Halloween. Ever since she was little, she loved it with all her heart. Her favourite movie when she was little was *Coraline*, which didn't make her overly popular.

Piper noticed the girl wasn't even in a costume. She was in black jeans and a faded flannel. She really didn't like Halloween.

"No costume?" Piper prompted.

The girl smiled and shook her head. "Not really my thing."

"It's Halloween!"

"Just another Monday to me."

"That's so sad."

The girl laughed and Piper swelled with pride.

"Maybe you can help me find one here," she said. Piper felt her cheeks and ears heating up. She swallowed and nodded wordlessly. Something about this girl made it impossible for Piper to do anything. To talk, or listen or generally function as a normal human being. It was a good malfunction, though. If there was such a thing.

They were next in line. Piper was ahead of her, so she assumed she'd be let in alone. But the man in front of the entrance opened the curtain and said, "Go on in, ladies."

They exchanged a look, but didn't protest. They walked in together, side by side as they were engulfed in the darkness of the tent. The lighting was very low, only a few fake candles to light their path. They had cheesy decorations like angry jack-o-lanterns and skeletons, but some of their stuff was actually scary. They had lage (barely moving) animatronics of clowns and demons and creepy children. Piper was fully ready to make a fool out of herself.

"Is it just me, or is this way scarier than you expected?" the girl said. Piper laughed and nodded in agreement. The girl took a step closer to her, and Piper lost her breath again. "Stay close. I hope we make it out alive."

Piper had a hard time focusing on the haunted house all of a sudden.

They walked through slowly, trying to avoid stepping on the motion sensors. Whoever set everything up did a bad job hiding them. You could see the words "Step here" on the black pads on the ground. There wasn't a lot of room though, so they were bound to step on them anyway. They stepped on a sensor and didn't even notice until a large animatronic spider leapt out at them. They both let out a shriek. Piper jumped away from it and ended up knocking shoulders with the girl beside her. For a second, she was going to apologize for it. Then she heard her laughing and her worry melted away. Without realizing, Piper started laughing with her.

As they ventured their way through the rest of the haunted house, they were more overcome with humour and joy than fear. Every time they set off an animatronic they still screamed, but they also burst into a fit of laughter, leaning on each other to keep themselves from doubling over. By the time they made it out, Piper's throat hurt from laughing and her cheeks had streaks of tears on them.

"Holy shit," the girl said. Her voice sounded scratchy. She definitely laughed as hard—if not harder—than Piper. "That was fucking awesome!"

"I know! That giant clown was terrifying! I thought it was a real person!"

"I couldn't tell if he was going to kill us or make us a balloon animal."

Piper rolled her eyes playfully. "What kind of terrifying clowns came to your birthday parties?"

"Let's just say I had an eventful childhood."

There was a beat of comfortable quiet between them, even if the festival around them was loud and chaotic. Their little part of it was a still pond without a single ripple.

The girl took a breath before she broke the silence.

"So… are you still up to help me find a costume?" she asked. Piper tried not to let her smile split her face in half. She nodded eagerly, watching the girl grin. "Perfect. Let's do it."

The crowd was even more dense on the other side of the haunted house, probably because of the sheer volume of people who went through the tent. They walked side by side through the crowd toward the booths. They managed to weave through all the people so they could get a good look at the items up for sale.

Piper looked through all the accessories. None of them really suited her new friend. The girl definitely didn't look like someone to wear animal ears and her hair was cool enough on its own, so she didn't need a wig. Piper took a good long look at all of the options before she found the perfect non-costume costume: a small black witch hat with purple lace wrapped around it.

Without hesitating, she picked up the hat and laid it in front of the saleswoman. She dug through her pockets for some money and dropped it onto the table. She told the lady to keep the change and turned around excitedly to the girl but—

Where did she go?

Piper realized she hadn't kept a very good eye on her companion. Somewhere between the haunted house and the booth, the girl had been swallowed up in the crowd, leaving Piper alone but completely surrounded.

CHAPTER TEN

When Piper got home that night, her mind was totally preoccupied. She slinked through the front door like a zombie, her mind buzzing from her headache. As much as she loved the Halloween festival, the aftermath was exhausting. Especially with school the following day.

She found her dad and his girlfriend, Laura, sitting on the couch watching a horror movie. All the lights were off in the house, so the only light was coming from the television. She also noticed the empty candy bowl sitting beside the front door. They must have had a lot of trick-or-treaters. Either that or her dad just got impatient and hungry. That was way more likely.

She planned to sneak past the two of them so she wouldn't have to talk to them (mostly Laura. She wouldn't mind talking to her dad by himself). However, her dad had other plans. Right as she was about to make it past them scott-free, he called her name.

"Piper," he called, "You're home. Come in, tell me about the festival."

She mentally cursed him for being such a dutiful father, but managed to paint on a smile and do as she was told. She turned on her heel and stepped into the living room, turning on the light fixture above them. They paused their movie and looked at her expectantly.

"It was great," she answered honestly.

Her dad didn't look satisfied with that answer. He gestured for her to go on and she shrugged.

"It was fun. They had all the usual stuff that's there every year. You should have come." She knew that was a little underhanded, but she didn't really care.

Her dad, Samuel, was supposed to go to the festival with her. He usually made an appearance, even if he did leave early (especially since he had met Laura). but this year, he didn't go at all. To make it worse, he didn't tell Piper he wouldn't be there. Not that she noticed his absence much, anyway. She certainly didn't miss him at the haunted house. But still. It felt like this woman was ruining their family traditions more and more all the time.

She noticed her dad bite his tongue. She was almost proud of herself for leaving him speechless, but she also felt guilty. Laura, surprisingly, was the one who spoke up.

"We'll have to go next year," she said, "All of us together. That would be fun, right?" She looked at Samuel for approval, but he was definitely not the one she should have been asking. Piper tried to swallow the angry tingling in her stomach.

"That'd be great," Samuel agreed. The tingling was turning into a pain so Piper huffed.

"It's been a long day," she announced, "I'm going to bed."

She could see both of their reactions. Laura was mostly oblivious, but Samuel knew something was wrong. His daughter was polite. Bubbly. She didn't abruptly leave in the middle of a conversation. At this point he knew very well what Piper's opinion of his girlfriend was, even if neither of them had the guts to say it.

She left the living room and made her way into her bedroom. She shut the door and collapsed into her bed. She wasn't lying when she said it was a long day, even if it was only an excuse to get away. She wanted some peace and quiet. Some silent time to reflect.

That lasted thirty seconds.

She heard a knock on her door and groaned, burying her face in her pillow. She heard the door open and shut and a moment later, she felt the bed sink as someone sat down beside her. She begrudgingly turned around to face her father.

"Are you upset that I didn't go to the festival with you?" he asked. She hated when he used that voice. It was the voice of a single parent, stretched thin. She knew that, reasonably, he couldn't do everything. He had his own life. He couldn't keep tagging along with her like she was a little kid. Still, it hurt. It wasn't so much that she was growing up. It was the fact that he was.

She sighed and shook her head. "No."

"It's okay if you are," he insisted, "You can tell me."

But she wasn't. It wasn't about the festival. It was about that woman and everything she stood for.

"I'm not upset," she said. He pushed some of her hair away from her face gently, laying a hand on her cheek the way he did when she was little. Back then, his hand would cover the side of her face. The calluses on his palm seemed massive, almost the size of her eye. Now, she hardly noticed them.

"You're so grown up," he said. She smiled sadly at him. She didn't like the reminder, but she couldn't imagine how hard it must be for him. To watch your child grow up. To feel their independence growing and them slipping away from you. She hoped he never felt like she didn't need him. Because she did. More than he could ever know.

"I remember going to the Halloween festival when you were too small to go on any of the rides, and way too picky to try any of the snacks," he laughed at the memory. "All the other kids your age wanted to leave early in the night. But not you. You wanted to stay and see all the costumes and go through the haunted house over and over."

Piper didn't really remember the night in question, but she remembered how she felt. She remembered the magic and euphoria of this unknown world. She remembered clinging to her dad's arm whenever something jumped out at them. It wasn't that she was scared. She just didn't want to lose him.

"We'll go next year, I promise," he assured her. He went to get up, but she grabbed his arm, her face serious.

"Just us, right?"

He hesitated for a moment. Maybe it was an unfair request to make, but she wasn't ready to give up everything they shared. Not yet.

She thought he'd sigh and have a serious conversation with her about her stubbornness, but instead he leaned down, kissed her forehead and affirmed, "Just us."

She smiled and released him. He was on his way out when he stopped and turned around in the doorway.

"I almost forgot. Your mom called while you were out. She's going to call you back on your phone in the next couple of days."

Her stomach dropped.

CHAPTER ELEVEN

To say Piper was waiting by the phone would be the understatement of the century. She left her ringer on during school hours to make sure she wouldn't miss the call. She slept with it on the pillow so it would wake her up if it rang. She wished she wouldn't obsess over it so much, but this was a rare occasion. She assumed the worst; *could she be in serious financial trouble? Was she in the hospital? Could she be in prison?* She rarely got phone calls from her mother that weren't serious or, on the off chance she remembered, a holiday. Halloween wasn't a holiday that her mother called her for. Could it be early Christmas? Was she trying to scope out what to get her daughter? That would be better than a crisis call.

She must not have been hiding her obsession very well because Hally pointed it out when they were supposed to be studying together in the library. Piper was checking her phone to make sure the ringer was on and she hadn't missed any calls.

"Expecting a call?" Hally prompted, clearly suggesting something that most definitely didn't apply. Piper let out a breath and turned her phone face down so she'd stop staring at it.

"My mom called while we were at the festival," she said. "Dad said she's going to call me back in a few days."

"A few days? That's vague." Hally closed her textbook and rested her chin on her hand, effectively giving up on studying. Piper loved when her best friend gave her all of her attention like this. Even if it didn't ease her mind in this particular moment. "Do you know what she's calling about?"

"Nope. And it's driving me fucking insane. I don't know what she wants."

"Is it possible she doesn't want anything..? That she's just calling to check in?"

Piper shook her head. "No way. Not my mom."

Hally nodded in understanding. After all, if anyone would understand, it would be her. She saw the dramatic highs and lows of Piper's relationship with her mother. It was frustrating and sad and long. Very long. Never-ending, in fact. Her father kept pushing for them to mend the relationship and as much as Piper wanted to, she didn't think it was actually possible. Too much had happened.

There was a silence between them. There really wasn't anything to say. There wasn't much consoling you could do in a situation like this. But Hally had the perfect answer, unsurprisingly.

"Do you want to come over after school?" she asked. "We can rent *The Outsiders*. Dad is probably cooking something awesome."

Piper managed a smile. Hally took her hand and laced their fingers together to comfort her. The small gesture was enough to make her breathe easier.

"That sounds perfect."

As the day went on, Piper had that shining beacon of

hope to get her through the dread swallowing her up like a black hole. Whenever a problem seemed too big to solve, she always had her favourite book—and movie—to fix it. She knew this wouldn't be the exception to that rule.

She was still clinging to her phone for dear life, though. She was wandering the hallways like a ghost, waiting for school to end. She was staring down at her phone when she bumped into someone and immediately wished she phased through them.

She took a moment to regain some composure before she looked up to face Brent. He gave her a toothy grin the moment he met her eyes. She wished she could have done the same. She was more concerned with picking up her phone, which she'd dropped upon impact.

"Hey, stranger. Long time, no see," he said. That wasn't the most appropriate greeting. It hadn't, in fact, been a long time without seeing each other. Their date was still fresh in her mind. She assumed he just said that because of how awkwardly they left things.

"Uh, yeah. How was your Halloween?" she replied. She tried to pay attention to him while also scanning the floor for her cellphone.

"Kind of boring. Yours?"

"Mine was cool."

"Did you go to the festival? I was disappointed when I didn't see you there."

He was disappointed he—

Oh no.

No, no—

"Yeah, I was there."

He nodded his head slowly, looking even more disappointed, though he had a smile on his face still.

"Oh. I was hoping to see you there but I hadn't heard

from you after our date so I thought you might've needed some time."

Piper raised a brow, turning her full attention to him. "Needed time..?"

"Yeah. I mean our date was great, I definitely feel like we have a strong connection, you know? But I totally understand if you need to process this so we don't move too fast."

She couldn't believe what he was saying. Was she body swapped with a different girl? Was she on a totally different date than he was? Because that date was terrible. Terribly awkward and terribly uncomfortable. What '*strong connection*' was he feeling?

She opened her mouth to speak but he misinterpreted her hesitation.

"S-Sorry, I know this isn't the time or place. You take all the time you need to process, I'm patient. In the meantime, I'll be planning our next date. I was thinking… a picnic. What do you think?"

"Actually, I—"

The bell rang, cutting her off at the worst possible time. Realization passed his face before he said, "Shit, I've got a huge history test right now. I'll catch you later."

He started walking away and she began to follow him so she could say her peace.

"Brent, wait. I—"

There was a crunch under his shoe and he stopped, bent down and turned back to her.

"Hey, this is your phone, right?" he said. He handed it to her, smiled and then kept walking, leaving her in the dust. She paused. She looked down at her phone, which was close to unrecognizable with a shattered screen. She cursed as she tucked it into her pocket and decided that was a conversation for another day.

"What do you think about love?" Piper mused, laying flat on Hally's bed. Hally was sitting on a fluffy stool in front of her elegant vanity, using a flat iron to turn her hair into ringlet curls. The vanity before her was about as organized as the rubbish filled disaster formerly known as Piper's thoughts. They'd already watched *The Outsiders* (it did not disappoint) but it wasn't a permanent cure to her strife. She had multiple different apprehensions going through her head, but she only wished to voice the ones that were unrelated to her mom.

"That's a pretty broad question, P," Hally mumbled, tilting her head to one side as she rolled a thin chunk of hair around the iron. "Care to elaborate?"

"Do you think it's real?" she asked quickly. As soon as it left her mouth, she felt stupid for saying it. What kind of a question was that, anyway? The answer seemed obvious and yet she was completely in the dark. What was she meant to believe? And more importantly, where did she fit into the concept?

Hally scoffed at her, amused as she clipped a perfectly curled section to the top of her head. Piper remembered when her mother would do that, on the rare occasion that she was sober and willing to leave the house.

"Of course it's real," Hally declared confidently.

An opinion so strong, Piper thought, *and yet she has no room for doubt. How the hell does she do it?*

"But... how do you know?" Piper pressed on. Hally already seemed tired of the topic. Piper could imagine why; to her, it was like trying to convince someone the sky was blue.

"I don't know, Piper," she said. "I can feel it. Like the

stars. Even though I can't see them all the time, I always feel that they're there. Waiting for me."

Piper fell silent. *Could it be waiting for me too?*

Perhaps that was her curse: to never be satiated. Never fulfilled. Perhaps she'd spend the rest of her life—seventy years still, if she was as healthy as her grandparents—awaiting this mystical thing that everyone else had already found. She didn't see it; not the way Hally did. Love always eluded her, and her family for that matter. Love escaped the Evans family like a clever rabbit, fleeing a hungry fox. Maybe she never had a chance in the first place, since she was doomed to that bloodline. It was also possible that Hally was wrong, even if she'd never entertain the idea. It was possible that love was just a fictional concept, fabricated by the likes of Shakespeare and Jane Austen. A conspiracy-theory-like ploy made to woo little girls and boost little boys. Just another bullshit '*meaning of life*' perpetuated by every television show, novel, movie and perfume commercial that people ingested every day.

But it also struck Piper that, just because a concept was made up, didn't mean it wasn't real. If she wanted to be nihilistic, she could say everything was made up. It's not like the language and society they lived in today had always been that way. It was created, then developed constantly since humans first walked the earth. The only thing that could be created from nothing was Nothing. If love was Nothing, it was Something still, because enough people believed in it. Right?

Essentially, love is Tinkerbell?

She squeezed the bridge of her nose with her fingers. She'd thought herself into such a spiral, she was getting a headache.

"Aw, babe," Hally said, turning around on her stool to

check on her friend. "Are you alright?"

Maybe love was like a headache: you did it completely to yourself, yet it hadn't occurred to you that it was there until it already hurt.

CHAPTER TWELVE

She stared at her broken phone sadly. It still worked, but the screen was covered in cracks, making it hard to see anything it was displaying. It would still ring, though. That was what counted.

Two days later, she still had no word from her mother. It was getting to be more frustrating than it was distressing. Surely, if it was urgent she would have called by now.

Piper and Hally sat down in the cafeteria for lunch. She wasn't particularly hungry. She hadn't had much of an appetite since the night of the festival. The anticipation was killing her. She was overthinking it and that feeling was eating her alive.

"You have to eat something," Hally insisted. "I know you're upset, but you'll be more upset if you feel sick."

Piper didn't answer. It wasn't that she didn't want to eat, but her stomach turned whenever she was upset. Hally didn't experience that the same way Piper did. Her emotions didn't envelope her every sense. Her emotions didn't fill her stomach and ring in her ears and cloud her vision.

Piper would kill to be that way.

Hally silently pushed a container of apple slices toward Piper. She gave Piper a short pat on the back before turning to scrolling through her phone. Piper hesitated, but reached out and took a slice and ate it. Her stomach grumbled at the taste of it. She hadn't realized how hungry she was until she got something to eat. She dug in, pushing that sick feeling to the back of her mind.

She could feel the smugness radiating off of Hally. She decided it was best to ignore it.

She heard footsteps approaching the table. She cringed at the sound, trying to focus entirely on her apple so the rest of the world would cease to exist.

It didn't work.

The table rattled as two people plopped onto the seats across from them. Piper looked up at Brent and Drew.

I don't have the energy for this, she thought. She looked to Hally for help, but it was too late. Hally was knee deep in Drew's eyes by then.

"Is that your whole lunch?" Brent asked, drawing Piper's attention. Her lips felt tight so she just nodded. He furrowed his brow and said, "That's not a very big lunch. You'll be hungry later. Do you want something else?" She simply shook her head in response, but he wasn't convinced. "Are you sure? It's no problem, I don't mind going to buy something from the cafeteria." She shook her head again. He still didn't take it. "Don't be stubborn, it's not a big deal. Seriously. I'll go get it now and—"

"Brent!" she interrupted. Her voice came out louder than she expected. The conversation beside her halted immediately and she felt eyes scalding her skin. She shrunk in her seat, staring at her lunch, which suddenly looked more brown than before. "Drop it, okay?" she muttered. The silence stuck around, heavy, like they were waiting for something. *But what?* She couldn't offer them any-thing. She didn't have anything to give.

She stood from the table, slung her backpack onto her shoulder, and scurried out of the cafeteria like the fright-ened little mouse she was.

She gripped her backpack straps until her knuckles turned white and her hands cramped. She hated this. She hated what her mother made her do—

No, I can't blame my behaviour on her. That's not fair.

She hated how angry she felt in response. She never considered herself an angry person. At least, she hoped she wasn't. But when Brent was insisting after she'd said no, she felt a small snap. Like putting so much stress on a rubber band that it stings your skin when you release it. Her only comfort was that she controlled herself despite it. She didn't let herself be awful to him. He didn't deserve that.

For some reason, she went to her locker. Her next class wouldn't start for fifteen minutes so there was no sense in getting her books and going there now. So she dropped her backpack on the floor and sat down. The hallway was empty, therefore she felt no shame laying her head down on her knees.

She steadied her breathing. She was so frustrated. She was frustrated that her mother called during the festival. If she was a good mother, she would have known Piper wouldn't answer. She was frustrated that her father didn't call her the minute he got the call. If he was sensible, he would have known his ex wouldn't call back until it was convenient to her. Mostly she was frustrated that she expected more. If she wasn't so stupid, she would have known that having expectations was useless. It only broke her heart.

The echo of footsteps made her ball herself up more. She heard them get closer and closer and sighed.

"No, I don't want to talk about it," she grumbled, expecting to look up and see Hally. But when she did, she saw Brent. He stood sheepishly, one hand in his pocket and one on the back of his neck. He gave her a nervous smile. She widened her eyes. "Oh. Sorry, I thought you were Hally."

"Yeah, she was going after you but... I thought I should. Is that okay?"

Not really.

"I-I guess."

He took her reluctance as willingness. He sat beside her but left a comfortable amount of space between them. Well, as comfortable as a space can be when you want to be alone.

"I'm sorry," he said. "I didn't mean to be pushy."

She surprised herself when she managed a smile. It was shy and unsure and totally involuntary. But she appreciated what he'd said.

"It's okay," she said.

He paused, like he expected her to say a lot more. She didn't. He cleared his throat. "Is... is that it?"

"Yeah."

"You're not mad?"

"Not at you."

Instead of delving more into that, he just sighed in relief and let his head fall back against the locker door behind him.

"Thank fuck."

She wanted to sigh heavily and express just how much he missed the mark. But she couldn't expect him to understand what she didn't. So instead she stood up and opened her locker, as if she had something to get. He stood up with her.

"By your reaction, I thought you were totally pissed," he said. She didn't react to that. She didn't feel there was an appropriate way to react to such a claim. "Good thing you aren't. You're a real cool girl, Piper."

Cool girl, she thought. *That's a funny way of saying complacent.*

"Oh yeah, you leave your phone around a lot," he said. "Here. I think you missed a call." He held her phone out to her. She hesitated. Not because she didn't want it, but because she felt like snatching it out of his hand at rapid speed and scolding him for letting it ring and not picking it up. But she recognized that as an irrational thing to be mad about. She gently took it from his hand and thanked him. Then he went back to the cafeteria.

She turned on her phone to check who called and saw *"No Caller ID."* Which meant it was probably her mom, who was probably calling from someone else's phone, as she probably still didn't have one of her own.

Piper resisted the urge to throw her already broken phone in frustration. Instead she slipped it into her pocket and sat back down on the floor.

CHAPTER THIRTEEN

Piper didn't want to see anyone that weekend. Hally had invited her out but Piper didn't want to go. Luckily, Hally understood her situation pretty well so she didn't mind spending the weekend alone. Meanwhile, Piper was avoiding her father's girlfriend. She'd been in her room since Friday doing all manner of idle activities to keep her mind off of life, in general. The only thing keeping her moderately sane was one recent, pleasant memory; Halloween night.

She wished the memory hadn't been tainted the moment she got home, but she tried to separate the events. That way the good parts remained pure.

She wondered where that girl was now. She wished she'd gotten her name, at least. Everything about her was a huge question mark. She looked about Piper's age, but if they went to the same school, surely she would have stood out. Someone like her wouldn't slip under the radar very well. Unlike Piper, who was the human embodiment of the colour beige, she was radiant. The type of beautiful that sucked the air out of the room, with the type of charisma that filled it with sunshine. Or at least, that was what Piper thought of her in the short amount of time they spent together.

She didn't fully understand this feeling. She'd definitely had it before. It wasn't uncommon for her to be lost in a daydream. An idealized version of a person, especially a chance meeting such as this. So far, she had a 100% fail rate with that feeling. She wanted this time to be different. She wanted to solidify all these thoughts, that she hadn't twisted them to be better because she was sad and craved that person she made up.

But, I didn't make her up, Piper thought. *She's real. I remember her just as she was. I didn't change her.*

She glanced at her dresser, where the witch hat she'd bought sat. She took a breath and shook her head at herself. She grabbed the witch hat and dropped it into Hally's pink duffle bag (which she hadn't returned) and kicked it under the bed. She decided to keep it for her costume next year. She also decided to disregard any narrative she'd created in her head about the girl from the coffee shop. Two chance encounters didn't mean anything. At. All.

She let Saturday absorb her like a sponge. She stayed in her pyjamas and watched mindless television to fill the silence. She ate junk food and didn't do any of her homework. It was a refreshing way to spend a day, especially after the stress she was—and continued to be—under. It was a nice way to ignore what was actually going on and live in an isolated world for a little while.

She was enjoying this life, until her phone started ringing.

That familiar sick feeling returned to her stomach. She picked up her phone quickly and cautiously, like her actions would determine whether they'd hang up or not. She read the I.D. and confirmed her suspicion.

"No Caller I.D."

She took a breath. She was mostly scared that something awful had happened. Something she should have known about, if she was a good daughter who visited regularly. Some part of her really wanted to pick up the phone, though. Even if what she heard would be entirely disappointing.

She took a grand leap and answered, pressing the phone to her ear with white knuckles.

"Hello?" she managed. She heard a heavy breath on the other end that sounded like relief.

"Hi, Piper. It's your mother."

There was a shake in her hands, whether from excitement or anxiety, she couldn't tell. "Hi, Mom."

"Sorry I took so long to call you, I called you a few days ago but I couldn't reach you."

"It's fine." There wasn't any urgency in her mother's voice. That was good, right? That meant it probably wasn't something too terrible.

"How was the festival? Your dad said you were there when I called him."

"Good," Piper answered. She didn't realize she was smiling as she spoke, but it made sense. Her mother didn't usually care to ask a lot of questions, especially when she called with a purpose. "It might have been the best year yet. Even though dad didn't come."

"I'm surprised he didn't. When I called, I expected to get the voicemail."

"Yeah, he should have gone. He was at home with his girlfriend." Piper cringed. She didn't think about it before she said it, but when she did, she immediately realized it was probably a sore spot. In fact, she wasn't sure her mother even knew about Laura.

When her mother hesitated in answering, Piper said, "Sorry."

"No, it's okay," her mom said quickly. "He mentioned her on the phone, I already knew."

Piper paused. She wasn't sure what to say. Was this the point of the call? To talk about Halloween? That was unusual...

"I'm glad your father met someone, Piper," her mom went on. "I want him to be happy. And I want you to be happy, too. That's why I called."

Piper raised a brow, even though her mother couldn't see her expression. She cleared her throat and asked, "What do you mean?"

"I want to see you," she said. "I know it's been a while and I haven't been there for you. But I want to be in your life, if you'll let me."

Piper almost dropped the phone. That was totally out of left field. She wanted to... but why? What changed?

Before anything else, Piper started to ask, "Are you...?"

Her mother understood immediately. "I'm sober. I have been for a few months now."

"Really?" Piper pressed on.

"Yes," she said seriously. "Really. I promise. And I totally understand if you're not ready. Don't feel pressured to see me if you don't feel ready."

"When?"

"I'm sorry?"

"When did you want to see me?"

"Christmas break...? I already discussed the idea with your dad and he said it's fine with him if it's fine with you."

It seemed too good to be true. Everything was so easy.

Certainly something wasn't right. There had to be something to ruin it. Something to come out of nowhere and ruin the simplicity of it all. There always was.

Her mother got sober before. Her mother wanted to mend their relationship before. But obviously it didn't work out. If it had, this whole thing wouldn't mean anything. But this time, something in her voice sounded different. And it was a bold invitation if she wasn't confident in her abilities. Piper wasn't sure what to do. Was she ready? That was the biggest question in her mind.

Realistically, she wondered if she'd ever be ready. Would she keep putting it off and putting it off and never get the chance to fix things? She'd regret that forever, no doubt.

"I'll come," she said.

She could hear her mom let out a quiet gasp. It sounded like excitement. That warmed Piper's nervous heart.

"Okay! Wonderful! I'll see you in a few weeks?" Her mom replied, her voice shaky. Piper's smile widened a fraction.

"Yeah. see you then, Mom. Bye."

"Bye, Piper."

Piper hung up the phone and laid it down on her bed. She stared at her trembling hands. She wasn't sure what was going to happen, but this felt like the start of something. She didn't know if it was good or bad, but it was something, and that was what mattered

CHAPTER FOURTEEN

November was full of anticipation for everyone. It was a lull in the school year. A month with no good holidays, with normal length weeks and totally devoid of decorations. December was right around the corner and it taunted everyone. Whether they were excited for Christmas, Hanukkah, winter break or just the cold weather, December was the promiseland. It was quite literally the moment they'd all been waiting for. But November trickled out mind numbingly slow, like a leaky faucet.

"My dad listens to Christmas music every day while he's getting ready for work," Hally said. They were settling into class on time, for once. They were early, in fact. That was probably just because Hally didn't want to add to Piper's stress any more. Little did she know, most of that stress had been replaced with excitement.

Piper hadn't told Hally about Christmas break. She didn't want to tell anyone until it was set in stone. Part of her still expected her mom to call and change her mind any minute. It wasn't worth telling people when it was still up in the air.

"He's just excited," Piper replied. Hally plopped into her seat with a frown.

"Well, he's driving me insane. If I have to hear Mariah Carey's All I Want For Christmas Is *You* one more time pre-snow, I'm going to lose it."

Piper laughed. "Good luck with that. I'll remember that exact quote for the court hearing."

"You better not testify against me."

"I wouldn't dare. You'd come for me next."

Hally broke her grumpy look and let out a laugh. Piper sat down in the desk beside her, getting out her notebook now that she could focus on something other than her phone. Her mind was still occupied. It usually was, but at least now, she had some positive ideas. Even if they still felt unreal.

"What's up with you?" Hally asked. "You're certainly cheery. That's a big twist from last week."

Piper shrugged, though she couldn't wipe the smile off her face. "Nothing, I just had a really refreshing weekend."

"Refreshing?" Hally repeated incredulously. "What did you do, get a massage?"

"No, I just hung out."

Hally nodded, but she still looked suspicious. It was obvious Piper wasn't telling the whole truth. Piper couldn't keep anything hidden from her best friend. That was like trying to hide an elephant behind a telephone pole.

"Did your mom call?" Hally asked, changing the subject. Judging by the look on her face, she didn't seem to suspect a correlation between her mother and a good mood. That was valid, considering their past.

"No, she didn't," Piper lied. She felt bad, like she should have told the truth. She probably should have. But she would be disappointed enough by her mother cancelling. She didn't need the humiliation of admitting it to others.

"That sucks," Hally huffed. "Do you think she's going to?"

Piper shrugged. She hoped she wouldn't receive another call from her mother, unless it was a here's-what-time-you-should-arrive call.

Their teacher strolled into the classroom, drawing their conversation to a close, though Piper had a feeling it wasn't over. Hally was stubborn. It took a lot for her to drop something she was keen on knowing. She would prod and prod until she got what she wanted. It was as admirable a quality as it was obnoxious.

They settled in as the teacher pulled up a slideshow and the class let out a collective sigh of boredom.

At lunch, they had a full table again. Hally, Piper, Joseph, Drew, and Brent were all sitting together. Piper sat beside Hally and Joseph, with Drew and Brent on the other side. The topic of the day was the same topic on everyone's mind; Christmas.

"My parents are crazy about Christmas," Brent was saying. "They go all out every year, and we spend Boxing Day visiting all of our extended family. Christmas day is cool, but the rest of it is totally exhausting."

"We never visit anyone," Hally said. "My Dad says the holidays are for being with the people you love and he loves me, so why visit anyone else?"

"You don't have any other family?" Drew asked. It was clear to Piper that him and Hally hadn't done much talking since they started going out.

"I do. They just suck."

Drew nodded. "Fair enough."

"What about you, Joseph?" Piper asked. "What are your holiday traditions?"

"Well, my older sister is in New York for university so she'll fly in whenever her holidays start. We don't visit a lot of extended family, but my grandparents usually come over for Christmas dinner," he explained. Piper smiled.

"That sounds nice."

"It's always fun, even if my sister and my parents fight the whole time and my grandparents are the worst gift-givers ever. We have to save up a lot of money months before so we can actually afford a gift or two each and my parents act like they don't have money problems but still argue about it every Christmas Eve. I guess that's just how the holidays are. They're... messy."

Everyone unanimously agreed to that. Even Brent and Hally who were the more fortunate of the bunch to have both money and a somewhat symbiotic family dynamic. Piper didn't think about money very much around the holidays. She didn't really have to. Her dad bought the presents, decorations and all the fixings for Christmas dinner. All she had to do was dig in.

She never asked for much for Christmas. She didn't want a lot of stuff. So instead of him wasting money on a ton of gifts she didn't love, he only got her a few things she'd adore and get a lot of use out of. Hally always got piles of presents, and a small fraction of them were actually of use to her. She imagined it was the same for Brent.

Piper didn't miss how her friends didn't ask her or Drew about their Christmases. She understood why Joseph and Hally wouldn't ask her. Even if Joseph didn't know everything—not even close—he knew enough to not ask too much about her family life. She wondered why Brent and Hally hadn't asked Drew, but judging on their reasoning for not asking her, she thought it was safer to leave him alone.

"Last year, my mom got into a fight with her sister because she hung holly instead of mistletoe," Brent said. "It was ridiculous. It was a total screaming match and they never resolved anything. Then ten minutes later, they were baking cookies together like nothing happened."

Joseph nodded in understanding. "Yeah, my family will find any excuse to fight during Christmas. Last year, my sister didn't make her bed so my mom wouldn't look at her for three hours until the bed was made so neatly you could bounce a quarter off it."

"Those Hallmark movies make Christmas look way more simple than it actually is," Drew commented. He had a melancholic look in his eye that confirmed Pipers suspicion: like her, the holidays would be especially different for Drew.

"Yeah," she agreed. "Not all of us can be business women who return to their hometown for the holidays, meet a small town man with simple values, fall in love with him and move into his small town home forever."

Drew smiled. "Maybe one day."

The nearer it got to Christmas holidays, the more Piper knew she had to tell Hally about her conversation with her mother. She was less nervous about her mom cancelling since the date was rapidly approaching, but that didn't make it any less stressful. Hally didn't have a positive opinion of Piper's mom. Piper was hoping she'd understand. She couldn't be sure, though.

Piper decided when and where she was going to tell her. She settled on telling her in her car on the drive back from school. That way they would be alone and if they got into an argument, Piper would go home and they would try again the next day. Besides, Christmas holidays began in three weeks. She had to get it over with or she'd be sick over it every day until then.

When three o'clock hit, Piper was the first person to leave. She was waiting by Hally's car when her friend left the school, smiling when she saw her like the rockstar she was. She was twirling her car keys around her index finger, illuminating the monotonous parking lot. Hally dressed well in any weather. As it got colder, she still couldn't abandon the short skirts. She had on a tan knitted turtleneck and a plaid skirt with a pair of thigh high black boots. Layered over her sweater was a black jacket with a faux fur hood. She definitely had fewer layers than Piper, who was still cold even though she was wearing a blue flannel with a white sweater and a black jacket over it, a pair of thick jeans and chunky black boots. Yet she was as careless as she'd been in summer.

"How are you not freezing?" Piper asked. She was sure she could feel her teeth chattering together. She wished she would have brought a hat and a scarf. Tomorrow, she definitely wouldn't leave without them.

"I'm too hot to get cold," Hally declared proudly. She unlocked the car doors and Piper didn't hesitate before hopping in and blasting the heat the minute the car started. Hally wasn't as eager. She took off her jacket standing outside the car and threw it into the back seat and settled into the front seat. She scrolled through her phone for a song to play while the car heated up and they both thawed.

Hally played some pop song that Piper wasn't really paying attention to when they pulled out of the parking space. She was ready to tell Hally. In fact, she was even excited. She hoped Hally would be happy for her.

"Hey, Hals?" she prompted.

"Yeah?"

"I've got to tell you something."

"Uh oh."

"No, it's a good thing. My mom called."

Hally screwed up her face at that. "Since when is that a good thing? I thought you were dreading her call."

'I was," Piper admitted. "But it was actually good. She wants to see me."

"Really? When?"

"Christmas."

"Christmas?" Hally repeated. "That's kind of short notice isn't it. When did she call?"

"A little over a month ago," Piper said. "Early November, when she said she would."

Hally hesitated. Something caught her off guard along the way.

"Was this before or after I asked you if she called and you said no?"

Uh oh, Piper thought. "After, I think."

Hally didn't say a word but she turned down the music until it was almost on mute.

"Why didn't you tell me?"

Piper shrugged sheepishly.

"I mean, I tell you everything, Piper," she said. "You coudln't tell me this one, fucking massive piece of info?"

"I didn't know what you'd say. I wasn't sure if she'd cancel or not."

"What do you mean?"

"I mean if I told you, I knew you wouldn't be totally down with the idea and I didn't want you to say '*I told you so*' if she cancelled."

Hally laughed humorlessly. "That sounds an awful lot like you don't trust me."

"I trust you," Piper said, "but you love being right. And I didn't want you to be right about that."

"I wouldn't *love* being right about it," Hally threw back. "Do you think I'm rooting against your family? No way. I want you to be happy."

"I never said you didn't," Piper corrected. "But I know you don't trust her."

"You clearly trust her a lot, considering you wouldn't tell anyone she called in case she changed her mind about you."

"Stop, I don't want to hear it anymore."

Hally sighed and softened a little. "You know what I meant."

"I don't care what you meant," Piper retaliated. "I thought you'd be happy for me. Actually, no. I wanted you to be happy for me. I thought you'd act exactly how you're acting now."

"That's not fair, I—"

"Don't talk to me about fair. My mom called me asking to mend our relationship and you couldn't show an ounce of happiness for me? That's exactly why I didn't tell you. I didn't want you to ruin it for me. And I certainly didn't want you to make it about you."

Hally bit her lip, but Piper could tell she was itching to say more. Piper was curious to see what she could possibly have to say in response, but when the car stopped in front of Piper's house, she didn't pause. She left the car immediately, only hearing the first part of her name leave Hally's mouth before she slammed the car door shut.

CHAPTER FIFTEEN

December fifth. That was the day Piper saw her Coffee Shop Girl again.

The air was getting colder and colder by the day, but there was no sign of snow yet. It felt close, though. The dry chill that stuck around from morning until night was the main indicator. The constant goosebumps and shivers were a close second. Winter was marching in like a grand army, but it had the courtesy to give warnings.

She was lucky it did because she wanted to savour the last moments of fall weather before everything was frozen solid. After school, she hauled her bicycle out of the garage, strapped on her helmet, and made sure to bundle up. It was a little warmer than it'd been for the majority of the week, but that didn't mean it was warm. The sky was clear and blue, with hardly a cloud in sight. It was the perfect fall day for a bike ride, especially since the temperature kept most people inside, so the road she usually biked on was only occupied by her.

It was the perfect chance to clear her mind. She'd been listening to nothing but her own thoughts for far too long now. She still hadn't told Hally about her mom. She wanted to now. She wanted to hear a second opinion. Piper couldn't tell if she was seeing the situation through rose-coloured glasses, or being paranoid. Probably a terrible cocktail of both. She was spinning in circles between being excited, dreading the whole thing and expecting it not to happen at all. She needed her best friend to kick her ass for being irrational. But this wasn't like being scared for a test or a presentation at school. This was different. More important. And the history there spoke for itself. Would Hally support her at all?

Piper focused her mind on the scenery around her and the feeling of the bicycle beneath her. It felt like she was flying, in a way. It felt freeing, to get out of the house all on her own. She definitely needed it. She'd been alone plenty, yes. But always confined to her bedroom. She thought it was her sanctuary. Maybe she'd made it her prison in the past week.

The ride didn't feel very long. She could have kept going until she was far away from her town and the sun set behind her, but she stopped at the coffee shop she and Hally visited months prior. The crowd was bigger than she expected. In hindsight, she should have seen it coming. It was right when school let out. It shouldn't have been surprising that people would have the same idea as her.

She stopped her bike and climbed off, pulling a bike chain out of her jacket pocket. She peered in through the large windows in the shop. The line was long from what she could see. There were plenty of vehicles parked around it, too. It was almost entirely cars, but there was one thing that stood out; a black and purple motorcycle. Piper admired it from afar. She may not know anything about them, but she definitely loved the look of motorcycles. They were sleek and powerful. Very confident machines. Nothing she could drive, for sure. She couldn't imagine the disaster if she tried.

She chained her bike onto the bike rack and walked into the establishment. The moment she stepped in through the door, she was hit by two things; the wave of heat and the welcoming smell of coffee. She got in the back of the line and took it all in. All the tables were occupied, rightfully so. Almost everyone in there were young people, like her. There were some older people, seemingly fresh off of work and feending for a pick-me-up. But their energy didn't match the building very well. While the students were holding large mugs with two hands and smiling between sips, the adults were checking phones or laptops or drinking their coffee like it contained a powerful cure. *And they say we're disconnected*, she thought.

She didn't mind the wait. While some people would be chafed about a long line, she enjoyed the calm moment. It was the perfect amount of time to scan through the entirety of the menu (even though she knew what she wanted) and count her pocket change to make sure she had enough. She definitely didn't mind having some time to warm up and catch her breath after the ride over. She didn't realize how cold — and exhausted — she was until she was resting inside.

It was a few minutes before her turn came. The boy behind the counter seemed swamped with the crowd. He was moving a mile a minute, spraying whip cream, blending drinks, writing names, wrapping treats. He couldn't have been much older than her. She suddenly felt bad for adding to his workload, but it was too late now.

He finally righted himself in front of her. He had brown, disheveled hair and an eyebrow piercing. His eyes looked tired, maybe a little bloodshot. She gave him a reassuring smile, to which he huffed out a heavy breath and gave her one in return.

"Sorry for the wait," he told her.

"Don't worry about it. It was just a chance to warm up," she replied. She noticed his sleepy smile widened in relief. She imagined customer service was a constant gamble between pleasant customers and terrors.

"That's a nice way of looking at it," he quipped. "Now, what can I get you?"

"A medium hot chocolate to go, please," she said. He typed it into the register and nodded.

"Coming right up. That'll be two dollars."

Piper planned this to be very smooth and fast. She planned to have the amount already counted out before she finished her order and have it in his hand right when he asked. But when she grabbed her change from her pocket, she moved her hand too quickly and dumped it all on the floor. She cursed and apologized before crouching down to pick it up. She had about twenty cents (in nickels, of all things) in her hand when she felt someone standing closely beside her and heard a familiar voice.

"Hey, Marshall. I'll cover hers and I'll have a medium black coffee as well."

Piper looked up and saw her. The purple hair, the cheeky grin, the hazel eyes. The room suddenly felt slow and quiet as she stood, ignoring her change completely.

At first, the girl wasn't looking at her. She was watching the boy behind the counter as he made their drinks. But it didn't take long for their eyes to meet, just like Piper knew they would. Piper was conscious of the fact that she was wide eyed, like she was looking at a celebrity. But she might as well have been. The girl in front of her always felt... unreal. She was mysterious and beautiful.

Piper opened her mouth to speak right when both drinks were held out in front of them, cutting her off. The girl must have paid somewhere in between this time, but in the haze Piper was in, she didn't notice it.

The girl didn't say anything. She took her drink and started walking toward the door. Piper stepped out of line so she wasn't in the way and watched as the girl left, wordlessly. She thought the girl would leave without a single word but right as she reached the door, she turned around to push it open with her back and said,

"What? No thank you?"

Piper chuckled a bit and held her cup up as if she was making a toast.

"Thank you, Mystery Woman," she said. The girl grinned and tipped an imaginary hat before disappearing through the door as if she didn't just steal all the air from Piper's lungs.

CHAPTER SIXTEEN

The next morning, Piper got up early. She took a shower, got dressed, ate her breakfast and waited for her dad to be ready for work. When he was ready, she told him Hally wasn't going to school that day so she needed a ride.

They got into his car and the air felt heavy. Maybe it was just another indicator that snow was just around the corner.

There was still no snow on the ground, but everything was covered in a thin layer of frost. Walking on grass sounded like stepping on dried up leaves. Fall had been totally left behind at this point, nothing but the odd spot of orange on almost-leafless trees to show for it. The sky was grey and so was Piper's head.

Her and her dad were quiet as they left the driveway. She didn't have much she wanted to say to him. She had a sneaking suspicion he felt the same way. The cold had settled into everyone seemingly overnight. Or at least, that was how it felt.

"How's school?" he asked.

"Okay."

"And your friends?"

"They're okay."

"Did your mom call?"

"No."

"Was she supposed to?"

"No."

There was silence after that. Unlike in Hally's car, the radio didn't come on automatically, so all they had to listen to was the engine and each other's breathing. It was still, but it wasn't calm. Not on her end.

"Laura is coming up for supper tonight," he said.

"Oh."

The drive to the school felt longer that morning. Maybe it was because her dad drove considerably slower than Hally, or because there was nothing to distract her from the drive so she just stared out the window and saw the same view she saw every morning, only clearer, since it wasn't whizzing by.

The school looked the same earlier in the morning. Only emptier, like a ghost town. She could even see the teacher's cars pulling in as her dad stopped the car in front of the entrance. She could feel him staring at her as she collected her things and unbuckled her seatbelt but she didn't acknowledge him.

"Are you feeling alright?"

"Yep."

"Are you sure? If you're sick, I can take you back home and—"

"I'm fine, Dad," she interrupted. "Thanks for the ride."

Without another word, she left the car. She walked in through the front entrance of the school. It wasn't much warmer in there than it was outside, but she took her jacket off at her locker anyway. She got her books for class and checked the time. Her class wouldn't start for a half hour yet. In the meantime, she wandered the empty school. It was rare to get a chance to see it without the chaos of hundreds of students.

She walked the hallways. There wasn't a whole lot to see around the classrooms. Most of them were empty, or had a teacher preparing for their class inside. Not overly exciting. So she headed to the gym and peered in through the window in the door. There was a junior volleyball practice inside. The game wasn't overly energetic, which Piper found totally understandable. She wasn't good at volleyball anyway, she couldn't imagine how bad she'd be at it first thing in the morning.

The slow volleyball wasn't any more interesting than the empty classrooms, so she moved on. She strolled down the halls toward the auditorium. She wasn't sure if there'd be a practice going on in there, but there was usually something to see in there regardless.

She opened the door quietly. The music flooded out of it the second it opened. Someone was playing a Christmas song on the piano and there were students in elf costumes dancing across the stage. Piper assumed it was the rehearsal for the Christmas concert. She watched as they spun and jumped along with the music. They were all going full-out. Matching each other's energy perfectly. If this was only the rehearsal, she couldn't imagine the actual performance.

They had matching green elf costumes, with pointed shoes and ears. She was captivated by the dancing, but was interrupted when she was trying to watch them.

"Hey, you in the doorway," a woman's voice said. Piper scanned the room until she laid eyes on a woman she could only assume was the director, sitting in the centre of the audience. "If you want to watch the rehearsal, you have to help with the set."

Piper furrowed her brow. "I'm sorry?"

The woman pointed in front of the stage, where two people were painting a massive canvas. "You can't just watch. Help with the sets or go to class, please."

It was still too early for class so Piper walked down the aisle to the front of the stage. There were two people sitting on the floor, both of them holding paint brushes and working on the same thing. Now that she was closer to it, she could make out what it was. It was a piece of cardboard they were painting to look like the front of a house, covered in snow. She sat with them, feeling awkward at first but one of the two immediately turned to her.

"Hey, I'm Maya. This is Locke. What's your name?"

"Piper."

"Cool name," Locke commented.

"What grade are you in? I don't think I've ever seen you before. I'm in grade eleven but they're in grade twelve," Maya rambled, pointing her thumb toward Locke. Piper suspected Locke would be older than Maya the moment she saw them. They had the sides of their hair shaved and the rest of it chopped just above their shoulders. They had black hair and blunt bangs that stopped just above their eyebrows and contrasted greatly against their pale skin. They had on a knitted sweater and a pair of baggy, light wash jeans. Maya, on the other hand, had a thick afro that circled her head like a halo. Her dark skin, unlike her companion's, was sprinkled with freckles and tiny moles. She had a colourful cardigan and a black, lace skirt that went well past her knees. Compared to these two, Piper looked like a blank sheet of paper; devoid of artistry and care.

"I'm in grade eleven, too," she said.

"Oh, cool! I wonder how we missed each other. I guess

we aren't in any of the same classes. I take mostly AP but all my electives are arts related. Like music, theatre, art. I want to study the arts in university, that's why."

Locke smiled to themself. Piper had a feeling these two were close.

"Yeah, I don't take any art classes," Piper said. Maya nodded in understanding.

"That makes sense. Locke doesn't, either. They think they don't have a creative eye, but I think it's exactly the opposite. You should see their drawings, they're incredible."

"Maya," Locke warned, their face covered in a blush that definitely wasn't makeup. Maya giggled.

"They hate when I brag about them, but how can I not, you know?"

Piper smiled. She was quickly warming up to them. Maya fished a paint brush out of a mason jar they had filled with brushes and water. She patted the water off in a paper towel before handing the brush to Piper.

"Here you go. I know it's lame you have to work to watch the rehearsal, but honestly, it's pretty fun. Me and Locke have been coming in early every day for the past week to paint and watch rehearsal. It's a positive start to the day," Maya said. She moved the paints over so they were closer to Piper and went back to painting her own section, though she wasn't done talking quite yet. "The set is close to being finished already, which is great. We've been working on it for a short while but I guess we work pretty fast. Do you paint?"

"Not really," Piper muttered. She dipped the paintbrush in the white paint and started in on the snow on the roof, taking extreme caution as not to ruin what they had done.

"That's okay, the whole set is planned out already and the hard part is already done. The hard part was mostly the sketch, which is under all the paint so no one can even see it. That took the longest. The painting part is easy, it's just tedious. I don't mind though. I think it's relaxing."

"It's relaxing to you because you're good at it," Locke huffed. They seemed to be getting frustrated with one area of the set, but Piper couldn't tell exactly what it was, since she was looking at it upside down.

"You're using the wrong size paint brush, that's the problem. Give me that." Maya took the paint brush right out of Locke's hand and plopped it into the water. She got them a new paintbrush with a smaller tip, pressed the water out of it and laid it in their hand. "There," she said. "All better."

Locke tried the paint brush before they replied. They dipped it in the paint and went back to what they were doing. Piper watched as the frustration melted away.

"Thank you," they said.

"No prob, Bob."

The three of them painted for a while, Piper and Locke remaining quiet and instead listening to Maya's many ramblings. It was pleasant. A much needed peace to defrost that sour feeling Piper had since yesterday. But, eventually, the bell rang, signalling that first period just began. They all had to rush out of the auditorium to make it to class, each of them going their separate ways.

By the time school ended that day, Piper hadn't found a way home. She didn't want to go with Hally. She didn't think she'd be welcome, even if she did. But her dad was working and she wasn't sure who she could ask. She could probably ask Brent. There was no doubt he'd agree, but she didn't want to deal with how painfully awkward that'd be. She still hadn't talked to him about their non-mutual feelings. That was a problem for a different day. She couldn't put up with that now.

She was trying to find out which of the school buses would get her home when her new friends appeared out of nowhere.

"Piper!" She heard Maya's bouncy voice squeal behind her. She turned to face the two of them, Maya hanging off of Locke's arm. They looked like they were in their own world.

"Hey, Maya," Piper greeted. They'd only just met, but Maya was looking at Piper like they'd been best friends in another life.

"Are you getting the bus?"

"Yeah, if I can find the right one," Piper replied. Maya shook her head.

"Screw that, come with us. We'll bring you home."

"Really?"

"Yeah, of course! Come on, my car is over here." Maya released Locke to lead the two of them through the parking lot to where her car was. It was a rusty old yellow hatchback with a rainbow bumper sticker and a gingerbread air freshener. "It isn't technically my car," she said as she took out her keys and unlocked the doors. "It's my mom's but her work is a short walk from our apartment and the bus is majorly packed. I rode it for a week and there were so many kids that some of them had to sit on the floor. It was nuts. So she walks to work when the weather's okay and lets me take the car to school."

Locke sat in the passenger's seat beside Maya and Piper sat in the back. They all buckled their seatbelts and settled in for the ride. The car was almost silent as it started but made a squeaking noise as they pulled away from the parking lot.

"The radio works but the sound quality is shit," Maya explained, "So we usually listen to music on this awesome bluetooth speaker that I've had forever. It looks like Hello Kitty. It's adorable. But I left it in the car overnight and now it doesn't work. I have no clue why. I'm not very good with tech stuff. The most I know how to do is hook my phone up to the speaker. Beyond that, I'm pretty much useless. But Locke, you knew what was wrong with it, didn't you? What did you say was wrong with it?"

"It's probably just because you left it out in the cold," they said simply.

"Right, the cold," Maya went on, "It was super cold last night but I didn't think about it very much. I mean, I didn't know regardless, so I couldn't have avoided it I guess."

"You could have brought it inside," Piper pointed out. She saw Maya smile in the mirror.

"Fair point," Maya conceded. "I'll definitely do that next time."

Piper thought that was the perfect time for a beat of silence, like she was used to. Sure, Hally talked a lot, but she always allowed for space. Probably because Piper didn't chime in all that often. She allowed time for Piper to speak. Or just sit in. But Maya and Locke were very different.

"I haven't seen you around school much, Piper," Locke commented, looking at Piper through the mirror. They didn't say anything else. They were probably used to their company going on tangents all the time without being prompted, so they expected Piper to do the same.

"Yeah, I'm not in any extracurriculars or anything," she replied. "I don't branch out much."

Maya chuckled. "You and Locke have that in common."

"I branch out more now," Locke argued.

"Yeah," Maya agreed. "Because I make you."

"Still counts."

Maya dropped off Locke first. When they pulled up, Piper was surprised to see that they were parked in front of the skinny apartment buildings she recognized from the city. They were as gloomy as they always were, with broken shutters and faded siding. Still, the block had some life. There were a couple skateboarders practicing on the sidewalk and Locke's place had plants on the window sills.

Maya stopped in front of their apartment and leaned across the middle console of the car to kiss them on the cheek. They collected their things, said goodbye, and climbed out of the car. Maya watched them jog up the stairs and waited until they were safely inside before she turned to Piper.

"Hop in the front, Piper," Maya said. Piper did as she was told, settling into Locke's place and buckling her seatbelt again."I hope you don't mind that I had to drop off Locke first. Their brother and sister get off school the same time we do and someone has to be home to make sure they both get home safe. Their parents don't get off work until five."

"No, I totally understand," she said. "They have two siblings?"

"Oh, yeah. Absolute angels. Locke thinks the world of those kids, even if they're a lot to handle sometimes. They have to babysit a lot since both of their parents work."

"I'm sure they're glad to have Locke around all the time."

"They definitely are," Maya said with a small laugh. "You've never seen two kids love a person more. I'm the youngest, so I never got to do the whole Big Sibling thing, but I just think it's so cute. Now, where am I headed?"

Piper gave her the best directions she could, especially since she didn't know the neighbourhood around Locke's apartment. But Maya managed to get on the right track, anyway.

"How long have you and Locke been together?" Piper asked in the short seconds of silence. Maya smiled.

"Half a year," she answered. "Best six months of my life."

Piper couldn't help but grin. The hopeless romantic in her was jumping up and down.

"I moved into the apartment right beside theirs. Me and my family are total extroverts, so we went over to introduce ourselves and invite our neighbours to a home-cooked meal. My mom's an excellent cook. Locke and his family came over that night and we talked the whole time. A week later I invited them to a picnic—because picnic dates are the ultimate dates."

"And the rest is history," Piper said.

"Exactly," Maya agreed.

"They're pretty quiet."

"Yeah. it takes a while for them to get comfortable. But don't be fooled. They may not say much, but they're always listening. They're the smartest person I've ever met. And the most observant."

"You're lucky to have found each other."

"Definitely. It just goes to show that, even in a shit town like this, you can find your people."

They pulled up to Piper's house, the engine rolling as Maya put the car in park. Piper didn't get out immediately. She enjoyed the sound of the whining car and the kind company.

"If you want, I can pick you up tomorrow. We always go early, so we can work on the set," Maya offered. Piper inhaled and nodded.

"Sure," she agreed. "I'll see you tomorrow."

She got out of the car and walked up to the door. Maya beeped the horn rhythmically as Piper let herself in, feeling a mixture of peace and conflict.

CHAPTER SEVENTEEN

For the remainder of time before Christmas break, Piper went to and from school with Maya and Locke. She spent her mornings painting with them, and her breaks and freetime with Joseph. It was a very different environment, going from them to Joseph. He was more reserved. Unlike all of Piper's friends, he left the majority of the space just for her. Like he was expecting her to have a lot to say. But she didn't.

She felt guilty for avoiding Hally, but she didn't feel like Hally was looking for her anyway. Piper wasn't hard to find. Her auburn hair made her recognizable, and she wasn't one to be in a crowd, so she couldn't get lost in one. Plus, if Hally really wanted to find her, she could ask the one other person she knew who hung out with her. But Joseph never mentioned Hally, so she mustn't have tried.

Some part of Piper wanted to mend things with Hally before she went to her mother's. It would be one less thing to worry about, for sure. But it was too late, as the final bell rang and signalled the end of school. *Maybe it's for the best*, she thought. *Maybe we just need a break from each other.*

Maya dropped Locke off first, just like every day, and then brought Piper home. Maybe it was only Piper's imagination, but since she started riding with Maya every day, she noticed she smelled like ginger bread all the time. It was a good way to get into the Christmas spirit.

"Merry Christmas, Piper," Maya said with a grin. Piper offered her a smile in return.

"Merry Christmas." She left the car and shut the door. She was leaving for her mother's place shortly after school, so she didn't hesitate too much before she left Maya. When she got inside, she finished packing her things and laid her bag by the door. She lingered for a moment, staring at it. She'd packed up her stuff in Hally's duffle bag. She didn't have a bag big enough for her stay, so she had to use it. It stung a little, even if she was aware that the rift between her and Hally wasn't permanent.

She did the bulk of the packing over the course of a couple days. The final things she added to the pack were her charger, toothbrush, hairbrush and any other stuff she needed that day, so she couldn't pack them early.

All that was left to do was wait.

Her dad got home a couple hours later. He was hardly in the door when he carried Piper's bag out to the car and told her they were leaving. He waited for her in the car while she double and triple checked to make sure she had everything. She knew she could always have her dad drop off anything she forgot. She just wanted to be sure.

Once she was satisfied, she walked out to the car and got in the passenger's side. As they drove, her dad tapped on the steering wheel idly.

"What are you going to do while I'm gone?" Piper asked.

Her dad said, "Laura's parents invited me up to their place for a couple of days. I think I'll go there."

"Nice," she muttered. She didn't hide her lack of enthusiasm, but he didn't pick up on it anyway.

"Are you excited to see her?" he asked.

Piper hesitated. She was. She definitely was. But she was equally as nervous. She was still expecting the worst.

"I think so," she said.

"She sounded different on the phone, huh?"

"Yeah, really different."

"Better?"

"I think so. Will you come in and see her?"

He hesitated. Their relationship had a messy end so she wouldn't be surprised if he decided not to, but against all odds, he agreed.

"I think I will," he said. "I'd like to see how she's doing for myself."

They pulled up to her house and parked in front. The neighbourhood was very different from the small suburb they lived in. The houses were far apart. Every one of them was perverse and narrow with faded siding and crooked shingles. None of them had proper lawns. The grass was yellow and patchy with a dirt path leading to the door. But her mom's house was different from the rest of the houses for one reason: decorations. The roof and windows were framed with multi-coloured Christmas lights. She had a poinsettia wreath on the door and two banners on either side of it. One said 'Merry' and the other said 'Christmas.' Piper and her dad exchanged a look before they both got out of the car. He carried her bag to the door with her trailing behind. She noticed him pause for a breath before knocking.

Her mother answered the door immediately. She was wearing a Mrs. Claus apron that had a splash of flour on it. She'd let her hair go grey since the last time Piper saw her, and yet she looked younger than ever before. She was only a little older than Piper's father but it was in her family to have grey hair at a young age. Piper found grey hairs on her own head all the time.

She beamed at the two of them the moment she saw them.

"Oh, good! You're here. Perfect timing, the cookies just came out of the oven. Come on in," she said, opening the door wide and stepping aside to let them in. Piper's dad let her go first and she took it all in like a gulp of water.

The house was cleaner than Piper had ever seen it. The hardwood floor was spotless and shined like it'd just been mopped. There was tinsel garland wrapped around the railing leading up the steep staircase. There was a small nativity scene on the table that Piper remembered used to be home to a bowl full of dusty fake fruit. The whole house smelled like fresh cookies and firewood. She couldn't help but let her jaw go slack with surprise.

Her dad stepped inside behind her and seemed to be in the same state of shock as he set the bag down by the door.

"The place looks great, Judy," he commented. Piper watched her mom swell with pride.

"Thank you, Samuel. I've had a lot of free time on my hands recently. Plenty of time to clean and decorate," she said. She wiped her hands off in her apron, leaving flour handprints on the bottom of it. "I'll make you a cup of tea."

"That's alright," he said, "I'm not staying very long."

She shook her head at him. "Nonsense. I just made some cookies, the kettle will only take a second to boil. I won't keep you."

Samuel looked at his daughter for a moment before

nodding his head and agreeing. He followed Judy into the kitchen with Piper on his tail. The smell of cookies intensified as they walked in and sat down. The kitchen was tiny, but it seemed a lot bigger than Piper remembered it. There was a radio sat on the counter playing soft Christmas music and a nutcracker beside it. A tray of cookies with steam coming off of them was on a cooling rack beside the stove, under an open window that dulled the heat of the oven. Judy clicked on her kettle and took out three mugs. Piper was about to speak up when Judy turned to face her.

"You like hot chocolate, right?" she asked. Piper blinked in surprise and nodded. "Perfect. I just picked up some for you yesterday." Judy turned back to the kettle. No one spoke, but it didn't feel tense. Maybe awkward, but not tense. Judy was humming. Piper and her dad watched as Judy plopped teabags into two of the mugs and then grabbed a packet of instant cocoa and poured it into the final one. The kettle clicked as it turned off. Judy grabbed it and poured a generous amount into all three mugs. She laid a tea in front of Samuel and the hot chocolate in front of Piper. Then she got a large plate from the cupboard and laid all the cookies on it in an organised tower. She laid it on the centre of the table for them before she got her own mug and sat down across from them.

Piper and her dad said thank you. They blew on their drinks, waiting for them to cool as they listened to the quiet music. Piper didn't know what to say. She didn't know what she was expecting when she walked in. To be honest, she didn't have a whole lot of expectations. But this felt like an alternate reality. It felt too... normal. So normal it was abnormal. For Judy, at least.

Judy laid down her mug and looked at Piper and Samuel, her eyes serious.

"I know I made a lot of mistakes over the years," she said. "But I'm done. I'm ready to be a good Mom and a good friend. I promise."

Piper looked at her dad for a moment, trying to see his reaction, but he was looking at Judy. She seemed as serious in real life as she sounded on the phone. Piper wasn't sure how to react. No one was speaking. Judy was giving them plenty of room to get whatever they had built up out. But Piper didn't have anything to unload. Not this long after. It wasn't worth it.

It was worth it to restart, though. If they could do it, she was more than willing to try. Even if it was a little weird.

She wrapped her fingers around the handle of the mug and held it up in the air.

"To starting over," she said. Her mother smiled tearily. Her dad was more reluctant, but he bucked up and smiled as well. The three of them clinked their drinks together, signifying their collective hope for the future.

Once her dad left, Piper and her mother finished their beverages and cookies. They were better than she expected. Better than she thought a woman who never baked in her life could make. They put their dishes in the sink and Judy wiped off her hands in her apron once again, more out of habit than anything else.

"I'll show you to your room now," Judy said, "I'm sure you want to settle in."

"I know where my room is," Piper said.

"Right. Of course." She noticed her mother sink a little at that. She didn't think before she said it. Sure, it'd been a while, but she still knew her way around. The house was only tiny. It was virtually impossible to get lost. But still, she should let her mom do some mom stuff.

She awkwardly cleared her throat. "Uh, can you help me with my bag, though?"

Judy perked up at that. She smiled and nodded. She grabbed Piper's bag from the doorway and led her daughter up the stairs eagerly.

While the house was cleaner and a lot prettier, it was still the same house. The paint on the walls was still chipped and faded. The stairs still croaked under your feet. You could still hear the water running through the pipes over your head.

The upstairs was even smaller and more narrow than the bottom floor. The hallway was just wide enough for one, relatively slim person. There were only four doors up there; two bedrooms, a bathroom and a closet. Piper's bedroom was the last door on the left. It still had a light lavender do-not-disturb sign hanging from the doorknob, just the way she left it. Judy opened the door and walked into the room, laying Piper's bag down on the floor.

"Your bag is pretty light," she commented. "You didn't bring a lot with you?"

Piper shook her head. "I'm low maintenance. I don't need a lot."

Piper followed her mother into the room. Nostalgia hit her like a pound of bricks. The room hadn't changed a bit. She had the same canopy twin bed, with the same pink and blue polka dot duvet and the same mermaid vanity. There were still teddy bears strewn on the floor and clothes that certainly wouldn't fit her in her closet. The room was cleaner, though. As if it was cleaned thoroughly, but everything was returned to its place immediately afterward.

"I didn't move around your stuff too much, I wasn't

sure what stuff you'd want to keep and what stuff you'd need to get rid of," Judy explained. "I did wash your sheets and your clothes but I don't think they'll fit you now."

Piper chuckled. "Definitely not."

"We can go shopping for new clothes, though," she offered. "Just so you can have clothes of your own here."

Piper nodded, not sure what else to say. Everything was so different, but so eerily familiar. Like it was a completely different life ago, when she used to stay there, spending time with her mother. She gave that up a while ago. She gave that up when her mom gave up on her.

She made sure to stress that to herself so she wouldn't forget. She didn't abandon her mother. She was abandoned.

There was a delicate silence, both of them looking around the room to avoid looking at each other. You'd think after all this time, they'd both have plenty to say. But they were the same in the sense that they were often left speechless.

"Alright, I'll leave you to it," Judy announced finally. "I'll call you when supper is ready."

Piper gave her mom a small smile. "Thanks."

She left the room, leaving Piper alone with her thoughts.

She couldn't deny things were off to a pretty good start. Sure, the bones of what happened before were still there, but they didn't try to sweep them away. It felt like both of them understood. Like both of them might be ready to move on. At last.

CHAPTER EIGHTEEN

Piper offered to do the dishes once they'd finished eating, but Judy refused. Piper really didn't mind. She liked having something to do. She hated being idle for too long. But her mother wouldn't let her help out at all. So, she went for a walk.

She shoved on her boots, coat and hat. It somehow still wasn't snowing, which was incredibly disappointing. It was getting close to Christmas and the idea of a green Christmas was hardly appealing.

Still, there was frost on the windows and a chill in the air that was promising. Perhaps today was the day. She announced to her mother that she was going and stepped out into the bitter air.

She didn't walk around her mother's neighbourhood very much before. It wasn't the safest place to wander around alone. She was semi-familiar with the area, but she knew it best from the passenger's seat of a car. If that even counted.

She listened to the sound of frozen grass crunching under her feet. It was the only sound around. She was the only one out, it seemed. She could just barely hear the sound of traffic from behind her, though. She didn't know exactly what road that was. Her dad never took it to get to her mom's place.

She decided to follow the sound. She looped back behind her mother's house. There was a small backyard with a worn down swing set and some sad, forgotten toys. The grass was as yellow as in the front, only more overgrown and the weeds were more plentiful. Surrounding the yard was a tall wooden fence with chipped paint and some broken boards. Piper approached the fence, where a jagged piece of wood stuck out. She used it to prop herself up, standing on it with one foot and throwing the other over the side of the fence. She straddled the fence like a horse as she built the courage to throw her other foot over and jump off to the other side.

Her feet hit the ground rough and she wobbled. She wasn't the most graceful girl in the world. She was amazed she even managed to get over the fence in the first place.

The ground sloped on the other side of the fence, leading down to a dirt road behind a few buildings. Piper walked down the slope, careful not to slip.

The path was slim, only fit for two or three people to walk at once. The dirt on it was dusty, so when the wind blew, it sprayed up into the air in a tan cloud. She was careful when she stepped not to kick the dust around too much. She didn't want dirt in her eyes.

From the centre of the road, she could see that it connected to the street on both sides. It was a small alleyway, fit with lowlights and a creepy, narrow entrance. The alleyway itself wasn't all that creepy, though. The sun was directly over it and the buildings it cowered behind were yellow and blue. Not the most threatening colours. But the idea of an alleyway was creepy no matter where it was or how it looked.

She couldn't decide which side to explore. The left was a wide, paved road with cars racing down it and a narrow sidewalk on the side. The right was another community, with houses and roads fit for two small cars, side by side. They both seemed intriguing and, in theory, she could explore them both. But her fingers were so cold they felt like they were going to fall off. She had to choose only one.

Or neither.

As she was caught up in her own thoughts, she heard footsteps rounding the corner of the left side. For a moment, she was frightened. Footsteps approaching an empty alleyway couldn't mean anything good. But then, the one approaching spoke just as Piper saw her face.

"Hey, stranger," the girl said. The very same girl Piper had in the back of her mind for some time now. She looked just the same, maybe better. The front parts of her hair were tied back in an elastic behind her head. She had on a thick black jacket and a red hoodie underneath. Her long legs were covered by a pair of black cargo pants and she had on heeled boots that made her even taller. Piper wondered how different in height they'd be if they were both barefoot.

"Hey. I'm starting to think you're stalking me," Piper teased. The girl smirked.

"Funny, I was going to say the same about you," she declared. Piper was glad she wasn't the only one thinking about the crazy coincidence of them seeing each other four separate times, totally unplanned. "What are you doing here?"

"My mom lives around here," Piper said, "I'm visiting her for the holidays."

"For how long?"

"Until boxing day," Piper answered. "What are you

doing here?"

"I live on that road," the girl said, pointing to the right exit of the alleyway. "I had to run some errands for myself and my roommates." She neared Piper as they talked until she was standing right in front of her. She was certainly tall in her boots. Her cheeks were flushed from the cold but her hair was immaculate, yet carefree. If that was possible.

"Christmas shopping?"

"You can say that."

"So mysterious."

The girl chuckled. "It's nothing that interesting. Just looking to make a proper meal for once. It is the holidays after all."

"You said you're shopping for your roommates?"

"Yeah. I live with a couple folks who are taking courses at the community college up the road. They make my rent cheaper so I don't mind splitting a meal with them."

Piper laughed, though she was perplexed. She could have sworn they were the same age.

"Anyways," the girl said. "I'm sorry we lost each other on Halloween."

Piper's heart clenched. *She remembered? Keep it cool. Don't be an idiot. Jesus, I can't believe she was thinking about me.*

"It's fine," Piper dismissed, trying to be nonchalant. It definitely wasn't working. Her stomach was doing jumping jacks. Fun, happy jumping jacks, but jumping jacks nonetheless.

"The crowd was so dense. I couldn't believe the amount of people there. I mean, it's such a small town. Where did they all come from?"

"People come in from everywhere for that festival,"

Piper replied. "I thought I made it clear that it kicked ass while we were there."

"You definitely did. But still. What a wild fucking turnout."

"I think that every year."

They smiled at each other. The air was getting colder by the second but for some reason, Piper hardly felt it. It was the most distant thing from her mind. She did feel a little silly, in layers of clothing that didn't match and a thick woven hat, knitted with sparkly yarn.

"I looked for you, you know," the girl said. Piper felt her cheeks flush for a reason totally unrelated to the weather.

"Really?" Piper's voice was sheepish and quiet when she replied and she saw the girl's expression soften.

"Yeah. I didn't leave after we split up. I was looking for you but I couldn't see much of anything in the dark and the crowd. I would have called your name, but I didn't know it."

Piper smiled. "It's Piper."

The girl nodded, a toothy grin on her face. At first, Piper was worried she was going to laugh at the name. She didn't know why she assumed that. It was just the first thing that popped into her head. But the girl met her eyes with a genuine twinkle that made Piper's palms sweat.

"That's a beautiful name," the girl said. "It suits you."

Piper hoped she could blame her red face on the temperature.

She didn't dare try to accept the compliment. She couldn't imagine the embarrassment of her voice shaking with nervousness or coming out quiet and shy. Instead, she bit her lip to contain her smile and looked down at her shoes. She heard the girl chuckling at her and chose to ignore it.

"You said you'd be here until boxing day, right?" the girl asked. Piper looked up at her and raised a brow.

"Yeah, why?"

"I'll see you again soon, Piper." The girl looked smug as she brushed past Piper's shoulder toward the street. Piper turned around at her, smiling at the ridiculous mystery she always left behind.

"Wait, you didn't tell me *your* name."

"If I don't tell you, will you be intrigued enough to come see me again?"

"I'll come see you either way."

Seemingly persuaded, the girl turned around. She inclined her head at Piper like a gentleman in an old film as she said, "It's been a pleasure meeting you. I'm Autumn."

Before Piper could get another word in, Autumn was strutting away.

"*Autumn*," Piper thought in her wake, *it suits her perfectly.*

CHAPTER NINETEEN

Things were good between Piper and Judy for the next couple of days. It was quiet, but good. She did normal mom things, like cook and ask about school and reminisce about things she did as a kid. It was weird, but nice.

Piper was trying to keep her focus on the here and now; her mother, Christmas, Autumn. She was ignoring calls from Hally which was easy enough, except for the horrible guilt that she felt every time she saw her contact pop up. She wanted to talk to Hally. She wanted to fix things. But she couldn't imagine trying to talk to her at her mom's. She didn't want it to blow up like it did the first time. She'd cross that complicated, painful bridge when she got to it. For now, Christmas was the only thing on her mind.

That day, Judy was wrapping some presents downstairs in the living room. Piper hadn't done any Christmas shopping. Her and Hally didn't get gifts for each other and her dad never wanted material gifts. He wanted quality time; seeing a movie, going out to lunch or simply spending the day lounging at the house, just the two of them. He wasn't a man who wanted a lot of things. It made him impossible to shop for, but easy to please if you have a few spare hours to listen to him talk about his favourite show, *River Monsters*.

Judy offered for them to wrap presents together, but Piper didn't have any present, nor any skills with wrapping. As much as she wished she did.

Instead, Piper was reading some old books that she'd left in her room the last time she visited while she waited for her mother to be done so they could do something together.

Midway through her favourite part of *Tuck Everlasting*, she received a text. She expected it to be Hally again, but it was Joseph. The text read,

"Hey."

Piper texted back,

"Hey. What's up?"

"Nothing. You busy?"

"Nope. why?"

"Wanna do something?"

Piper didn't hesitate. While she hadn't read it in a while, she'd read that novel countless times. She never hung out with Joseph outside of school. Seeing him would certainly be better than sitting around, waiting for her mom.

She texted Joseph back quickly and got dressed. It was way below freezing, so she made sure to layer up, since she suggested they go to the park. It probably wasn't the most practical idea but it felt festive. A walk in the park with a friend in the holiday season sounded like exactly what she needed. A cherry on top of this already fantastic Christmas break.

Once she was dressed, she left her room and bounded down the stairs. She found her mom, sat on the floor in the living room, surrounded by wrapping paper and bows.

"I'm going to meet a friend. Is that okay?" she asked.

Judy looked up at her and nodded.

"Yeah, of course. Do you need a ride?"

"No, I'm okay. I'll be home soon."

She left the house after that. Boots, mitts and silly hat equipped.

When the sun hit her, she had an urge to run. A sudden, delicious burst of energy. She took a deep breath and took off. She felt the wind in her hair and listened to the rhythm of her footfalls. She felt at peace. In the moment, for once. She felt every step through her whole body. Every crunch of frost and rocks under her boots. Every heavy, warm breath.

She kept running until she got to the park.

When she finally got there—panting and tired but beaming like an idiot—she found Joseph leaned up against a silver Toyota in the parking lot. Piper assumed it was his parents'. You didn't see a lot of teenagers with such expensive, practical new cars. Maybe that was a generalization, but he'd also mentioned his family having money problems. There was no way they could afford two cars.

He looked up, saw Piper and immediately straightened up. He gave her an awkward wave and waited for her to approach.

She gave him a smile—the best one she could manage between breaths—and stood against the car with him.

"Uh, did you run here?" Joseph said with a quiet laugh.

"Yep." She chuckled with him. It was rather silly. Like something a child would do. But she didn't care.

"Why?" he asked.

She shrugged, brushing her hair out of her face. "I just felt like it, I guess."

"Good day?"

"Going on a couple, actually."

"I'm glad."

When he said that, she knew he wasn't lying. He wasn't just saying it to be polite like anybody else would. In just two words, she could feel the sincerity in it. She was lucky to have him.

The conversation dissolved. It was a little odd, but not unpleasant. Piper was too calm for unpleasantness.

"Do you wanna, like, walk around...or something?" he asked.

"Sure."

And they proceeded to do so. They walked around in near silence, making quiet commentary about the people they saw, or the way the sky looked, or the fact that there was no river in Riverside Park, but there was a lake. A large one that had a thin layer of ice over it.

"How many idiots do you think will try to skate on it when it's about as thin as a fingernail?" Joseph quipped. Piper chuckled.

"At least ten. It's a good thing the water is shallow."

"Amen to that."

It wasn't very exciting, or interesting, but it was comforting. She was glad to have Joseph.

"Why did you want to come here?" he asked. "Isn't there a park closer to your house?"

"There is, but I'm staying at my mom's," she admitted. It didn't stop feeling weird to say. Even though this wasn't her first time saying it.

"Oh." The air felt a little heavier. "How is she?"

"Better. A lot better, honestly."

He looked over at her. She could feel him scanning her face but she didn't look over. She knew he was only looking for confirmation. For safety.

Once he got it, he said, "Good. That's great, Piper."

She smiled. "Yeah, I'm pretty happy about it."

There was a lull in the conversation before Joseph awkwardly asked, "How's your boyfriend?"

Piper rolled her eyes, assuming he was teasing her. "He's not my boyfriend. Why do you ask?"

Joseph shrugged. He was picking at his fingernails idly. She hoped she didn't make him feel awkward.

"I was just curious," he said. "You guys broke up?"

Piper shook her head. "We were hardly together."

"He looked at you like you were married."

"Well then it was one-sided."

She noticed Joseph make a face and sighed. She turned to face him, both of them pausing their steps to look at each other.

"Look, I like him," she said. "He's a nice guy. But I don't like him like that. I don't mean to lead him on. I thought we both felt the same but now it's pretty clear he doesn't and I'm not sure how to tell him."

Joseph's face softened and his shoulders relaxed. Something she said must've comforted him but she had no idea what.

"Can I offer some advice?"

"Go for it."

"Be upfront. Tell him the truth, you owe him that much. Do it as soon as you can. Believe me, a broken heart feels better when it's a quick smash and not a slow melt."

Piper shook her head. "I seriously doubt I'm breaking his heart."

"You're too modest," he insisted. "I can't imagine what it'd feel like to have you and lose you. It'd be enough to kill a man."

He carried on walking, leaving her laughing incredulously at him before speeding up to walk at his side.

It began to get colder—it was December after all—and she wished she would have brought a warmer jacket when she left her house.

Joseph noticed her shiver and slipped off his jacket, wrapping it around her shoulders. She was a little shocked, and tried to protest, but he ignored her.

"You're going to freeze to death," she argued.

Joseph shook his head. "I'm alright. I like the cold," he murmured.

She said nothing for a moment, and just enjoyed the warmth he provided her with. All the elements were there; it was a little cloudy, freezing cold and the air felt so still and dry. Piper could practically taste it. It was going to snow.

Joseph wasn't shivering. Piper had no idea how he was totally okay in the weather. She wanted to see how he fared when the snow began. Because it would begin soon. She just knew it.

They sat down on a bench by the lake. It was metal, so the cold seeped through her pants and chilled her thighs. Joseph didn't seem to mind, if he was even feeling what she was. He certainly didn't show it.

"Can I be totally sappy for a second?" Piper asked. Joseph peeled his eyes away from the lake to look at her.

"Shoot."

She turned to look at him, one leg folded up on the bench so she could direct herself entirely on him.

"I'm really glad to have you," she said. "I feel like I don't say it enough to people. Most of the time I expect it to be implied. But I feel the need to actually say it this time. I fucking love you, man. Thanks for... sticking around. Even if I'm distracted ninety percent of the time.

I appreciate it."

He grinned at her. He might've been awkward some-times, but the one thing he was fantastic at was making you feel heard. Seen. Listened to.

"Barf," he muttered with a laugh. "I fucking love you too, man."

She chuckled, turning forward again and watching as the first snowfall of winter drifted down.

CHAPTER TWENTY

On December 25th, it felt as bizarre as it did natural to wake up in her kid-self's bedroom to the sound of her mother singing along to Christmas music. She stared at the ceiling for a moment, a faint smile on her lips, enjoying the feeling of home in a place that wasn't her home (or her best friend's car).

The first thing she did when she kicked her blankets off was look out the window. Since the first snow, it had snowed a lot. The ground was covered in a thick layer of sparkling snow and every window had icicles dripping down from the top. The house was cozy and warm and it was a white christmas. Piper believed that most things couldn't realistically be perfect (even if she used the word a lot to describe things) but this seemed like a pretty perfect Christmas under the circumstances.

She left her room after that, staying in her pyjamas and marching down the stairs. She almost felt like a kid again. She felt the magic of Christmas, even if it wasn't for the same reason children do. She just felt childish in her happiness.

"Piper!" Judy said as Piper emerged in the living room. "Merry Christmas!"

As excited as Piper was for Christmas, she definitely couldn't beat her mom. She was glowing in a Santa hat and her pyjamas. She was laying breakfast out on the coffee table in the living room. She had *Elf* queued up on the television and pillows on the couch to make the whole room look comfier.

"Merry Christmas, Mom," Piper replied. Her cheeks already hurt from smiling and it was only 9 a.m. Judy sat down on the couch and patted the cushion next to her so Piper would join her. Piper did as instructed, sitting down and sinking back into the couch.

"Before breakfast," Judy said as she reached for the table beside the couch. She opened the drawer in the table and took out a small rectangle wrapped in snowflake paper. She closed up the drawer and turned to Piper proudly. "Your gift."

Piper stared at it. She hadn't really thought about that. She knew her mom was wrapping gifts but for some reason it hadn't dawned on her that she got her one. Her mother placed it in her hand. It'd been so long since she received a gift from her mother. She wasn't even sure what to do with it.

"Go ahead," her mother said, "Open it."

Piper did as she was told. She tore off the wrapping paper (though it was wrapped so nicely, it felt like a crime) until she could see what it was. It was a book, and Piper turned it around to read the title.

The Outsiders.

Piper inhaled and stared at the novel.

"Do you like it? Your dad said you like to read and I'm not sure what you've read. I don't read much but I read that years ago and I liked it so I got you a copy. It's the anniversary edition. If you don't like it, we can pick something else out—"

"I love it," Piper said. Her smile had wavered for a moment but she managed to keep herself together. "Thank you, Mom." She pulled her mom into a tight hug, and it took a moment before Judy hugged back. When she did, she held Piper close but carefully, like she was equally afraid of losing her and breaking her.

They held each other for a moment, as if it would erase everything that happened before. Then, they could have a proper restart without any biases. But as Piper pulled away, she knew she didn't want that. She was proud of her mother for the change she'd made. She was grateful for this light on the other end of the tunnel.

They both sat back and Judy turned on the movie. They watched it together and ate breakfast and laughed like any other mother and daughter.

After the movie ended, Piper went upstairs again. She was rummaging through her bag for something to wear. It occurred to her she hadn't brought anything festive besides an abundance of neutral coloured knitted sweaters, which wasn't matching the energy of the day.

She was taking clothes out of the bag and laying them down on the floor beside her. It was a lost cause. She knew what she packed. She didn't know why she was still looking. But it felt like fate when she pulled out the witch hat she'd bought two months ago.

She remembered throwing the hat into a bag under her bed but she hadn't thought much about it since. She had no idea she'd brought it. But it worked out pretty well.

She went to the window. There was no one in the alleyway but then again, over the course of her stay at her mother's, the only people that have been in the alley were her and Autumn. And that was only one time.

She laid the hat on her dresser and got dressed. She waited a little while. Maybe it was stupid to try to meet Autumn on Christmas day. She was probably seeing family. But it was worth the try. She didn't want to leave the next day without a trace.

She left the house, scaled the fence, almost slipped on the slope and waited in the alley. There weren't a lot of cars passing by on the nearby roads. She could hear music coming from one of the buildings in front of her. It felt different than before. She blamed it all on the day.

She waited a few minutes, freezing her ass off but being too stubborn to go anywhere. It all paid off when she saw Autumn round the corner.

Autumn didn't look festive at all, but the snowflakes in her dark hair were magic enough for Piper.

"You didn't open your present?" Autumn asked. Piper scrunched up her nose in confusion. Autumn chuckled and walked over to the buildings. There was a small space in between them, like a tiny, dark alley for mice. She pulled out a gift bag with a purple, glittery bow on it.

"I don't blame you," she said as she approached Piper and held it out to her. "I hid it really well."

"God help your children on Easter," Piper said with a laugh.

"Open your present, smartass," Autumn muttered playfully.

Piper smiled as she took the gift and opened it up. There was red gift paper inside which had something wrapped up in it. She shed the paper from it until she got to the centre. It was a small plush deer on a keychain, with wide glass eyes with sparkles in them. Piper's grin widened at it and she looked up at Autumn, still confused.

"I couldn't not get it," Autumn said. "It reminded me of you."

Butterflies fluttered against Piper's stomach and she stared at the plush with more affection than any inanimate object could ever feel.

"Thank you," she said sincerely. "I love it."

"I'm glad. I was worried I wouldn't see you before you left so I hid it here. Now that I'm thinking about it, you probably couldn't have found it without me."

"Definitely not."

Piper was distracted for a short moment until she remembered why she went to find Autumn in the first place. She had the hat tucked into her jacket pocket (it really was a comically small hat.)

"I have something for you, too. Close your eyes."

Autumn did as she was told, eyes closed and hands out in front of her. She tapped her toe, feigning impatience and making Piper laugh.

Piper pulled out the hat and made sure it hadn't been squashed in her pocket. She felt dumb giving her such an outdated present, but she needed to give it to her.

"Sorry I didn't wrap it," she said. She laid the hat in Autumn's hands. She watched as Autumn opened her eyes and her face split into a smile. "Two months late, but I found you a costume."

Autumn held up the hat and turned it over, taking in all the little details. She happily put the hat on her head and posed.

"How does it look?"

"Fantastic."

"That's what I thought. Thank you, Piper. It's perfect."

"No problem."

There was a silence, both of them admiring their respective gifts, before Autumn checked the time on her phone.

"Fuck. I have to go," she said. Piper visibly sank.

"Oh."

"Merry Christmas, Piper. I'm sure we'll bump into each other again."

She went to walk away, but Piper wasn't ready to finish the exchange yet. She didn't want fate deciding anymore. She had to take matters into her own hands.

She called after Autumn, "Hey, I still owe you for that hot chocolate."

Autumn kept walking—she must've been in a big hurry—but she turned around so she was walking backwards.

"Don't worry about that, I—"

"No, I owe you," Piper insisted, over enunciating each syllable. "I should return the favor."

Autumn stopped in her tracks and Piper assumed she got the message from the smile on her face.

"Okay," she said. "You're right. Sunday, twelve o'clock."

"Where?"

"You know where." She turned back around and waved as she went. "Catch you later, stranger!"

CHAPTER TWENTY ONE

The next day, Piper's dad picked her up. His car smelled familiar, like a pine tree air freshener and his cologne. Her dad had the heat on blast, which was welcoming, especially considering the weather outside. Snowflakes were falling in small, fast clumps. Her dad said the smaller the snowflakes, the more snow. So far, that was proving to be true. The ground had almost a foot of fresh powder already and the snow had just started.

Samuel told Piper to get in the car to stay out of the cold while he got her bag and put it in the back. She watched him walk up the steps, where Judy was standing with Piper's bag. She couldn't hear them but she saw their mouths moving as they spoke. Both of them smiled and to Piper's surprise, Samuel opened his arms to her. They embraced for a moment. Piper didn't miss how tightly her mom squeezed her dad's shoulders.

After a moment, they both pulled back and Samuel picked up the bag, waved goodbye and returned to the car.

When he got in the front seat, the snow from his jacket wafted off into the car, melting rapidly in the heat. He turned to Piper.

"Did you have fun?" he asked. She nodded.

"It was great."

"She seemed to think so, too." He buckled his seat belt and pulled away from the house and onto the main road. "She was very glad you went. I am, too. I think it was good for both of you."

"I think so, too. How was your Christmas?"

"It was pretty good." He had a big smile on his face so she knew he was holding something back. She assumed it was only because she didn't like Laura and he didn't want to make her uncomfortable.

"How was visiting Laura's family?" she asked.

"It was nice. They're good people, I think you'd like them."

Piper shrugged. "I might."

That might be the most acceptance Piper has ever expressed toward her father's relationship. He seemed awfully pleased with it. His smile widened but his eyes stayed focused on the road. Part of her Christmas present to him was going to be not being an asshole, for as long as she could manage it.

They pulled up to the house. Piper could see the twinkling of the lights on their tree through the window. She always loved her dad's Christmas decorations. They were as understated as they were magnificent. He didn't use a lot of tinsel. He thought it was tacky. Instead he used a lot of lights and pine cones that smelled like cinnamon and nutmeg. His presents were all decorated in the same wrapping paper, with different coloured bows. He was extremely neat and tidy, which was probably why Piper had the same, pin straight bob haircut since she was five. Consistency and neatness are very important in the Evans family.

They got out of the car and went inside. In the few moments between the car and the house, they already got coated in snow, which they proceeded to track onto the pristine hardwood floor. *Mother nature must be making up for starting so late*, Piper thought.

As much as she enjoyed spending time with her mother, she missed her house. Her mom's house was so small and the walls were so thin that the whole house moaned on windy days. Her own house was much stronger and because of the way her dad had always taken care of it, every inch of it was deliberate. No chipped paint. No scratched floors. No squeaky doors. She understood that living in her house was a great privilege and she was never not grateful for it.

"By the way, Hally came by earlier today. She told me to tell you to give her a call once you got home," Samuel said as he took off his coat and draped it over the radiator to dry. He took Piper's from her and did the same, the two of their jackets displayed side by side.

"Okay."

Piper went to her bedroom. She decided it was time to bite the bullet and reconcile with Hally. But that didn't mean she had to do it immediately. So she put away her things and hopped in the shower.

She took an extra long shower that day, both to procrastinate and to relax. She did like staying with her mom, but over the course of her stay, she never fully conquered the shower controls. Every shower she took was either boiling hot or freezing cold. No inbetween. It was as frustrating as it sounds. She was relieved to get into a satisfyingly lukewarm shower she was entirely familiar with.

After she got out and wrapped herself in a towel, she looked at herself in the mirror. She looked different for some reason. She couldn't pinpoint what changed. It could've been nothing in her appearance. Perhaps she was just seeing herself differently. Whatever it was, she liked it. She felt less conflicted when looking into her own eyes.

As she got dressed in her room, she opened her phone and called Hally. It only rang once before she picked up.

"Piper! Finally! Jesus, I thought you fell off the edge of the earth," Hally exclaimed. Piper smiled.

"The earth is round, you know that right?" she responded snarkily.

"Har har. That's the asshole I know and love. I missed you. How was your Christmas?"

"It was really good."

"Good. That's awesome. Really." Hally sighed heavily into the phone, which sounded more like a puff of static than an apologetic exhale. "I'm sorry I was such a dick. You were right. I should have just been happy for you. I want you to be happy. You know that, right?"

Piper paused midway through zipping up her jeans to pick up the phone and sincerely say, "I know."

"You better. Cause I love you, Evans."

She chuckled. "I love you, too. And I'm sorry, too. I should have told you before. We both fucked up."

"I'll totally forget about it if you do."

"Sounds good to me."

Piper laid the phone back down on her dresser so she could finish getting dressed. She zipped up her jeans and grabbed a shirt to pull over her head.

"Got any plans for tonight?" Hally asked. "We have a little over a week before school starts again so we have to make up for lost time A.S.A.P."

"I'm down for whatever."

"Cool. I'll pick you up at six?"

"See you then."

Her phone beeped three times, signalling that Hally hung up. That was the easiest reconciliation anyone had ever experienced. Piper didn't know what she expected. Her and Hally didn't really fight, so they definitely didn't hold grudges.

She finished getting dressed and dried her hair. She didn't have a lot to do to get ready. Some lip smacker, a pair of stud earrings and her phone and wallet in a small backpack was all she had to do to be ready for anything.

She ate supper with her dad and heard a horn honking outside at approximately 6:15 p.m. Closer to being on time than Piper expected.

She said goodbye to her dad and left the house with her hood up to block the snow, which was still falling in blankets.

Piper spent the following two days with Hally. They mostly did things Hally wanted to do. Not because Hally was being pushy. Piper just didn't have a preference, so whenever Hally suggested something, Piper went along with it. So they ended up going to tiny, locally owned restaurants for every meal, exploring shops full of gorgeous handmade clothing and trying to stay out of the snow. Hally made every outfit look good, but still, the cold wasn't entirely her friend. She chose fashion over functionality often, meaning she was often freezing and complaining. Piper may not have looked like a model (frankly, she looked like she picked out her clothing in the dark) but she was warm. And she took every opportunity she got to rub it in Hally's face.

Sometime in the afternoon on day two (Saturday), the

subject of the boys arose.

"Brent's been asking about you a lot, apparently," Hally said. She was picking at a fancy chocolate eclair. It looked beautiful, but Piper tasted her own eclair (which was vanilla and strawberry) and it didn't live up to her astronomical expectations. *Why make food beautiful if it tastes like shit?* She pondered.

"Oh yeah?"

"Yep. I don't know what you did to that boy, but he's seriously obsessed. Have you talked to him at all since school ended?"

"Nope."

"You're driving him insane, Evans."

Piper huffed. "I know. I don't know what to do."

"Well, I may have an idea that I'm already in the midst of executing."

Piper frowned. This didn't sound good. "What did you do?"

"I found a club that won't card us."

Piper leaned back in her chair, crossing her arms and shaking her head like a disapproving father. "No way. Bad idea."

Hally rolled her eyes. "Oh, come on. It'll be fun. We're teenagers, we have to do crazy, stupid shit every now and then."

"That's more than crazy and stupid," Piper retaliated. "It's dangerous. We're kids, Hally. We could get in huge trouble. What if our dad's found out?"

"You're so stressed all the time," Hally whined. "It's not that big of a deal. We'll go out with the guys. We'll dance, maybe drink a little and then we'll sober up and get you home before curfew. Cool?"

"No. Not cool. We shouldn't drink. What if we don't

sober up in time?"

"Then we'll get a cab and you can crash at my place. Cool?"

Piper scrunched up her nose. She still wasn't convinced it was a good idea. Especially considering that she wanted to end it with Brent as soon as humanly possible. She didn't want to lead him on any more than she already had.

Hally, sensing her reluctance, reached across the table and grabbed her friend's hands.

"Trust me," she said. "It'll be a night to remember. Plus it's totally casual, no strings. Maybe it can be a good chance to transition Brent from loverboy to acquaintance..?"

She wasn't making a very compelling argument. To Piper, it seemed like she was grasping at straws for a good excuse to go. But she gave Piper the puppy dog eyes that she always fell for.

Piper groaned loudly and nodded.

"Fine. but if we get arrested or our parents find out, you're going to tell them you sedated me and dragged me around *Weekend At Bernie*'s style."

Hally beamed. "Deal."

CHAPTER TWENTY TWO

Sunday morning, she hopped out of bed the second she opened her eyes and rushed to the bathroom to shower. She washed her hair thoroughly, and used way more conditioner than she needed. She couldn't help it. She wanted to be as thorough as possible.

When she was done, she got dressed in a pair of black jeans and a blue collared shirt with a white jumper over it. She checked the time, and it was still two hours before she had to meet Autumn. She was both relieved and restless. She dried her hair with the blow drier and brushed it out. She put it up, then took it down, then put it half up, then took it down again. Frustrated, she finally decided on a ponytail and tried not to second guess herself.

After she was done with all of that, she still had an hour and a half. *Damn it*, she thought. *What now?*

She bounded down the stairs and got herself breakfast consisting of dry Cinnamon Toast Crunch and a glass of chocolate milk. She ate slowly, hoping to prolong the experience so she wouldn't have so much anxious energy as she waited around.

"Good morning, Piper," her father sang as he walked into the kitchen, turning on the coffee maker to make himself a cup. "How did you sleep?"

"Good," Piper replied, though it wasn't entirely true. She tossed and turned from nervousness. But she was in a good mood, and she wasn't going to let her lack of rest change that.

"Want some coffee? Or tea?"

"No, I'm actually meeting a friend for coffee at twelve."

He turned around and gave her a look. "Really? Is this a guy friend?" he said this in a way that was both teasing, and extremely fatherly. Piper rolled her eyes.

"No, not a guy friend. A girl I met. Her name is Autumn."

Her father nodded, accepting the answer and turning around to make his coffee. Piper assumed the conversation was over, so she finished her breakfast and put her dishes in the dishwasher, checking the time yet again. There was still a half hour before she had to go. Maybe if she walked really slow, she wouldn't make it there too early.

So, she pulled on a jacket, grabbed her phone and wallet, put on her boots and left the house.

The snow let up, which was good. It must've rained sometime that night because the snow that remained was scarce and slushy. It was definitely less pretty than the winter wonderland they'd had for the past couple days but it sure was warmer.

The walk to the coffee shop wasn't a very long one, but it was boring, because there wasn't much to see. Or at least, it felt like that way. Probably because she was totally preoccupied. She was taking a shortcut off the main road since she didn't have her bike this time. But still, it felt like she was walking forever in limbo.

But, Piper kept walking through the boring scenery,

and the sound of vehicles. She walked slow, her phone in her hand as she tried to put on a song to help her along. Something to dim the boredom.

She picked a personal favourite of hers—*Cigarette Daydreams*—and let it play, no headphones to stop a passersby from hearing her music. She felt like skipping, but she knew she'd look more ridiculous than she already did.

She saw the coffee shop come into view, and sitting outside the shop's entrance was a motorcycle. She recognized it from before. It was such a distinct vehicle, she couldn't not recognize it. Something like that stood out in your mind, even if you'd only seen it once in passing.

Leaning against the motorbike was none other than the owner herself, Autumn. She grinned at Piper and leaned off the bike to come greet her. They met in the middle of an empty parking lot.

There was a silence, just the two of them. It felt like they were the only two left. In the shop. In the town. In the world.

Piper smiled sheepishly. "You'd think there'd be more people here on a Sunday, huh?"

"Well it is the Lord's day," Autumn quipped. Autumn seemed to break from a reverie when Piper spoke, coming back to earth with a start. Piper understood that feeling well.

"Um, is the bike yours?" Piper asked, looking it over a bit. She couldn't imagine riding a motorcycle. She'd be much too scared.

Autumn glanced back at her bike for a moment before focusing on Piper and smiling proudly. "Yeah, he's mine. He was in the shop for a couple days for repairs. I just got to pick him up yesterday."

Piper tilted her head at Autumn inquisitively. "He?"

she repeated. Autumn nodded in confirmation.

"Yeah. People always call their bikes and boats '*she*' and frankly I think that's kind of weird and it probably has a misogynistic origin, so I've decided to call my bike a *he* as a middle finger to that."

Piper chuckled. "I like that."

"Why, thank you," Autumn replied. There was a beat of time where they just stood there, isolated and distracted by each other, until Autumn spoke up again. "Well, are we going to stand out here or are you going to buy me a coffee?" she teased. Piper's smile widened.

They walked into the shop side by side, and Piper let Autumn order her coffee, then ordered herself a hot chocolate. Piper paid for them both with a ten dollar bill she had crumpled in her wallet. She shoved the change into her pocket, and they sat down across from each other in a seat near the window.

They sipped their drinks in mutual comfort, faint smiles on both of their faces. Finally, Autumn put down her cup to speak.

"Can I ask you a question?" she said, her eyes piercing Piper's.

Piper gulped anxiously and laid down her mug. "Uh, sure," she mumbled.

"You're gay, right?"

Piper felt a jolt. There was no signal in her brain yelling yes or no. *How do you answer a question that you definitely should have an answer for, but just don't?* She cleared her throat and stared up at Autumn.

"I—I don't know," she muttered. "I didn't think so."

Autumn looked disappointed with her reply. She sat back in her seat like she wanted to sink into it and disappear. She was making an effort to hide it, nodding like she'd swallowed a sigh. if she was doing it for Piper's sake, she was failing. It was obvious. "Oh. uh, sorry. I thought you liked me. I mean, why else would you make an effort with someone you didn't even know?"

Piper nodded. She was a little embarrassed that it was obvious that she had more than just platonic feelings for her. "I—I do like you," she admitted. "It's just…confusing. And there's also this boy…"

Autumn tilted her head. "A boyfriend?"

"No, not really. Just a boy that I went out with a few times."

Autumn accepted that answer better. She seemed to perk up when Piper admitted she liked her. Piper waited in agony for Autumn to pick apart her awkward reply, but she didn't.

"I like you, too," Autumn admitted. Piper exhaled, feeling exhilarated. She was overjoyed, but perplexed. How could Autumn like *her*?

Piper swallowed her immense joy and said, "Good. Um… I'm glad."

Autumn laughed and shook her head. "Good. That makes two of us."

Autumn took a long sip of her coffee but she looked like she had more to say, so Piper didn't say a word. As she laid down her drink, Piper watched her carefully.

"So this not-boyfriend," Autumn started, "Do you have feelings for him?"

Piper thought about it, but ended up on the obvious answer. She inhaled and shook her head. "No. I just haven't cut it off yet."

Autumn nodded. "So… this isn't a date?"

Piper smiled. She couldn't help but think that was a ridiculously stupid next question but she appreciated that

Autumn wasn't angry at her for her confusing and complicated relationship.

Piper picked up her mug and raised her brows at Autumn teasingly. "Not this time."

The rest of their time together was comfortable. More than comfortable. She was comfortable with Hally. She was comfortable with Joseph. This was something completely foreign to comfort. This was like a drug, and she was just getting her first taste. This foreign comfort dripped from their silence like a broken faucet. No, like a broken spout spewing liquid gold. No, like a broken railway cart spilling whole diamonds. No, like a broken girl, realizing she'd been wrong about Shakespeare.

CHAPTER TWENTY THREE

That's it, Piper thought, pacing her room on that rimy mid-evening. *I have to talk to Brent*. She was supposed to meet up with Hally, Drew, and Brent in a few minutes to go to some lame dance club that would let them slip in, even though they're underaged.

She knew that today, at some club, with both of their friends there was definitely not the time to break up with someone, but did it really matter? They weren't actually in a relationship, they'd only been on a couple of dates. They hadn't even kissed. It didn't matter to her, and he could have anyone he wanted. She was merely trivial to him, anyway. He couldn't be horribly heartbroken to lose her. After all, between all the girls in the school, she certainly wasn't a front runner as the best in any meaning of the word. She wasn't the prettiest. Nor the smartest. Nor the most interesting. Nor anything else for that matter. She wasn't special. He would move on.

"Piper!" Hally shouted from the bottom of the stairs. "I've been waiting outside for ten minutes! Hurry your nerdy ass up!"

"Chill, I'm coming!" She grabbed a pair of ankle high black boots Hally lended to her over a year ago and checked her purse (which she also borrowed from Hally) for the third time to make sure she had everything she would need. She had all the reasons in the world to stay home. She didn't want to go and she seriously doubted she could have any fun while planning her breakup in her head all night.

She bounded down the stairs, feeling nervous and insecure. She whole-heartedly believed this was Hally's worst idea yet.

Hally was wearing a dark purple lace top, and a black miniskirt with silver zippers circling it. For shoes she had a pair of purple heels, so tall that Piper pitied her feet. Her hair was french braided on one side to create the illusion that section was shaved. Her makeup, extravagant as always, was done in a dark smokey eye with purple glitter with black lipstick to match. She looked incredible, as always, if not a little inappropriate for negative-ten degree weather. Piper admired Hally's confidence to wear whatever she wanted, and look incredible in it. Piper also knew she didn't have to worry about Hally being treated poorly for dressing in a way that showed off her body. She was a proud feminist who would knock anybody's teeth in for degrading her.

"You look like you're going to your cousin's baptism," Hally commented, giving Piper a once over. Piper rolled her eyes.

"Don't forget, this dress is yours," she retaliated.

"Yeah, from fifth grade."

Piper ignored the comment and left the house, Hally trailing after her, to the red convertible that they seemed to never leave.

Piper was wearing a red dress that ended right below her knees. She had a black belt around her waist with a gold clasp. The sleeves were long and mesh and the neckline was a thin V with a sheer layer of mesh in the gap in material. She was going for comfort more than anything else. The dress was thick enough that she wouldn't be too cold and it wasn't tight on her, so she could still move comfortably. It definitely wasn't Hally's style anymore.

Hally picked up the boys, and when Drew said he wanted to drive, Hally insisted that she wouldn't be caught dead in Drew's truck, especially not going somewhere as nice as the club they were on the way to. When Drew offered to drive the convertible, Hally basically laughed in his face.

"No one drives this baby but me," she said, turning the radio up as a sign to Drew that their conversation was over. Piper knew that Drew had no chance driving the convertible. Still she thought it was a little cruel that Hally made him sit in the backseat.

Piper stared out the window, and ended up catching Brent's eye in the mirror. He gave her his usual charming smile, and Piper thought about how hard it would be for her to break up with this boy.

They pulled into a parking lot of a dark building, the only lights being the gentle yellow ones above the door, and the colourful ones peaking through the tall, tinted windows. She stared at the building for a moment too long, because she didn't notice everyone getting out, and Brent holding the door open for her.

She shook her head to clear it and stepped out, following him up to the door and pretending she wasn't uncomfortable with his hand on the small of her back.

A giant man stood at the door, his black leather jacket making his fiery eyes stick out and making him look double his size. He had a tiny, bald head that was riddled in tattoos. His hands were clasped in front of him, three times larger than Piper's. Piper felt herself shiver in fear, and Brent looked uneasy, but Hally strode up to the man with Drew on her arm and all the confidence in the world.

She smiled at the bouncer, confidence seeping out of her perfect posture and persuasive eyes. "Excuse me," she said simply. He gave her a once over, then stepped aside and let her in. Piper stared in astonishment, and Hally turned to look at her.

"Act like you belong, and they'll think you do," her best friend whispered, passing by the bouncer. She tugged Drew in with her, but when Piper tried to pass by, she was stopped.

"Where do you think you're going?" his voice boomed and made Piper want to shrink away from him.

Hally popped her head out again. "They're with me."

And, inexplicably, the bouncer let them pass.

"Hally, that was incredible!" Piper exclaimed once they were inside. Hally didn't seem fazed.

"I think you mean *I* am incredible." Her cheeky smile made Piper relax a little. Hally and her were complete opposites, but Piper always felt relaxed when her friend let loose.

She pulled Piper over to a bar and ordered two drinks Piper couldn't dream of being able to pronounce. She took them from the bartender and handed one to Piper. She was about to take out her wallet, when the bartender waved his hand and winked at her.

"They're on the house. Have a good night, ladies."

Hally grinned at him. "Thank you. We will."

She raised her eyebrows at Piper cheekily, and they scuttled away, drinks in hand.

The music was louder as they got closer to the dance

floor, where hopping bodies glimmered under the flamboyant lights. It seemed, Piper observed, that everyone in the room was beautiful. Not an unpleasant face passed her, not one unhappy fool on the floor. She liked it, though she still felt shaky. She was worried that it was obvious that they didn't belong there.

The two of them found the boys, talking amongst themselves and sipping on a beer each. They seemed to be waiting for their girls to return, and the way Brent beamed at Piper when she approached stung her.

Hally downed the rest of her drink and grabbed Drew by the hand, announcing that they were going to go dance.

Then, Piper turned to Brent.

"Hey," she breathed, and it was so soft that there was no way he heard her. But, he understood anyway.

"Hi."

"Brent, I need to talk to you."

He made a face at her and said, "What?" His lip reading ability wasn't good past one word, apparently.

She stepped a little closer so he could hear her properly. She leaned into his ear and, taking a deep breath, she repeated, "I need to talk to you. I need to say—"

"I know what you're going to say."

She felt a wave of relief wash over her. Maybe this wouldn't be so hard. "You do?"

"Of course," he wrung his hand through hers, their fingers intertwined. He looked at her fondly, making her think he didn't know what she wanted to say at all. "You're going to apologize for disappearing on me. But, that's okay. I don't blame you. Sometimes, you just need some time away. I understand completely. However, I really did miss that pretty face of yours." He tapped her nose playfully, smiling at her. She felt infinitely more guilty. *That's it*, she thought. *I can't do it tonight.*

So, she smiled back at him. "I... missed you, too."

She wished she didn't lie. She hardly thought of him.

"Good. That's your punishment."

She didn't want to talk to him anymore. She didn't know what to say. So, mimicking Hally, she finished off her drink and pulled Brent off onto the dance floor.

She was definitely too sober to dance like the people around her, so she did an uncomfortable bob along with the music, looking at anything but Brent. She couldn't believe she chickened out. She wanted to get the whole thing over with in one night but she couldn't. She was too scared. She didn't want to upset him.

As the night went on, she began to loosen up, but she owed that to the alcohol.

She had plenty of drinks as the time passed. It seemed there was always some fruity, strong smelling drink in her hand, even after just finishing one. She'd totally forgotten her apprehension about drinking.

She felt groggy, and the more she drank the more she realized she had never been drunk before. She'd drank—being friends with Hally made for a handful of convenient opportunities to—but she'd never been drunk.

The more blurry and uncoordinated everything seemed, the more confused and disoriented she got as well. She couldn't remember how many drinks she'd had, and she had no concept of time. How long had they been out? What part of town were they in?

She was dancing more than she usually would. The fears of being judged had left her when the alcohol entered her system. Part of her felt great—careless, excitable—but she mostly just felt... ill. The club felt cold and she was nauseous and her breaths felt slow and uneven.

After who-knows-how-long of dancing and drinking, Brent took her aside.

"Hey, maybe you should slow down a bit," he said. He sounded concerned, but she didn't see why.

"Why would we? We're having fun!" she exclaimed. She was slurring when she spoke, which made her laugh. Brent sighed.

"I know, but maybe we're having too much fun."

She rolled her eyes, but she couldn't stop him when he took the drink from her hand and laid it on a nearby table. He tugged her by her arm to a single stall bathroom across from the bar.

When both of them were inside, he shut and locked the door. Her eyes stung from the fluorescent light in the bathroom. His scanned her face and, even in her haze, Piper noticed that he looked worried.

"You look sick," he commented. He laid a hand on her cheek carefully, but she swatted it away. He furrowed his brow. "What's wrong with you?" he asked, his voice barely above a whisper. The bathroom blocked out almost all of the music. All she could hear was a ringing in her ears, her heavy, irregular breath and the booming bass through the door.

One thing was clear; her usual filter was gone. So, when Brent asked her that question, she couldn't resist admitting what she wanted to in the first place. The words came out of her mouth before she even thought of them.

"I'm gay."

He stared at her, and he must have been drunk too because he seemed to think she was joking. A quiet, nervous laughter racked him for a moment. When he saw she wasn't laughing, he asked, "What?"

"I think I'm gay. I want to break up."

He looked hurt, and her mind was shouting at her to shut up. Caught under the influence, she didn't listen.

"Well, I do like you, but not the way you want me to. I'm sorry I led you on, but I only want to be friends."

It settled with him that she wasn't kidding, and he started to shout. She couldn't decipher what he was saying, but she knew he was angry. His words were melting together in her brain and they didn't mean anything. She felt numb and lost. That wasn't the way that should have happened. She should have been respectful. She should have been nice. But she wasn't herself. She felt like she was going to throw up.

Absent-mindedly, she left the bathroom with him yelling after her. She closed the door behind her and engulfed herself in the sound of raging music. She saw stars. The wall of sound hit her like a bus and her eyes wouldn't focus. She found Hally crying, mascara staining her face, running outside.

She followed her, trying not to stumble. But, through the door, she did, and the bouncer took her arm to steady her.

"Careful, Miss," he said gently. "Do you have a ride home?"

She made no move to reply. She pulled her arm away from him, waved him off and fell on her knees. The dizziness and sick feeling in her tummy overtook her and she emptied her stomach. Her throat tingled and her eyes watered with the burning sensation of bile and liquor coming up. It took her a moment to be able to stop throwing up, but when she could, she followed after Hally.

Hally was standing next to her convertible, pulling her keys out of her purse and unlocking the doors.

"Hally," Piper said, finding her own voice through the alcohol. Hally turned to look at her and sniffled. Hally, for once, wasn't perfect. Black streaks ran down her cheeks from her makeup and her face was flushed from crying. Piper managed to snatch the keys from Hally's hand. "What are you doing?"

"I'm going home!" Hally sobbed. Piper, somehow, still had some sense. She shook her head, though the slight movement made her want to vomit again.

"You can't drive," she mumbled. She wanted to sound more forceful, but she felt too dreadful to raise her voice. "You've been drinking all night."

"I don't care!" Hally snatched the keys back and clicked the unlock button again, though the car was already unlocked. She was going to get in but Piper grabbed her arm.

"You'll get into an accident," Piper argued.

"I'm a good driver!" Hally shouted. Piper exhaled. The ground below her was spinning.

"You're drunk."

Hally rolled her eyes. "I've driven myself home drunk before. I can do it again."

Piper opened her mouth to speak, but Hally ripped her arm away roughly, hopping into the driver's seat. Piper stared.

"Are you getting in or not?" Her best friend croaked. Piper thought for a moment. She had no other ride home. After what happened with Brent, she couldn't ask him for help. She thought about calling her dad and pulled out her phone, only to find it dead. She couldn't remember using it at all that night.

She put her phone back and nodded. She got in the passenger's seat and laid her head back. She knew a car ride would only make her queasy stomach worse, not to mention the life or death consequences of her driver being inebriated. However, her brain was too slow to think about the true consequences fully. All she knew was that she wanted to go home.

"Just… be careful," she begged. Hally brushed her concern away with a wave of her hand.

They pulled onto the road and found that it was mostly empty. Piper managed to relax a little. Any thought of getting into an accident left her. There weren't any cars to get into an accident with.

She stared out the window, shutting her eyes and trying to keep whatever was left in her stomach down. She was freezing, but she felt too tired and sick to move to turn up the heat.

"What happened?" Piper asked her friend sheepishly. Hally sighed.

"Drew was flirting with some chick at the bar. I went looking to the ladies room and when I got back, this random girl was all over him." Her voice was weak, and made Piper want to hug her. She loved her friend so much that it broke her heart to see her upset. She looked at Hally. She wanted to spew on about how he wasn't good enough for her anyway, and how she was way too beautiful to let some guy hurt her. But she couldn't form words very well, so she laid a trembling hand on Hally's shoulder.

"I'm really sorry, Hal."

Hally sniffled and managed a bitter laugh. "It's partially my fault. What was I thinking? Taking a boy like him to a club. Of course he'd go looking for some college girl to replace me."

Piper frowned. "It isn't your fault," she said. Hally took one hand off the wheel and twirled her hair with it.

"Thanks, P." She let out a long breath and shifted in her seat so she wasn't slumped over. "What happened with you and Brent after?"

"Bad stuff," Piper murmured. "Very bad."

"Ah, that sucks. Don't fret over him too much. He's a big boy. I'm sure he'll get over it." She looked away from the road to make eye contact with Piper. For a short moment, Hally managed a genuine smile that made Piper feel better.

"Thanks, Hal—"

As if from nowhere, the sound of a honking truck blared, and Piper couldn't turn her head fast enough to see the source. The car collided with something huge, accompanied by the sound of Hally screaming. Someone else screamed, but Piper couldn't make out who. It could have been her. Piper felt her head snap back against her seat as the airbag hit her and she blacked out to the sound of smashing glass and metal.

CHAPTER TWENTY FOUR

When Piper awoke, she wasn't in her bed. She lay on a thin mattress with stiff covers in a narrow, pristine bed. She looked around, the fluorescent lights feeling like needles in her eyes. The sight of them alone was enough to make her head pound.

She was in a hospital. Her wrist was wrapped in a cast. It felt sore beneath the layers of bandages. She wiggled her fingers, just to make sure she still had control of them. She didn't remember the events of the night before, but she vaguely saw headlights and smelled alcohol as she thought back.

A doctor walked into the room, and she recognized her as Dr. Benson, her family doctor. She was a kind woman, with greying hair and blue eyes. She was tall and thin with a crooked nose and skeletal hands. Despite her cold appearance, she was as warm as they come. She was always kind and gentle with Piper, so Piper didn't feel particularly unhappy to see her.

"How are you feeling?" she asked, picking up a chart from the bed and looking it over. Her eyes looked beady as she squinted to read it all. "You got into a pretty bad accident. Do you remember much?"

Piper shook her head. She remembered it vaguely. As if it was a story someone else told her months ago. She got the gist of it, at least.

"Well, it should all come back to you soon. You're lucky you got off with just a broken wrist. It was quite the crash. Although when you got here, you were experiencing severe alcohol poisoning. We had to perform a gastric suction to alleviate it."

"Gastric suction?" she repeated inquisitively. Dr. Benson nodded.

"Stomach pumping."

Piper felt herself go pale. How much had she drank? Far too much, quite obviously, but was Hally okay? Did Hally have as many drinks as she did?

"In the meantime, you have some visitors," Dr. Benson said. She moved away from the topic too quickly. There was a lot more to explain. "Do you feel up to talking?"

Piper, feeling awkward but, not willing to be alone, nodded her head.

Dr. Benson left, and after a few short minutes, Piper's eyes widened.

Hally rolled into the room in a wheelchair, her left leg propped up with a cast. Somehow, the girl still managed to smile like a beauty queen, even in the dreadful conditions before them.

"Hey, Lightweight," she said, rolling up to the side of Piper's bed. She sighed and turned suddenly serious, which was unusual for Hally. "I'm so sorry."

Piper huffed. "It's okay."

Hally shook her head stubbornly. "No, it's not," she argued. "I hate that you're so goddamn understanding all the time."

"Really, you were drunk," Piper said. "You didn't

know better. Besides, I chose to get in the car with you."

"I pressured you," Hally said. She took a shaky breath and Piper noticed her best friend's hands shaking. "You looked really pale last night," she added quietly. "You looked... out of it. And, your breathing... It was scary, but I didn't really think anything of it. I just thought you drank a bit too much. I thought you would sober up once I got you home." A tear fell from her cheek, and Piper wanted to reach out and hug her, but they were so far away from each other. "I'm sorry. It was my fault. I was selfish and I wanted to get out of there to spare my own stupid feelings. I never wanted to hurt you, Piper. I love you, you know that?"

Piper felt herself crying, too. That kind of crying that snuck up on you when you were least expecting it. The kind of crying that felt built up and smashed through the dam like a tsunami. The same kind of crying that made the whole room look blue. Her chest shook in quiet sobs and she nodded. "I love you, too."

Hally swiped at the tears on her own face but it was no use. New ones kept replacing the ones she got rid of.

"I hate that you're here," she whispered. Her voice was so desperate and weak. Piper put out her hand and Hally took it and squeezed it tightly. "Some part of me knew that one day, I'd fuck up bad. I've had it too easy for too long. But I never expected that I would hurt you in the process. It's my fault you're here. I might as well have broken your arm myself and drowned you in alcohol."

"Stop it," Piper scolded. "You didn't force me to do anything."

"I didn't stop you either, though. Did I? I mean, Jesus! I made you come out with us when you didn't want to. I got you the first drink. I was driving the car!" Hally shrieked.

Piper remained quiet. Hally sniffled and pushed some loose strands away from her face.

"I remember, right when the car stopped moving, my leg hurt so bad but I didn't even care. I looked over at you and... a—and you were so... still. I thought you were dead or something. I couldn't even hold your hand because your arm was squished in between you and the airbag" She stared at Piper's cast and shook her head to herself. Piper's vision was cloudy with tears. She didn't know Hally was awake during the whole accident. *That must have been awful.*

"I'm so so s-sorry—" Hally whispered, but her voice broke and she erupted into sobs. Piper pushed off her covers and swung her bare legs off the side of the bed. She leaned forward and wrapped her arms around Hally, hugging her friend tightly. Hally clutched to her, her hands eager as cries shook her whole body. She held onto Piper for dear life, her hands wrapped up in the hospital gown Piper was wearing.

"I don't blame you, Hally," Piper managed to say, her voice more level than she expected. "I know you would never deliberately hurt me. It was all just an accident. Besides, think of it this way—" She pulled back from the hug to wipe some tears off of Hally's flushed, devastated face. "—If I'd just gone home, I would have gone to bed with a possibly lethal amount of alcohol in me. I'm not grateful we got into a crash. But I'm grateful you were there. And that we're both alive. The whole night fucking sucked. But no part of me blames you for me getting hurt."

Hally took a couple uneasy breaths but managed to stop crying. She was still disheveled, and looked like she was still in pieces. But her gasping sobs stopped and she managed to nod her head at Piper.

Piper wanted to say more to relieve Hally's guilty conscience, but Hally spoke before she could.

"I, uh, plugged in your phone for you," she said. Her voice sounded scratchy and wobbly from crying but Piper didn't mention it. "Some girl called when it turned on. I picked it up. I figured if she was a friend, you would want her to know what happened. I don't know if it was the right thing to do..."

Hally seemed different. She was less sure of herself. It wasn't common for her to question her own actions. She always knew what to do. It was unsettling to see her second guess herself.

Piper didn't think it was right to mention that either. Not yet, at least. Besides she was curious about something else anyway.

"A girl?" Piper repeated inquisitively.

"She said her name is Autumn. I told her you were in the hospital and I'd let you know she called but she insisted on coming."

Piper turned red and felt her breath catch in her throat. "A-Autumn's here?"

"Yeah. I tried to tell her you might not be up for visitors, but she was pretty stubborn. Who is she? Why didn't you tell me about her?"

Because she would find you a million times more attractive than me, Piper thought, but didn't say it out loud. It was a bitter, jealous thought and she hated to have it.

"She's nobody, really," she lied. "I hardly know her."

Hally looked skeptical. "She's nobody? Yet, she needed to drop everything and see you in hospital?"

Piper didn't know what to say, so she just shrugged. Hally scanned her face for a second before asking, "Do you want me to go get her?"

Piper shook her head. "No, you don't have to. You're not well, you should stay put."

Hally waved a hand dismissively. "It's only a broken leg. Besides, now I have a sick new ride."

Piper was astounded that Hally could make a joke about her situation. A second ago, she was bawling. Now she was borderline casual. Piper thought that Hally was trying to cover up her true feelings for her friend's sake. Piper didn't understand how she could. Piper felt like shit. She thought, *what are the odds that the first time you get drunk, you get in a car accident and have to have your stomach pumped?*

They couldn't have been this good, right? That was her gambling career out the window.

Hally wheeled herself out of the room, and Piper felt anxious in her absence. Butterflies floated into her stomach as she heard boots approaching her room. She quickly wiped away all the tears she could manage and tried to fix her hair. She hoped she looked okay.

What a ridiculous thought, she mused, *of course I don't look okay. Not after all of this.*

When the footsteps stopped, there stood Autumn, her hair pushed back in a black beanie. Her face against the harsh fluorescent lights was incredibly welcoming.

She looked at Piper closely, a sympathetic smile forming on her face.

"Hi," she breathed.

"Hey."

"How do you feel?"

Piper didn't know how to reply to that. How did she feel? Other than stupid and sore? "Fine, I guess," she mumbled. Autumn approached the bed awkwardly and sat.

"What happened? I mean, Hally told me what happened vaguely, but it didn't really sound like you."

Piper scrunched up her nose a little at the comment. "You don't know me," she retorted. Autumn's smile faltered.

"I guess you're right," she agreed. "So… was this all in character for you, then?"

Piper sighed heavily and conceded. "Not at all."

Autumn looked vaguely amused, but still concerned. She bit her lip, her usual confident vibes turning sheepish. "I hope it's okay that I came. I know we don't know each other, but I was worried about you."

She was worried? Piper's mind was working the way it always did: ten times too fast. She managed to smile, however. She was glad to see Autumn, but then again, she always was. It didn't matter that her and Autumn didn't really know each other, because it was comfortable and safe.

"I'm glad you're here," Piper admitted. She wasn't lying, which was a weird feeling. She felt like she did a lot of lying lately. "I broke up with the guy I was with."

Autumn raised an eyebrow. "Really?"

"Yeah," she answered. "But, not for you. I broke up with him because I wanted to." That time, she was only partially lying, so she told herself it didn't count.

"Oh, I see." Autumn had a teasing lilt in her voice. "So, you didn't break up with him because you liked me?"

Piper shook her head. They were dancing around the elephant in the room and that was just fine with her. She didn't want to think about it more than she already had to.

Autumn asked, "So, you wouldn't accept if I asked

you out on a date?"

Piper felt the butterflies having a mosh pit in her stomach, and a blush take over her cheeks. "Well, I didn't say that," she mumbled.

Autumn smiled and stood up. "Get some rest."

"But—"

"Did you think I would ask right now?" Autumn asked. She smirked at Piper, a cockiness around her that Piper just adored. "We need to have a better story than that, don't we?"

Piper was speechless, but she had so much she wanted to say.

"Take care of yourself, Piper," Autumn said and Piper watched with happiness, excitement, and just a little bit of sorrow, as Autumn winked at her and left the hospital room.

CHAPTER TWENTY FIVE

The next day, Piper was allowed to leave the hospital. They kept her an extra day for observation and since no additional problems arose in that time, she was given the all clear to go home.

Even though her father wasn't much of a disciplinarian, she was still worried about the consequences of her actions. She knew she couldn't get off with a slap on the wrist or a stern talking to. She couldn't remember the last time she got in actual trouble. She understood with great confidence that whatever punishment her father chose for her, she'd deserve it. She did a lot more than just staying out past curfew this time.

She had a feeling Dr. Benson talked her father down from being too upset with her, though. From the moment he stepped into her hospital room, he was nothing but worried. Only caring and protective. He wasn't angry. Initially, that was a relief. Now, Piper wondered if that would wear off the moment she was deemed healthy.

He brought her clothes from home, since her dress (Hally's dress, actually) didn't survive the crash in very good condition. It certainly wouldn't be missed. The vomit on it was enough to make Piper want to get rid of it, anyway. She also didn't mind having one less reminder of that night.

She got dressed in her room while he waited outside, discussing something with her doctor. She was overwhelmed by the guilt of it all. She couldn't imagine being a parent and hearing that something so awful happened to your kid. Especially since it was her fault. And then he had to see her in the hospital. He had to read her chart and discuss her condition with doctors. The pain in her arm was nothing compared to that.

Once she was dressed, she stepped out of the room. Her father and doctor were just finishing up their conversation. She stood by the door, cradling her cast in her other hand awkwardly. It felt uncomfortable and heavy. But strangely, she liked it. She'd never broken a bone like this before. When she was younger, tons of kids came into school with casts. Apparently, kids are prone to accidents. She never was. She was too careful. However, she was always jealous of their colourful bandages covered in drawings and signatures. And besides, her arm didn't really hurt. The most painful thing about it was the admonition it told her; to never be so stupid and reckless ever again.

They finished their talk with a firm handshake and her father saying, "Thank you very much, Doctor."

When her dad walked toward her, she felt the need to take a deep breath. Sure, he wasn't normally an angry person. But this wasn't normal. This was a massive, colossal, shitty series of events. She didn't know how he'd react.

He put his arm around her waist as a way to carefully lead her out of the building. It was a loving, fatherly thing to do. A way to express he supported her, even if they seemed like they were on opposite sides at the moment.

"Are you alright?" he asked gently. Piper nodded, but

felt as though she needed to say something to him.

"I'm fine," she complied. "I'm really, really sorry, Dad."

He sighed deeply, taking back his hand so he could rake it through his hair. "I know. And, you should be. You scared the hell out of me, and I'm sure your mother will be worried sick when she hears the message I left on her machine."

She agreed sadly. "I didn't mean to hurt anybody," she said. Her voice was more vulnerable than she thought it would be, but it was true. She thought the only one she would hurt was herself. Maybe getting into that car with Hally was an act of self-destruction, she thought. It was definitely possible. Looking back, she hadn't allowed herself much success in other aspects of her life. Maybe she was preemptively punishing herself for trying to make a change.

Or maybe, she was just stupid enough to give up on her beliefs once she had a few drinks in her.

"I know, honey." His tone was benign but sorrowful. She felt like she was a kid again. A kid with a guilty conscience who needed her dad to tell her everything was going to be okay. "Let's just go home," he said.

She nodded again. They left through the main doors of the hospital. Piper felt the sun on her face and cold air on her skin. It felt good to be outside, at least. Even if it was cold and the sun was shining directly in her eyes, she savoured the taste of the outside air. Everything in the hospital smelled like plastic and medicine and soap.

"You're still grounded, you know," Samuel teased. Piper managed to crack a smile and let out a playful huff.

"I figured as much."

Piper felt sad, for a multitude of reasons. One of

the more trivial being that she'd just given Autumn her number when they were at the coffee shop, and now she wouldn't be able to talk to her. She knew she deserved to be grounded. In fact, she probably deserved worse than a grounding. But she wasn't willing to lose Autumn before she had the chance to know her.

The biggest thing weighing on her mind, of course, was the accident. More of it came back to her, but she was unconscious for most of it. She hated that Hally witnessed it all, because now it would weigh on her. She could only hope Hally wouldn't bottle this up like she did everything else.

When they got home, Piper told her dad she felt ill. It wasn't a lie entirely. She did feel sick and uneasy, but she mostly wanted to go to her room so she wouldn't have to talk about what happened. She wasn't ready yet.

She retreated to her room. Samuel forgot to take her phone before she left, so she messaged Autumn and Hally that she was grounded and would have her phone taken away. She gave them both her email address. She had an old, barely functional Hello Kitty laptop tucked away in her room and she figured that would be the perfect way to communicate with them. She was lucky she never cleaned out her closet. Once her texts sent, she slipped her phone onto her bedside table and rolled over. The moment she shut her eyes, she was out like a light.

When she awoke, her phone was gone from the table. She expected it to be, so she wasn't worried. She glanced at the clock mounted above her door. It was 6 p.m. She'd slept for eight hours.

She could hear the murmur of the television downstairs through the walls. She pulled out her laptop from her closet, and started it up. She didn't even know if it would work. It was slow and ancient, and was only used for games when she was younger. It probably had a million viruses. She pondered if it would turn on at all.

But then the screen beamed to life (though the picture looked fuzzy) and it connected to the internet automatically. She found her way into her email account and saw an email from an unknown address. She opened it.

thepurplepunk@gmail.com: *Hello, Piper. How was your day? Is that a stupid question? You did just get out of the hospital and now you're grounded. I could probably assume how you're feeling myself, but you know what they say about assumptions. Anyway, here is my formal email, though I wish we were using anything but email. Email sucks considering it isn't the early 2000's anymore. Get back to me when you can. Hope you're well. Laters! ~ Autumn.*

She smiled at the message, and decided to reply. Her fingers floated over the keys before she settled on what she wanted to say.

xRedHeadPixiex@gmail.com: *Hello, Autumn. You hit the nail pretty much on its head, I'm not fantastic. And I agree, email sucks. But you did get your facts wrong. Email was popularized in 1980, not 2000. It was invented in 1971 by Ray Tomlinson. It gained momentum with users on Arpanet. It wasn't as casual then, though. If you're talking about the kind of email we use nowadays, you're still a few years off. Microsoft made an email platform in 1996 and in the same year, Hotmail and some other companies began offering free email you could use virtually anywhere (get it? virtually?) But, while the rest of the world is totally over it, email is all we have for now. Which would you rather? Crappy, laggy conversations, or none of me at all?*

Actually, after the random email facts, you probably shouldn't answer that question.

She reread her email a thousand times after it was sent before she determined that it satisfied her. She was going to close her computer, when she saw that her email was already opened. Autumn was waiting for her to reply. That warmed her heart.

Moments later, another email popped up.

thepurplepunk44@gmail.com: *Okay okay, you're right. I definitely want to talk, even if it is on the shittest platform available. Also, why the fuck do you know so much about email? Who knows that many facts about email? And even if you know them, why would you say them? Do you think you're going to impress me with your obscure knowledge?*

I'm not going to lie. It's working. Until next time, stranger~.

Again, Piper replied immediately.

xRedHairedPixiex@gmail.com: *Don't insult or underestimate my ability to know all about useless topics. Get used to it, because there's plenty more where that came from. Wait until I start on different kinds of beatles. Then you'll really be in for it. I hope we can talk soon. I'll be waiting, Coffee Shop Girl.*

She smirked to herself, and hit send.

CHAPTER TWENTY SIX

Laura wasn't over for supper that day. Piper wondered if that was because of her. As much as she didn't like Laura, she didn't want her dad thinking he couldn't have her over. Sure, Piper would prefer it if she wasn't around. But Samuel was an adult. He could date whoever he wanted. It was his house. He shouldn't let Piper dictate who could and couldn't come over.

She voiced her concern over her spaghetti.

"Where's Laura?"

Samuel looked up at her, clearly surprised. "Uh, she had a thing tonight. Why?"

"Is that true?" she asked. "Or did you not invite her for my sake?"

Samuel looked down at his bowl. That was answer enough for Piper but she let him speak anyway.

"I wanted to give you space," he said. "She understands. It's been a hard couple days for you."

Piper smiled, though the guilt that was sucking her blood like leeches grew stronger by the second.

"Thanks," she said. "But honestly, I'm fine. You don't need my okay to have your girlfriend around." She had a weird taste in her mouth after that so she pushed her bowl away. Before her dad said anything in response, she was already standing. "I think I'm going to go back to my room."

"You're not going to finish your supper?"

"No. I'm full. Goodnight, Dad."

He seemed hesitant but he said goodnight as well and watched her leave.

Piper retreated to her room. Her father didn't push her. He knew she was distressed after everything. She made it pretty obvious, even if she was trying not to.

That wasn't the only reason she wanted to leave supper early, though. She was also excited to see if Autumn had replied yet.

When Piper saw that she hadn't, she tried not to feel too sad. She liked Autumn. Everything was easy with her. It was like breathing. So natural, so simple, but it keeps you alive. It was everything, but most didn't appreciate just how significant a breath of fresh air can be. That's what Autumn was; the perfect breath of fresh air, after holding your breath. She was breathing in fridged, winter air after the first snow. She was a gasp after a bad dream, realizing everything was alright.

She was what Piper needed.

And, Piper found it funny that she had seen Autumn and thought she was beautiful. That's where this all stemmed from. Piper had seen a creature so beautiful, and so out of the ordinary in an ordinary place, that she was mesmerized. She craved seeing that perfect sore thumb again. Autumn made her believe in destiny. In fate.

It was weird. Piper could be such a cynic. She didn't believe in that kind of stuff. She felt it was a nice thought, but she never seriously considered it. She just thought it was a fictional concept and nothing more. But now, the way she felt about Autumn without knowing her, she knew that it was more than a concept. It was true, to some extent, at least. She wondered if Autumn felt the same. She wondered if—

She was cut off from her wondering when she heard a noise from her laptop. A notification. She opened her email again. *Speak of the devil.*

thepurplepunk44@gmail.com: *I'll have you know, I love beatles. I don't know jack shit about them, but I love them so beatle facts are more welcome here. On a non-beatle related note, how long are you going to be locked up in that tower, Rapunzel?*

Piper had to stop herself from typing out her reply too fast. She wasn't great with a keyboard (even before her accident), so the faster she typed, the more mistakes showed up. She wrote her answer as carefully as her fluttering heart could manage.

xRedHairedPixiex@gmail.com: *In that case, did you know that some beetles are carnivores? Dermestid beetles are known as "skin beetles" because they're flesh eating and can strip the carcass of an animal to bone. I watched a video of them in action. It looked like something out of a horror movie. I implore you to look into it.*
      As for my prison sentence, I'm grounded until further notice. Why do you ask?

thepurplepunk44@gmail.com: *That may be my least favourite beetle fact in the world. But it also might be the most rock and roll beetle fact in the world. I haven't decided yet. I will definitely look into it, but whatever trauma that leaves me with is your fault.*

I hope you're released sooner rather than later. I'm looking for a good time to properly ask you out on a date.

She felt her face go red, and the smile on her face grew twice its size. Now, she had another reason to regret her actions. She felt like her separation from Autumn was punishment enough for her misdoings. She would gladly have every bone in her body broken from that car crash to spend more time with this girl in person.

Well, that was probably an exaggeration.

She shook herself from her reverie and typed a message in response.

xRedHairedPixiex@gmail.com: *If I have to have the image of hundreds of beetles eating the skin off of a dead bird in my mind, then you have to. Those are the rules.*

But why can't you just ask me?

thepurplepunk44@gmail.com: *You deserve better than an invitation over email. Especially if it's in the middle of a conversation about flesh eating beetles. Don't worry. I'll figure something out.*

Piper tried to think of something to say in return, to no avail. Instead, she deemed the conversation over, and switched over to talk to Hally. She was about to type out a message when she saw that Hally sent her a link to a video call five minutes ago. She was glad her and Hally—despite their differences—had the same idea. She clicked on the link and saw Hally on the screen, picking at her nails idly. Piper couldn't imagine how bored she was.

"Hey!" Hally said excitedly when she noticed Piper.

"How are you feeling, Red?" She had her usually perfect blond hair tied into a messy bun. Her acrylic nails that she was so fond of were mostly cracked off or chipped. Her face was bare. Even her ears were without decoration. She hardly looked like herself.

"Fine. I'm more worried about you," Piper replied. "That broken leg suiting you nicely?"

"Definitely," Hally chuckled. "Surprisingly, I don't mind it much. I might bedazzle my crutches when I get them."

Piper smiled at that. She loved her best friend (which was a very redundant thing to point out) and she loved that that was such a Hally thing to say.

"I want to say I'm sorry, Hals. I feel kind of responsible—"

"Well, don't. It's not your fault."

"You can't take all the blame."

Hally didn't look completely convinced, so she moved on to a new topic immediately. She was the most deflective person Piper knew. It was no surprise that she wouldn't want to talk. Especially after she broke down in Piper's hospital room.

Hally asked, "I meant to ask, where were you before you followed me out of the club? I didn't see you anywhere."

Piper remembered what had happened and made a split-second decision: it was time to tell Hally the truth. She owed her best friend that much. "I broke up with Brent."

Hally looked taken aback. "Really? Brutal. I know you weren't in love with him or anything but why right then? Did something happen?"

Piper had to take a deep breath to prepare herself to

say the next sentence. "There's... someone else. And while I can't blame it all on her, she was the person to make me realize that I'm not who I thought I was. I was tired of pretending and avoiding a very necessary change. And I had to stop leading him on. I never really liked him. I just knew I was supposed to."

"That's... a lot to unpack, P."

Piper nodded in agreement. It was a lot for her to think about. She spent her whole life thinking she was someone else. Thinking that her life could be the same as everyone around her. But it couldn't. Not just because she couldn't find it in her to like guys like Brent but because, deep down, she couldn't stay cynical. If she wanted to be happy, she had to allow herself to believe in all that stupid shit that scared her. All that stuff that she thought she wasn't allowed to have, so she told herself didn't exist like destiny and magic and love.

It was time she stopped denying it. Change was inevitable and fearing it wouldn't make it slow down.

"Wait, did you say she? Are you..?"

Piper had her hands on the sides of her laptop, gripping it like it was weighing her down. She thought if she let go, she'd float to the ceiling like a helium balloon.

"Yeah," she said. "I'm gay."

Piper waited in tense silence for Hally to react. She couldn't even try to predict what Hally was going to do. She thought she knew her best friend inside and out but when it came down to it, she had no clue what to expect.

Piper went through every possibility in her mind in those short seconds. She imagined the call ending abruptly, or Hally giving some stupid, impersonal speech about being proud of herself. She imagined her friend distancing herself. No longer inviting her over, passing her in the hall without turning to look at her.

Instead of looking at her differently, weirdly, or even sympathetically, Hally smiled in a funny way, a realization passing her face. Piper, for a moment, was conflicted and upset.

"What?" she asked nervously.

"It's just.." Hally cut herself off with a soft laugh. "Cora Silverman told me she liked you last year and I told her you weren't gay and she looked like she really doubted me."

Piper's lips parted in a mixture of shock and relief. "Cora Silverman liked me?" she asked.

"Hell yeah!" Hally exclaimed.

"And, she knew I was gay before I did?"

"Apparently."

"Damn," Piper swore. "She's cute."

Hally laughed at that. Piper liked that Hally wasn't really making a big deal out of it. That was what Piper wanted. It didn't have to be a big thing. She didn't know why she expected it to change everything.

"So, tell me about the girl," Hally said then, catching Piper off guard.

"It's Autumn," she replied simply. "The girl you talked to while we were in the hospital."

Hally smirked. "She's pretty." Piper wholeheartedly agreed and was about to add something to that effect. Before she could, Hally continued, "But, don't get me wrong. If she hurts you, I will not hesitate to make her ugly. Make sure to tell that girl I'll be watching her."

Piper grinned. "I will."

CHAPTER TWENTY SEVEN

It was nine o'clock on New Year's Eve, and Piper was desperately trying to fall asleep. Most people would want to stay up to witness the new year, or at least be part of the celebration, but she was grounded. Her father left to go to his girlfriend's party. At first, he insisted on staying home with her so she wouldn't be alone, but she urged him to go and enjoy himself. She would be fine by herself until he got back the following day.

The hitch in the plan was that Piper couldn't sleep. That was probably due to the fact that it was nine o'clock, and who in their right mind goes to bed at nine o'clock on New Year's Eve?

With a sigh, she opened her laptop, hoping to distract herself. Of course, every page she opened was full of people who weren't grounded. Everyone else was taking in the final moments of the year. She saw pictures from the more wealthy kids, who were hosting massive house parties, all of them dressed like they just stepped off the red carpet. There were also pictures from celebrations in Maya and Locke's neighbourhood. The whole street was transformed for the holiday. While no one was very dressed up, they all looked so happy. They were sharing meals with neighbours and setting up for a firework show.

Apparently, whether they had money or not, everyone was ecstatic to hit the restart button.

As she scrolled (which was just an act of torture, since she couldn't take part) she recieved an email from Hally.

amandahugnkiss@gmail.com: *Hey hottie, you home?*

Piper laughed at the nickname as she replied:

xRedHairedPixiex@gmail.com: *I am, why?*

amandahugnkiss@gmail.com: *Looking for some company?*

Piper, confused, started to type out a reply, when she heard a sound at her window. She turned toward it, just as a tiny pebble clicked against the glass and fell away. She slid her laptop aside and walked over to the window. Cautiously, she opened it up and peered out.

Outside, she didn't find who she expected to.

She found Autumn.

She was wearing a white dress shirt and a tie with an open black coat on top. Her hair was half up in a bun, the rest of it in curls on her shoulders. She had a pile of pebbles in one hand and a bag in the other. When she saw Piper, she dropped the rocks and smirked.

"My lady," she called out, using a phony English accent to sound gentlemanly.

Piper smiled down at her. She was happy to see her, but her brow was furrowed in confusion. "What are you doing here?" she asked.

"Come down and I'll tell you."

Piper rolled her eyes playfully. "One second, let me change."

"Don't, just get down here!"

"But I'm in my pajamas!"

"Too bad!"

Amused, Piper grabbed a jacket and left her room, trotting down the stairs to the back door. She pulled the door open and stepped outside, where she found Autumn, standing beneath her window in the middle of the yard.

"What are you doing here?" Piper asked again.

"I wanted to see you," Autumn answered, "And your friend Hally was kind enough to accommodate me. Though, she did say she would murder me if I made you upset."

Piper laughed at that. "That sounds like Hally."

Autumn approached Piper and handed her the bag she was holding. "Go change."

Piper looked suspiciously at the bag but made no move to do as she was told.

"Don't worry," Autumn said when she hesitated. "Hally picked it out. She insisted she knew exactly what you would want."

Piper was about to stammer a response when Autumn gave her a gentle push toward the door.

"Go! We're on a schedule, here!"

"Okay, okay!" Piper laughed, but obeyed the request anyway. She walked back inside and into the bathroom, changing into the clothes Autumn had given her.

She looked into the mirror, and was astounded. It fit, better than any clothes she bought had ever fit her. It was violet, making her an accessory that would fit perfectly beside her companion.

The dress was form fitting from her chest to her waist.

It had off the shoulder sleeves, and the skirt went a little past her knees. Past the waistline, the dress was flowy with a very thin layer of tulle beneath it. Piper thought it was a beautiful dress. She wasn't sure if she looked beautiful enough in it. She was sure it looked stupid with her cast.

With the dress was a pair of matching heels. Naturally, Piper hated heels, but she slipped them on anyway. She would appreciate everything given to her by Autumn. Even if it was Hally who picked it all out. She made a mental note to thank Hally.

When she left the bathroom, Autumn was standing in the open doorway, and her grin fell away to astonishment. Piper looked down at herself self-consciously. The way Autumn was staring at her made her feel vulnerable.

"What? Does it not look okay?" she muttered, trying to fix nonexistent wrinkles in the skirt. Autumn stepped closer to her, fondness in her eyes.

"You look beautiful."

Piper blushed to her ears. She didn't trust herself to try and form words after that. Surely she'd stumble like an idiot if she did. Instead, the two of them left the house and Piper shut the door behind them.

Autumn put her arm around Piper, pulling her a little closer. She led her to the front of the house, where her purple motorcycle was parked.

"Have you ever been on a motorcycle before?" Autumn asked, detaching from Piper to approach the bike and grab one of two helmets from the seat. Piper shook her head. Autumn smirked and walked back to Piper, holding the helmet out to her. "You're going to love it."

Piper took the helmet from Autumn and raised a skeptical brow. Autumn turned and grabbed her own helmet, then sat down on the motorcycle, shifting forward for

Piper to get on the back.

Piper hesitated for a moment. She took a breath to gain some courage, but eventually hopped on the bike with Autumn. They both slipped on their helmets and secured them. Piper made sure hers was tight. One accident was more than enough for her.

"All good back there?" Autumn asked.

"Yeah," Piper confirmed, trying to mask the fact that she was nervous. Motorcycles were dangerous. Motorcycle accidents were more common and more dangerous than car accidents. She wished she didn't know that fact.

"Good. Hold on tight to me, okay?"

Autumn didn't have to tell her twice. Piper sat close to Autumn and wrapped her arms around her torso, locking her fingers together to make her grip as cemented as possible.

"Ready?" Autumn asked. Piper took a deep breath, promising herself she'd shut up her worries for a few hours. Or at least, she'd try to.

"Hell yeah."

Autumn revved the bike and before Piper even knew what was happening, they took off. At the sudden acceleration, Piper tightened her hold on Autumn, but it only took a few moments before she relaxed. It felt like they were flying. Or they were passengers on something mystical and alive. Like a dragon. It almost felt like the bike was breathing under her. The rumble sounded like a low, powerful growl.

Autumn was right; Piper really did love the motorcycle. It felt dangerous, but with the comforting feeling of Autumn against her, she felt safe.

They drove down the winding roads of their small town. Piper felt a smile behind her helmet, and made no effort to suppress it.

They took a back road, leading down to a park near the city. Autumn stopped the bike and hopped off, pulling off her helmet. Piper took hers off too, and Autumn helped her down from the bike. She didn't really need the help, but she liked that Autumn held her hand for a moment.

She looked around the park, confused as to why Autumn had brought her there, until something caught her eye.

The park was very open, with only a few park benches and structures around. One of the structures was a small, compact gazebo near the entrance of the park.

She'd been to this park before, and she'd seen that gazebo before, but never like this.

It had yellow fairy lights strung inside it, illuminating it in the night. In the middle, lay a red checkered blanket with a picnic basket beside it, and a palm sized speaker on top.

She stared for a moment, at a complete loss for words. What could she say? And even if she said anything, would she spoil the moment?

Surely not, she decided. *Surely nothing could spoil this.*

Autumn kept a hold of her hand and, with a cheeky grin, led her over to the gazebo, the two of them stepping in and sitting down on the blanket together.

"Autumn, this is…" Piper couldn't find the right word to describe it. She muttered, "Y-You didn't have to…"

"I know, but…" Autumn started quietly, her eyes on Piper like there was nothing else in the world. At the moment, that was how it felt. "You deserve to be treated like a princess."

Piper rolled her eyes at Autumn, even though her

cheeks were burning red.

"What?" Autumn said. "Too cheesy?"

"Just cheesy enough," Piper replied.

Autumn chuckled. She looked genuinely relieved, which gave Piper the insane notion that Autumn was nervous too. That was astounding on its own. What was it about Piper that brought this elegant creature to be humbled?

Autumn recovered easily. "Now, I have no idea how to cook, so there is McDonald's in here," she admitted, referring to the little, light brown picnic basket. "I hope that doesn't spoil the magic."

Piper couldn't help but laugh. "That's perfect."

They opened it up, digging into a nutritious meal of french fries and nuggets. When they released their hands to eat, Piper's hand felt abnormally cold without Autumn's to hold.

After they'd finished, they just talked, with music from Autumn's playlist playing in the background. While they were both talking, they weren't really saying anything. Talking was just a thing to do while they looked at each other and took in the fact that this was reality. They were really there. They were alive, for real this time. Everything before then felt like a demo.

Finally, a song came on that made Autumn's eyes light up.

"Oh, I love this song. Come on, Princess, dance with me." She offered her hand to Piper, and without a moment's hesitation, Piper took it.

As she let Autumn pull her to her feet, something dawned on her; she'd never danced like this with another girl before. How was she supposed to do it? She'd danced with boys, but that was different. When a boy and a girl dance, they both know where their hands are supposed to go, and who is supposed to lead. But, dancing with another girl, how would they know?

Autumn seemed to know, as she gently placed her hands on Piper's waist. Piper followed along and strung her arms around Autumn's neck, the same way the fairy lights were so delicately placed on the gazebo around them.

It took a second for Piper to recognize the song, but she was glad when she did. It was *Intertwined* by Dodie and Piper found herself being lost in the music completely, like there wasn't a sound outside of their bubble. She buried her head in Autumn's shoulder as they danced—swayed—to the music. She felt a sense of finality, like she'd been waiting for that moment her whole life without knowing.

"So, you're quite the romantic, aren't you?" Piper said, a playful note in her voice. Autumn rolled her eyes.

"Perhaps. What do you think?"

"I think it's amazing." Piper was honest, and her voice was as careful as the steps they took in unison. "It's so not what I expected. I can't believe you did this for me."

"This is nothing," Autumn said. "You deserve a million nights like this."

Piper looked up at Autumn. She stared into the other girl's eyes, captivated and conflicted, searching for an answer.

"Why me?" Piper asked quietly. "What's so special about me?"

Autumn pulled back a little so she could lay a hand on Piper's cheek. She had a dreamy smile on her face and Piper's face tingled from her touch.

"I can't explain it," she said. "There's just something

about you. I know it's weird. We're still strangers. But ever since I first saw you, I thought you were… significant." Autumn looked a bit bashful. She laughed nervously at herself. "I'm sorry if that sounds totally creepy."

Piper was quick to correct her. "No, it's not creepy," she insisted. "I feel the same way."

Autumn let out a sigh of relief. "Thank god." Piper was relieved, too. She was so glad that the magnetic pull she felt wasn't one-sided. She didn't really understand it, but she didn't care to. She was fine being confused. She was confused all the time anyway. At least now, she was confused and happy.

"So, you're like a proper bad girl now, huh?" Autumn prompted. Piper tilted her head in confusion. Autumn went on, "You went out clubbing, dumped your boyfriend, and now you snuck out while grounded."

At the mention of that awful night, Piper stiffened. She blinked away images of her stumbling out of a bar and took a small step away from the girl in front of her. With the step, she also took her hands back from Autumn's shoulders and crossed them anxiously.

"Let's… not talk about that," she mumbled, her voice unsure. Autumn frowned and shook her head.

"Oh, no, I didn't mean…" She looked like she couldn't find the right words. Her eyes danced around Piper's face for a moment before she exhaled. "Sorry. I didn't think before I said it."

Piper shrugged as if the sounds of ringing ears and crushing metal weren't clouding her brain.

"It's alright, I just don't want to talk about it," she said. Autumn nodded in understanding. The air around them was tense but neither girl seemed upset. They were both pondering on what to say next.

"If you ever do want to talk about it," Autumn said, "You can talk to me. But in the meantime…"

She reached into the basket in the gazebo and took out a sharpie before standing in front of Piper again.

"Can I sign your cast?" she asked cheekily.

Piper laughed and nodded. A final exhale was enough to wash away the high tide that crowded her skull. She held out her arm for Autumn, who held it gently with one hand and immediately got to work, as if she'd preplanned what she wanted to write.

"You know, I always wanted a cast when I was younger," Piper admitted.

"Oh, yeah?"

"Yeah. I thought it was so cool, having everyone you knew sign their name to it. It was just one of those special little things that I loved."

"This is your first broken bone?"

"Yeah. Have you ever broken a bone?"

"I broke my nose," Autumn said. She was scribbling a bit, and Piper looked at her instead of the cast so she could be surprised by what she got. "I was in middle school. I got into a fight with a girl called Fiona because she kept calling my best friend a geek. It wasn't the best insult but it pissed me off enough."

Piper smiled at the story. She could picture middle school Autumn, shorter and angrier with a bone to pick.

"So, she won?" Piper asked.

"Hell no! A broken nose wasn't stopping me. I had to teach her a lesson."

She laughed. She wanted to hear more, but before she could ask, Autumn said, "Voila! All done!"

Piper looked down at her cast. Autumn wrote her name in bubble letters and coloured them in black. Instead of a period at the end of her name, she drew a little crown.

"I love it," Piper told her. "Why did you draw a crown?"

"You're a princess, remember?" Autumn replied matter-of-factly. Piper looked up at her, and it was then that she noticed they were standing quite close. Piper was a little shorter, so Autumn looked down at her. Piper had a similar feeling to being on a stage with a spotlight over your head. She bit her lip. She couldn't think on what to say, but she didn't want to move. They were so close, Piper could feel the taller girl's breath against her skin.

"Can I kiss you?" Autumn whispered, and Piper sucked in an anxious breath, but didn't hesitate. She nodded, trying not to look too eager.

"Yeah," she answered. "Yes. Definitely."

Autumn smiled and leaned down to press her lips against Piper's. For a moment, Piper felt as though everything had fallen away from them. Piper closed her eyes, and they were standing in an open abyss, just the two of them. The ground under their feet dropped and reality crumbled and they were the only particles that remained. Autumn's hands were on either side of her face, and Piper could feel the warmth of her palms standing out against the hostile world they floated in.

When Autumn pulled away, Piper didn't feel ready for her warmth to leave her. Autumn moved her hands away from Piper's face, and Piper felt suddenly icy. Elated, but icy.

"Come on," Autumn said, grabbing the blanket from the gazebo floor and taking Piper by the hand. They took off, sprinting to the edge of the park, where the open grass sloped into a hill, elevated above the city. There was a thick row of trees to block the park from the city, so all they saw from that hill was greenery and an endless sky of stars.

Autumn laid the blanket out on the grass and the two of them laid down on their backs, side by side.

"Now, we wait," she said.

Piper turned her head to look at Autumn. "Wait for what?"

Her date shushed her. Piper rolled her eyes playfully, turning back up to look at the sky, where Autumn was looking.

A few seconds of nothing passed. They could vaguely hear the city folk partying on the opposite side.

A moment later, a spark glimmered into the air, giving birth to a sky of fireworks of all different colours. Piper squeezed Autumn's hand tighter every loud sound that hit her ears, but stayed where she was. She reveled in the feeling of her heart pounding with every explosion. She basked in the beautiful night, and the gorgeous girl beside her.

"Happy New Year," Autumn said wistfully.

"Happy New Year."

CHAPTER TWENTY EIGHT

Piper woke up that morning in her bedroom. She'd slept surprisingly well and her body felt looser and more relaxed than before. When her eyes fluttered open, the room was lit by streaks of morning light, peeking through her blinds. She was about to turn over in bed to check the clock, but found herself weighed down by an arm strung over her waist.

In a bout of forgetfulness, she tensed, but she eased up when she thought back on the night before.

After the fireworks, they didn't go home. It was much too nice a night for that, so they stayed out a while later. They listened to music and danced and star gazed without bothering to check the time. They were out for much longer than they intended. By the time they decided to turn in, it was already 3 a.m.

Piper's head was still a treacherous whirlpool. She didn't want to return to her house alone, so she invited Autumn inside. They cherished the final hours of their date, playing cards and sharing useless knowledge until dawn and at some point, they must've fallen asleep. Nothing beyond that transpired.

Now, Piper couldn't decide if she should get up, or

stay put and let Autumn sleep.

She pondered it for a moment but ultimately decided the first option was preferable if she wanted to explain the situation to her father.

She gently took Autumn by the wrist and lifted her arm so she could free herself from the bed. She wiggled out and let Autumn's arm return to the mattress as she stood from the bed.

She was still in her dress from the night before, so she had to change. As much as she loved the dress, she was relieved to toss on a pair of jeans and a t-shirt. The extravagances made her look unfamiliar. She preferred to look like herself, even if the dress made her feel a fraction more royal.

When she was out of the room, she trotted down the stairs and checked the time on the oven. It was one o'clock. They'd slept in.

"There she is." Her father's voice made her jump. She turned around to see him. He was dressed for work in a flannel shirt and a pair of worn out jeans, holding a newspaper at the kitchen table. He must've skipped his morning ritual of 'reading' the paper at Laura's place. "How was your New Years Eve? I feel bad for leaving you behind."

"Don't worry about it. I actually had a really good night." She took a breath, sitting down across from him at the table. He was distracted, paying more attention to the crossword than he paid to her. Normally she wouldn't care that much. But she needed his full attention in this moment. "Can you... put down your paper? I need to talk to you."

He glanced up at his daughter, a look of uncertainty on his face. He folded up his paper and laid it aside.

"What's wrong?"

"Nothing. I just have something to say." She fiddled with the edge of her sweater absently, unsure of how to phrase it. She muttered, "A... friend came over last night, and we went out. I know, I'm supposed to be grounded, but I couldn't refuse."

Piper had expected him to be disappointed, at least. After all, she betrayed his trust by abandoning the punishment she received for betraying his trust. That was pretty hardcore. But just like before, he was understanding. He simply sighed, and smiled at her. "That's okay," he said. "I'm just happy you weren't alone on New Year's Eve."

Apparently two wrongs do make a right.

"Wait," she added hesitantly. "There's more. We stayed out late and... they spent the night. Nothing happened, I swear, but they did sleep over. I'm sorry, I know I should have asked first but we just fell asleep and I didn't really think about it."

His face changed, but he didn't look angry. Just concerned. "Who was this? Was this that Brent guy? Because, I don't feel comfortable with you having boys sleepover—"

"It wasn't Brent," Piper interrupted quickly. "It was a girl. Her name is Autumn."

He relaxed and chuckled to himself. "Oh, I see. You made it sound like you'd gone on a date."

Piper sucked in a breath, staring at her hands in her lap. "I was on a date," she said, "With Autumn."

He scrunched up his nose—a habit they shared when they were confused—and watched his daughter. She, slowly and hesitantly, looked up to meet his eyes.

He was silent. He didn't say a word, he just looked at her. She couldn't tell what he was thinking from his face.

"Dad," she said softly. "Please say something."

It took him a short moment to recover. He gave her a stern, fatherly look. "The same rules apply with girls as they do with boys," he said. "No inappropriate behavior under my roof."

"Okay."

He stood then, taking his newspaper under his arm, his face returning to its usual sunny expression as if he'd snapped out of his concern completely. "I'd like to meet this girl. Whenever it's good for you." He rounded the island to where she was and put his hands on either side of her face. He looked at her for a second, the way only parents did (like he was trying to immortalize her in that moment) before leaning down and giving her a kiss on the forehead. As he retreated, he said, "Thank you for telling me. I want to hear all about it when I get home from work. I love you, Kiddo."

Her fear melted completely. "I love you, too."

She felt dazed as he let her go. She watched as he gave her a big smile, grabbed his keys and left through the front door. She smiled to herself in his absence. She was lucky to have him.

She walked back up the stairs to her room. She opened the door quietly, but realized she didn't have to when she saw Autumn sitting up on her bed, rubbing sleep out of her eyes. She looked toward the door as Piper walked in.

"Hey," she mumbled, her voice heavy with sleep. "It's late."

"We slept in," Piper commented, sitting beside her. "You, a little later than me, but still."

She lay her head on Piper's shoulder, though Piper was shorter so she had to hunch to do it. Regardless, they huddled together.

"Your house is quiet," Autumn commented, her eyes closed as she wrapped her hand in Piper's.

"There's no one home."

"Ah, that explains it."

With Autumn's hair brushing against her neck, Piper felt a powerful urge to lean down and kiss her. Instead, she occupied herself with finding something to say.

"You should get dressed," she said. "You know, in something you haven't been wearing since yesterday."

Autumn turned her head to look up at her and smiled, then sat up straight. Piper immediately missed the feeling of the other girl against her.

"Here, I'll find you something to wear." She stood up and walked over to her wardrobe, filing through her clothes. She had a lot of baggy clothes, which would have to be what she gave Autumn. Autumn was taller than Piper and she was certainly made up of more muscle than Piper too.

As she rifled through her belongings, she said, "I told my dad. Y'know, about our date."

"Oh? Was he mad?"

"Nah, my dad doesn't really get mad," she chuckled. "I told him about you. Not much, just that you're... you."

"A girl?"

Piper nodded. She pulled out a baggy—incredibly nerdy—Nintendo t-shirt from her drawer along with a pair of dark joggers and handed them to Autumn.

Autumn barely looked at them. Her eyes were on Piper, cautious like she expected the worst. "What did he say?" she asked nervously. Piper smiled.

"He said he loved me," she replied. "Oh, and we can't do anything inappropriate here."

"So... no strippers?"

"Precisely," she laughed. "He also said he wants to meet you. I imagine that'll be more fun for you than for me, since you'll get to see where I get all of my charming, geeky traits from."

Autumn didn't laugh. She looked pensive, her eyes glittery like she was looking through Piper. The room suddenly felt small. Piper reached out toward her.

"Hey," she said, "Are you okay?"

Autumn blinked and met her eyes. She smiled hesitantly. Her hands clutched the folded garments tightly.

"Yeah, sorry," she replied. Piper wasn't convinced, but it wasn't her place to pry. As curious as she was, she didn't want to cross any boundaries. What they had was fragile and new. She didn't want to put any pressure on it.

The house creaked and wind whistled outside. Piper somehow forgot how cold it was outside. It was so warm where she was.

"I should go change," Autumn said. She wasn't totally broken out of her reverie, so she turned to leave Piper's room like an apparition. Before she left, she paused and held up the shirt in front of her. She hesitated, glancing at Piper with a cheeky smile and a teasing lilt in her voice.

"Starfox?"

"Shut up and get dressed."

CHAPTER TWENTY NINE

When school started back up, a lot of things Piper wanted to avoid became unavoidable. Brent and Drew were part of that. Everytime she passed either of them in the hall she got a prickly feeling like something was about to happen. But nothing yet. The main thing was the accident. Her and Hally were beacons, basically screaming *"LOOK HOW TRAGIC WE ARE!"* Their casts stuck out like sore thumbs, especially since Hally was on crutches. Piper could hear people talking about them. They weren't being very discreet in their gossip. They didn't understand that what they thought of as fun, juicy gossip was her life. It was getting hard to keep up with.

The story at school was different than how she remembered it. Then again, high school gossip was just a giant game of telephone. It always ended differently than it began.

She fully realized how out of hand the rumours got when she visited the auditorium to see her friends.

"Piper!" Maya screeched when she stepped inside. The girl took off in a full sprint toward her and tackled her in a hug. They hit the ground together and though Piper's wrist ached from the impact, she didn't want to interrupt the moment.

"Uh, hi Maya," she mumbled, disoriented by the embrace.

"Hi? That's all you have to say? I thought you were dead or something!"

"Why did you think that?"

"I overheard some guys talking about you," she said. "They said you were super high and drove into an intersection with two oncoming semi-trucks. I didn't think anyone could survive that." Maya propped herself up on her arms, looking down at Piper from on top of her. "You look great for someone who's supposed to be dead."

Piper rolled her eyes and pushed Maya aside so she could stand up.

"Yeah, that's not exactly what happened," she said. She offered her hand to Maya and pulled the girl to her feet. "But I appreciate the concern."

Piper noticed Locke coming toward them. They looked concerned, even though they had a fantastic poker face. They asked, "What *did* happen?"

Piper exhaled and shook her head. "It wasn't as glamorous as everyone thinks, trust me. I don't really want to talk about it."

Maya looked between the two of them before shaking her head.

"Consider it dropped," she said matter-of-factly. She grabbed Piper and Locke by their hands and hauled them down to the space below the stairs, where they were before. "Now that the Christmas play is said and done, we have nothing to work on. Which is totally lame but it's fine because our set was awesome. We did a great job, I'm so proud of us."

Piper wanted to comment that she hardly worked on

the set at all, but she kept quiet.

"My art class has a huge project, though. It's supposed to be a portrait, three people minimum. So I was wondering if you guys would be my subjects."

"There's only two of us," Locke said. Maya swatted at their arm playfully.

"I'll be the third!"

"A self portrait?" Piper asked. "That'll be pretty hard, won't it?"

Maya shook her head again. "Not at all. I've done a dozen before. I'm a master of self portraits."

Piper could never paint herself. She doubted she could be objective about how she looked.

"I'll be a subject," Locke said. Maya squealed with joy and looked to Piper expectantly. Piper didn't even like having her picture taken. She didn't know how she'd fare with getting her portrait painted. But with the way Maya was looking at her, she couldn't refuse.

"I'll be a subject, too."

After school that day, she returned home. She was expecting a call from Autumn on the landline, since her phone was still being held captive.

The moment she stepped through the door, she heard the phone ringing. She kicked off her shoes and ran over to answer it before it went to voicemail. She nearly knocked down the table it sat on when she barrelled toward it and snatched the phone up. She pressed it to her ear and exhaled.

"Hello?"

She heard Autumn laughing on the other end. "Hey. Did you run home or something?"

Piper rolled her eyes. She held the phone to her ear

with her shoulder so she could use both hands to remove her jacket. "I didn't want to miss your call."

"I'll call a little later next time," Autumn said. "Give you more time to get home."

"Good plan."

"How was school?"

Piper answered that question by groaning heavily and dropping her jacket to the floor.

"Sounds fantastic," Autumn quipped sarcastically.

"Oh, it was a treat," Piper agreed. "I hope the stories die down quickly. Its been one day and I'm already exhausted."

"I'm assuming you were the main topic of discussion?"

"You have no idea. Hardly anyone spoke to us, but I heard mine and Hally's name about a thousand times. And the story was completely twisted. I have no idea who spread it around."

"I might have an idea..." Autumn muttered this under her breath, as if it were more of a random thought than an addition to their conversation. But it piqued Piper's interest.

"Who?"

She heard Autumn sigh. "There were only two other people there. And one of them has a reason—albeit a shitty reason—to spread rumours about you."

Piper felt sick at the notion. "Brent?"

"I mean, you guys didn't end on very good terms. From what you told me, he probably felt embarrassed and angry. Maybe he wanted to humiliate you to get you back."

Even though Autumn couldn't see her, Piper was shaking her head. She knew he was angry. He had a right to be. It must've been embarrassing to be broken up with that way, both of them drunk in a club bathroom. But she didn't think he was capable of doing something so petty.

"That's not like him," Piper replied.

"How well did you know him?"

Piper didn't answer, because she hadn't known him very well. She knew the parts of him he was willing to share, and vice versa. They hadn't known each other on a very deep level. They knew enough to fill out the first section of their wikipedia page. Past that, they were both clueless.

"He's harmless," she said. She didn't know why she thought that. Surely, if he was as stereotypical as she thought, he would be anything but; however, thinking back on the things he told her—especially about his friendship with Drew—she was inclined to believe it was true. He was softer than the other boys. He required more care. And, he cared for her. One night couldn't throw that away.

Autumn didn't say anything. Piper got the impression that she was waiting for clarification or some evidence to support the claim, but a gut feeling was hard to put into words.

Piper decided the best approach was to change the topic entirely.

"How was your day?" she asked. Autumn hesitated before replying, clearly not finished with their initial conversation. She complied patiently, though. As she always did.

"It was pretty boring," Autumn answered. "I was mainly just waiting around for you."

Piper was grateful that Autumn couldn't see the blush on her face. "That makes two of us."

"What would you say if I asked you out on a second date?"

Piper furrowed her brow. "Now?"

"No, not now. Tomorrow night. We need to have a proper date."

"What? New Year's wasn't a proper date?"

"No way! Not a first date. A first date takes place at a cheap movie theatre, with sticky floors. We have to eat expensive popcorn, and have awkward conversations, and get shushed by some old lady."

Piper laughed. "I had one of those."

"Yes, well now you have to have one with me."

Piper could hear Autumn's grin when she was speaking and couldn't help but grin with her. "Alright. Tomorrow night."

"I'll pick you up at seven."

"See you then." She hung up, her heart soaring above the clouds. She felt like every teenage girl in every chick flick that had ever been made, all at once.

CHAPTER THIRTY

Autumn picked up Piper at seven o'clock on the dot. Piper expected no less. For someone who looked so edgy, she was as organized and level-headed as a person could be.

She wanted to come in. Do all the cliche date shit; shaking the father's hand, waiting in the doorway and watching as Piper walked down the stairs like a princess. But Piper told her it'd be better if she just pulled up outside. It would avoid the complication of her dad seeing the motorcycle. That was a conversation Piper was not up for yet.

Piper tried not to think about appearances too much. She didn't want to be the type of person who let that consume her. But Autumn looked so good, Piper felt like she wasn't even there. Autumn was a marble statue on display. Piper felt like the plaque underneath.

But still, the first thing that came out of Autumn's mouth was, "You look beautiful."

They paid more for the popcorn than the movie, which is to be expected. It was the cliche they were aiming for, after all.

They took their seats, in the middle of the sixth row.

They were perfectly centered. They had a perfect view on the screen. But Piper didn't care about the movie at all.

"Do you come to the movies a lot?" Piper asked. The beginning of the movie was playing and she was already zoned out, instead, focusing on the girl beside her. She was much more interesting, after all.

"Not really," Autumn answered. Their voices were low, as not to disturb the other movie-goers. "I used to, when I was a kid. But not anymore."

"Why not?"

Autumn paused and shrugged. She strung an arm around Piper's shoulders and Piper felt inclined to ask more. She could feel the words floating in the air. Something was left unsaid.

She asked, "Were you a movie buff as a kid?"

"Sort of," Autumn conceded. "But I didn't see a lot of mainstream movies."

Piper screwed up her face playfully. "Hipster."

Autumn let out a quiet laugh. "That's not what I meant," she said. "I just meant I didn't see the normal films that were out. I saw... different stuff."

"I think we're saying the same thing here."

Autumn shook her head incredulously. "Pipe down and watch the movie. Are you paying attention at all?"

Piper smirked. "Nope."

Autumn turned to look at her. She had a smile on her face but her eyes seemed closed off. Piper could feel the wall between them.

Autumn leaned over and planted a kiss on Piper's lips before returning to the movie. But Piper wasn't finished.

"You're so mysterious," she teased. "I feel like you know everything about me and I know nothing about you. Isn't that weird?"

"Not really."

"Come on, one anecdote. Then I'll be quiet and let you enjoy the film."

Autumn glanced at her again. Piper pouted, her round green eyes sparkling like a puppy begging for scraps. Autumn sighed.

"My favourite movie was *Cars*. I watched it so many times we had to get another copy, because our original one skipped so much we couldn't get past the first thirty minutes. Are you happy now?"

Piper thought of her many copies of *The Outsiders*. She beamed. "Very," she answered.

"Good. Now, shush."

They did anything but. For the duration of the movie, they continued to reminisce on their childhoods. Autumn left a lot unsaid. She hardly mentioned her parents or her home town. She didn't mention her school or friends. She talked mainly of shows and toys she liked, and games she'd play. Piper learned that her favourite show was *Spongebob Squarepants* and she carried a plush beluga whale everywhere she went until she was ten. It wasn't much, but it was something.

After almost two hours of sitting in a theatre, neither of them could even remotely explain the plot. They were shushed more than once, though. So that was another cliche crossed off their list.

As the credits rolled, they stayed in their seats. Everyone else was piling out of the theatre but they stared at the moving text, hands clasped together. It was nice to just sit there. The lighting was dark, save for some markers by the exit and the screen in front of them. It was all they had to illuminate the night. Piper thought Autumn looked elegant in the low lighting. Like she was glowing.

"You're staring," Autumn whispered, snapping Piper from her thoughts. She had a smug grin on her face that turned Piper's face red.

Piper looked away stubbornly, shaking her head. "I was not. I was just... observing."

"Likely story." Autumn stood up, collecting their empty popcorn bags and soda cups. She looked down at Piper and gestured for them to go with a nod of her head. "Come on," she said. "I'll drive you home."

Piper groaned. "Already?" she whined. "Can't we just run away somewhere? Get on your bike and drive into the sunset?"

Autumn smiled. "One day, princess. But not yet. Let's go."

Piper exhaled but agreed. She got up and followed Autumn out. They threw out their garbage and walked through the theatre slowly, stretching the date out as long as they could.

Their movie wasn't the only one letting out at that time. One across the hall from them had people flooding out of it, chattering on about how sequels are always worse than the original. Which was right, but it was as obvious as pointing out that it's darker at night than it is during the day.

Amongst all the people, Piper could make out only one conversation.

"The only acceptable sequel is *Toy Story 2*. Period." It was a guy's voice, one she found vaguely familiar. But the one that replied, she recognized immediately.

"What about *Toy Story 3* and *4*?"

Brent.

"Do they count as sequels if they're not the second movie?"

"I think so. What else would you call them? Tri-quels? Quad-quels?"

"Sounds like something from Harry Potter."

"Fuckin' nerd."

She listened to them laugh. She probably should have kept walking. She could have finished her date happy, in that puppy-love trance she'd been in all night. But curiosity and guilt, when combined, could overpower logic with ease.

"Piper?" She heard Autumn say a few steps ahead of her, but she'd stopped walking. She was standing there, letting the crowd go around her. She felt Autumn come up to stand beside her but she didn't move. She was on a mission. She was looking for him.

They were the final two, holding up the rear of the group. Drew had his arm thrown around Brent's shoulders in that friendly way jocks did. They were both smiling and it felt like the perfect time for her to say something. They were already in a good mood. She doubted she could soil it.

She took a step toward them, feeling the courage building up in her chest.

"Brent, I—"

He brushed past her, their shoulders bumping as he went. It was as if he hadn't heard her. She felt like a ghost. She was surprised he didn't move through her, since she was apparently incorporeal.

She paused. What was the logical next move here? She'd just embarrass herself if she went after him. She turned around, meeting Autumn's eyes.

Autumn put a hand on her shoulder, offering her comforting eyes.

"Give it time," she said. "You can't rush this stuff."

Piper nodded slowly. She hoped she didn't ruin their date with her drama but she didn't apologize. Even though she thought she should.

Autumn wrapped her arm around Piper's waist and steered her out of the theatre and into the clear, January night.

Autumn kissed her goodnight on the step and while it didn't fix Piper's problem, it did make her brain a little sunnier than it was before. At least now she could make out a path ahead of her through the thick fog.

When she was on the other side of the door, listening to the sound of her date's bike revving outside, all she wanted to do was lie down. She felt like she was moving fast lately. Quicker than she could keep up with, honestly. And she was ready to slow down.

Her dad had other plans.

He strolled into the foyer as she was taking off her shoes. He had his cell phone in his hand, carrying it low. For some reason, it looked very heavy.

"Hey, kiddo," he said, "How was it?"

Piper smiled. She had a great night, she couldn't deny that. She was always too quick to let one bad thing soil something perfect. She said, "It was fun."

"Good," he responded with a smile. The conversation was very casual, even when he asked, "Has your mom called since you left the hospital?"

Piper was taken slightly off guard. She shook her head and didn't voice what she was thinking; *Did she call while I was in the hospital?*

Her father nodded, showing no surprise or worry, which didn't ease her mind much. Maybe he improved his acting skills. He did say he wanted to try improv classes.

"Alright. Maybe give her a call and let her know you're okay."

Piper felt her eyes unfocus from her father's face. She must have shown some sign of agreement because he patted her shoulder and walked on. Before she realized it, she was in her room, staring at her mother's contact.

It all felt too familiar. The casualty of the conversation. The nervousness creeping up on her. The blank stare, focused on her mom's name. It was too real. It happened one too many times.

But, Piper had seen her mere weeks ago. Things couldn't spiral that quickly.

She pressed call and held the phone up to her ear. She didn't press it to her face. For some reason, she felt like it would burn her. She needed to keep a distance.

She listened to it ring once... twice... three times... four times... and then she heard a click.

She felt herself relax and almost laughed at her own nervousness.

"Mom. Hi. Sorry I didn't call earlier, I'm out of the hospi—"

Then a voice that was definitely too robotic to be her mother's spoke.

"Your call has been forwarded to an automated voice messaging system. *Judy* is not available. The mailbox is full and cannot accept any messages at this time. Goodbye."

CHAPTER THIRTY ONE

Piper's stomach was in knots. She definitely didn't feel confident talking to Brent that day. Frankly, she didn't feel confident doing anything that day. But she knew she had to. The world wouldn't pause for her to get her shit together. Even if that seemed fair, considering all the shit she had to put back together over the years. Or months.

She found Brent before he went to basketball practice at the end of the day. He didn't look the same. He didn't have a goofy smile or dreamy eyes. He looked like he had the colour sucked out of him. He was alone this time. He was collecting his things from his locker. She assumed his friends went ahead. Including Drew.

She walked over to him and, feeling like a child, tugged on his jersey to get his attention. He turned around and looked down at her, literally and metaphorically. His eyes scalded her skin and she averted hers in intimidation.

"Piper, what are you doing here?" he asked, his voice as low and menacing as distant thunder. Piper had a hard time finding the ability to speak

"I just…" She cleared her throat. "I need to talk to you."

"About what?" he spat in response. She thought that

was a stupid question, but that would definitely be the wrong thing to say.

Instead, she settled for, "You know what."

He huffed, turning back to his locker as if it were truly interesting and not just gym socks and torn textbooks. "Talk, then. Make it quick."

She sighed. She folded her hands in front of her, fidgeting with her fingers nervously. "I wanted to apologize. We ended things on a bad note and I didn't like that. I didn't get to say things the way I wanted to."

"Yeah, because you got loaded."

She felt like huffing in frustration but she didn't want to lose her temper with him. She had to keep her cool.

"Yeah," she agreed begrudgingly, "Because I got loaded. I meant to say that it wasn't anything personal. You're a good guy and any girl would be lucky to have you. I'm just the wrong girl."

She noticed his hands—which were busy rummaging through his locker—slow down and become still. He was hesitant to reply but when he did, he turned to face her and looked her in the eyes.

"I'm so sorry, Piper," he said. She felt her hands unravel in shock. Of all the things she thought he'd say, "*I'm sorry*" wasn't one of them. "I wish I would've reacted better when you told me... what you told me."

She wished he would have said it out loud instead of skipping around it. But she appreciated that he acknowledged it at all.

He was shaking his head, looking down at his shoes. His face was screwed up and for a moment, she thought he was going to cry.

"I guess I'm just a hopeless romantic," he said. "I thought we belonged together. But that kind of shit isn't real. And I never wanted to hurt you."

She smiled, her eyebrows downturned. She took a step toward him but he stepped backward.

He was shaking his head faster. Then her relief turned into worry but she kept her distance from him.

"I—If I hadn't bought you drinks, you wouldn't have gotten hurt. You wouldn't have broken up with me that way, and I wouldn't have reacted that way, and you wouldn't have left with Hally. And you wouldn't have gotten your liver drained or whatever."

"Stomach pumped," she corrected.

"It was all my fault," he muttered. She could tell he wasn't hearing her. He probably didn't know she was there anymore. He looked like he was somewhere else, a feeling Piper was very familiar with. "It was all my fault."

Piper shook her head. "It wasn't your fault," she said, even though she thought he couldn't hear her. He put his hands up by his head, tangling his fingers in his hair. He was breathing like he'd been running. Piper didn't know what to do. She had panic attacks before, but she'd never witnessed someone else having one. She had no idea how to help. Especially since this came out of nowhere. He was breathing steadily a minute ago. She knew he was a nervous person, but she never thought it was this serious.

Piper reached out a hand. She wasn't sure what she intended to do, but she wanted to ground him. He squeezed his eyes shut tightly and she froze.

Out of nowhere, she heard footsteps coming quickly toward her. She turned and saw Drew coming approaching them, worry written all over his face.

"Give him space," he ordered as he stopped in front of his best friend. Piper watched as Drew inspected Brent carefully, seeking injuries or cause. He didn't find any, of course. Physically, Brent was unharmed. "Jesus, what did you say to him?"

Overwhelmed, Piper couldn't form an intelligible response, so she muttered, "I-I don't know."

Drew wasn't listening anyway. He had a hand hovering over Brent's shoulder, not touching him. Brent must have noticed his friend because both of them kneeled together. Brent tucked his head, hands buried in hair, rocking his torso back and forth. Drew was sitting up with a flat back, eyes focused on his friend. He seemed to know exactly what to do. Like he'd done it a thousand times before. He was speaking, his voice low and careful. It was too quiet for Piper to make out, but it seemed to help Brent.

Piper stood there stupidly, watching the exchange until her fly-on-the-wall routine was interrupted.

"Why are you still standing here?" Drew asked roughly, obviously talking to Piper even though his eyes were trained on his friend.

"I—I don't know," she repeated. He waved a hand.

"Go home. You've done enough for one day."

"I was just talking to him—"

"I don't care. Go."

With one more glance between them, she nodded and began walking away. She wouldn't be useful to either of them anyway. While trying to do something nice, she pushed Brent and he spiralled out of control. What if she did the same with her mother? What if all this time she was blaming that woman for everything, when really it was all her fault? She pushed her over the edge again and again and again in a vicious, unending cycle.

Her worst fear was that it was her fault. That she had the capability in her to turn people into problems. She didn't want to have that effect on the people she loved.

But how would she know if it was truly her doing? And even if it was, did it even matter?

Her phone rang and, startled by the sound, she immediately picked it up.

"Hello?" she murmured, realizing she hadn't even checked the caller ID.

"Hey." It was Autumn. Though Piper knew she couldn't see her, she still made an effort to pretend she wasn't upset.

"Oh, uh, hi."

"I just wanted to see how you were. You seemed a little shook up after you saw your ex."

Piper covered the phone speaker, cleared her throat so her voice wouldn't wobble, and said, "I'm fine."

Autumn didn't sound convinced. "Alright, if you say so. Do you want me to come over, or—"

"No, I mean it. I'm fine. Don't worry. I'll talk to you later."

But, she didn't talk to Autumn later. She turned off her phone, locked her bedroom door, and laid down. When her father came to the door, asking if she was hungry, she said no, saying she felt ill. She listened to his footsteps descending down the hall.

By the time her alarm went off in the morning, she hadn't slept. She'd stayed up all night, thinking. She was definitely letting this get to her more than she should have. She couldn't help it. Her brain felt too heavy for her to do anything other than lay there, listening to her thoughts as if they were someone else's. The people in her life spiraled. Her mother was the first offender. Then it was Hally. Now Brent. There was only one common denominator.

The next morning, she told her father she was sick, and stayed home from school.

CHAPTER THIRTY TWO

She spent Tuesday calling her mother's cell phone over and over and over, hoping for an answer. Or at least a different answer than what she'd been getting. However, everytime so far, she got the same response:

"Your call has been forwarded to an automated voice messaging system. *Judy* is not available. The mailbox is full and cannot accept any messages at this time. Goodbye."

It was driving her insane. She was pacing around the empty house, getting the same message again and again. She just wanted some sort of conclusion. Something to answer her question. Just like when she was waiting on her mother's call before. It was the anticipation killing her. Only this time, she had a feeling it wouldn't be as simple. This time it wouldn't end with hot cocoa and presents.

The house had an echo when she was there alone. She couldn't stand feeling so isolated, but she didn't want to see anyone. Her dad would have stayed home with her, but she insisted that she was alright so he was at work and she was all alone.

Piper never had a lot of people in her life. She never had a big friend group. She wasn't close with her extended family. For a long time, it was just her, her dad and Hally.

Then Piper met Joseph, and Samuel met Laura, and their tiny bubble expanded. Piper wasn't accustomed to adding people to the bubble, so Joseph was special to have been invited by her. And Laura should have expected to not be welcome in the VIP area of her life. She was wary to add anyone to the inner circle, but when she did, she had a hard time letting them go. In a few short days, Judy pushed her way back in. Piper let her do it, too. She made the perfect slot for her to fit into. She let the relationship heal. She started over. But now she didn't know what to think. Maybe she should have left her bubble closed for good.

Then again, if she had, she never would have met Autumn.

The more phone calls she made, the more fruitless it all seemed. She was never getting an answer. Or a call back. Calling wasn't helping at all. She needed to do something.

She was going to call Hally, but she didn't want the "*I told you so.*" She didn't think Hally would actually say it. But she'd think it. And Piper didn't want that.

She called Autumn. Without giving her any of the details, she asked to be picked up at her house. All she said was, "I have to see something."

So, Autumn agreed. She was in front of the house, waiting for Piper on her bike. Piper didn't bother getting dressed. She left the house in her pajamas and she saw Autumn smile for a moment, but the smile slowly dropped as she saw the expression on the other girl's face.

"Are you okay?" she asked. Piper climbed onto the back of the bike, putting on the second helmet and clipping it under her chin.

"Do you remember the alleyway we met in a couple

weeks ago?"

"Yeah?"

"Take me there, please."

Autumn looked like she wanted to ask a lot of questions, but she didn't voice any of them. She put her helmet on and revved the bike. Piper wrapped her arms around Autumn's waist and they took off onto the street.

The journey felt longer than before, even though they were moving relatively fast and they weren't far away to begin with. It felt slow. Drawn out. Suspenseful. But in reality, the ride was only a few minutes and when Piper got off the bike, she was holding her breath.

Autumn parked the bike on the right side of the alleyway, on the side of the road. Right when it came to a stop, Piper got off and took off her helmet. She laid it on the seat and walked into the alleyway. It was empty, just as it was before.

She climbed up the slope to her mother's fence and hopped it. Her feet hit the dirt with a shake and she stared at the house anxiously. Now that she was actually standing there, she wasn't sure if she wanted to find out the truth. *Maybe I should go home*, she thought, *Curl up in my bed and try to pretend this never happened.*

But she had to know. She couldn't go home empty handed. She came for an answer and she was going to get it. No matter how much it hurt.

She went around to the front door and knocked. She waited impatiently for a response and when she didn't get one, she pounded on the door harder. The sound of her fist hitting the door echoed down the street but still, the door remained closed and locked. She was probably drawing attention to herself with such a racket, but her mother's neighbourhood was notorious for break-ins anyway. Her actions were par for the course.

Piper went around to the windows, peering in. The house definitely wasn't as pristine as when she was there. It was messy. There were dishes and garbage left around and Piper wondered how the mess accumulated so quickly.

She made her way around the house to the glass back doors. She tried them, but they were locked as well. She cupped her hands on the glass so she could see in properly and she finally caught a glimpse of what she went there to see.

Her mother was strewn out on the couch, glass bottles haphazardly laid on the floor and the tables beside her. She was using her Christmas gift to Piper as a coaster for a pint. She was sleeping with her mouth open and drool leaking down her chin. She looked old. She aged a lot in the short time since Piper saw her. Piper thought she was dead for a moment, but she noticed her chest rise and fall (her breathing was as steady as an even snowfall—she had plenty of practice to withstand whatever it was she consumed) so she relaxed ever so slightly. It was just as Piper suspected. She didn't know if that comforted her or not.

She took a step away from the door and kneeled in the grass. She had a real Mom for a week. Maybe less. She felt tears on her cheeks but she didn't remember crying. She didn't feel the sadness. It was just happening to her.

She didn't realize Autumn had followed her until she felt the girl's arms wrapped around her, holding her tight. She didn't ask why Piper was crying, which was for the best. Piper wouldn't have answered.

One thing was clear; anyone can spiral at any time if they were pushed. So what pushed Judy?

What pushed Piper?

CHAPTER THIRTY THREE

In December, Piper was spending every day wishing for snow. Now, she just wanted it to rain.

She read *The Fault In Our Stars* when she was in middle school and while she didn't catch the John Green fever the way everyone else did, one part stuck out to her after all this time. It was from a fictional book inside of a fiction book, which did fascinate Piper to no end. She remembered the paragraph was all about pain. How—no matter what else is going on—you still felt it. Piper didn't know if that was true. She thought about that section of that book every time she was upset and yet she still didn't believe it. Because she could distract herself from anything. She did it by accident constantly. Plus, people always told her she could do anything she put her mind to.

Piper thought it applied more to rain than to anything else. Rain demanded to be felt. To be heard. To be seen. It was cold and shocking at first touch, like electricity. It either roared loudly or pattered gently against your window. It glistened as it fell. It made everything shine. Rain was Mother Nature's attention whore. And Piper loved it with all her heart. After what she saw, she could use some rain.

That night, she sat at the dinner table with her dad and Laura. They were eating, but she was pushing a carrot around her plate absently. They must have felt the same tense feeling she did, because neither of them spoke. They even chewed quietly. Their forks didn't klink against their plates, either. Not even once. The only thing that connected them was the sound of the whirring refrigerator they were all abundantly aware of.

After a while, she noticed they both finished eating. But neither of them got up from their seats. They just sat there. Staring at her. Eventually, she had to say something.

"What's going on?" she asked. Samuel and Laura exchanged a look, a smile, then returned back to looking at Piper.

"We have some news," Samuel said with a grin. He took Laura's hand in his before continuing, "We're getting married."

So it wasn't tension keeping them quiet, apparently.

Piper felt her jaw drop. "You're..."

They ignored her futile attempt to speak.

"We haven't decided on when the wedding will be, but we want it to be soon. Why wait?" Laura chimed in, looking positively giddy. She must have noticed how Piper was looking at her, because she looked a little sympathetic. "I'm sorry that this is such a surprise. I asked your father to marry me last week but we wanted to wait to tell you together."

Piper closed her mouth and took in a breath through her nose. She let it out slowly, trying to stall for time before she said anything at all.

She had no idea what to say even after the stalling.

"Well," her father began to pry. "What do you

think?"

She cleared her throat, not sure if it would come out weird or shaky, and said, "That's awesome. I'm really happy for you guys." She was grateful she didn't choke on the words. They felt thick in her throat, like a milkshake. Or a mouthful of rocks. She pushed her untouched food away, feeling a little sick, and added, "Excuse me."

She went back upstairs, trying not to seem too anxious to get away, and back into her bedroom. She closed the door behind her and locked it, sitting down with a textbook in front of her in case her father wanted to come in. She could pretend she just had urgent homework. The lock was easy to pick, besides. He only ever did it when it was absolutely necessary. Like when she was eleven and he heard her crying. He picked the lock to see if she was okay. He was a good father.

But, he had kept something from her. She felt betrayed. Why hadn't he told her?

Maybe, it was because he had Laura now. He had a new life. One she wasn't a part of.

CHAPTER THIRTY FOUR

She went to school the next day in a haze. Someone picked her up. Probably Hally but it could have been Maya. She wasn't paying enough attention to notice. Everything looked like it had a thick film over it. She wasn't seeing things right. She didn't feel right. She felt like a ticking time bomb. She could hear the ticking against her skull as time passed. She was managing it the best she could but every time someone tried to talk to her or she got in trouble for not paying attention in class, she felt the ticking speed up until it was hammering her head. She wondered if there would be any internal damage.

If you asked her what classes she had that day, she couldn't tell you. She must have made it to them—in time, no less—because she was never reprimanded for being in the wrong class or showing up late. She was running on autopilot. She didn't feel like a person. She felt like a vessel, carrying around her memories and her experiences. She felt so heavy all day. She was tired of being full of sand.

She trudged down the hall like a zombie. She dragged her feet as she went. Tired and heavy and distracted. She knew she was sad but she couldn't actually feel it. Not deep in her heart the way she usually did. It was like her emotions were in a glass jar she was too weak to open.

She was walking down the hall with Maya and Locke. She didn't realize it was them until Maya linked arms with her and tried to get her to skip down the hall with her. For obvious reasons, the skipping never took off. But Piper thought she heard Locke laugh, so that was something.

They rounded the corner by the art room, where Maya was headed. They were going to separate. Locke was going to walk Piper to her final class of the day, but the three of them stopped dead in their tracks as Piper's eyes focused.

Her locker was straight ahead, only it had a huge crowd around it. She felt herself disconnect from her friends. Her feet were dragging her toward it. She pushed through the crowd, hearing her peers' voices distantly, like they were underwater.

She made it to the front of the group and saw it. Her locker was a spectacle. There were smashed dinkys glued to it and a sign that said "Don't drink and drive!" For a prank, it was pretty half-assed. But one of the tiny cars—a cherry red convertible—was utterly demolished and she felt like everyone was laughing at her and she couldn't handle it. The world went from being on mute to being on full blast and she couldn't take the pressure squeezing her head and clamping her chest. She felt breathless. Her heart was beating so hard it felt like it was going to tear through her skin. She fell to her knees. She clutched her chest, heaving for breath. *I'm having a heart attack,* she thought. *I'm going to die.*

She couldn't keep her hands steady. She felt her whole body trembling. The pain in her chest was making it impossible to breathe in. She was swallowing air but none of it was making it to her lungs.

She could hear the chaos around her but her eyes were screwed shut. She was focusing on staying alive. She couldn't breathe. Surely that meant she was dying.

"What the fuck is wrong with her?" a girl asked.

"Don't just stand there, get a teacher or something!" another shrieked.

"What the fuck would a teacher do?" It was Locke's voice, louder than Piper had ever heard it. "Call a fucking ambulance!"

Someone was sitting with her. There were footsteps happening all around her. She was gasping for breath so loud, she could make out the sound of it through all the shouting and pacing.

She heard a boy talking on the phone and teachers trying to get the crowd away from her and dinkys hitting the floor behind her. Her tears were so hot they burned her face and she couldn't sob because she couldn't catch her breath so she was heaving and crying and trembling and they were all staring at her.

The paramedics were there within minutes. She was being rolled out on a stretcher as she listened to her classmates' competing voices and a teacher calling her father. She was hyperaware, and yet, she had no idea where she was or what was going on.

An oxygen mask was strapped to her face. At the same time they were taking her blood pressure and hooking her finger up to a heart rate monitor. And she was crying. And gasping. And shaking. And she was saying something she couldn't hear that didn't actually mean anything. She could hear the siren vaguely. She wanted to go home.

CHAPTER THIRTY FIVE

The hospital felt different this time around. When she was there before, it felt like closure, in a weird way. Like something ended. But this time it was like everything was on stand still. The world finally did pause while she got her shit together. At least for a little while.

She was finally able to catch her breath and her chest pains went away. She was still shaking but it died down since the paramedics brought her inside. They managed to calm her down without any drugs. They had her sitting in Dr. Benson's office by herself. They gave her a bottle of water and told her her father was on the way. She had a weird sense of calm over her. People always talk about the calm before the storm, but what about after? When the world stops turning for a few short moments and it's finally over. You're not checking the damages or cowering under cover. You're just sitting in it. Soaking it up. You're grateful to be alive.

When she could breathe again, that was all she was thinking. She was glad to be alive. Life threw a lot of shit at her and now, she was on the other end of it. It wasn't over, exactly. But she had enough appreciation to realize how she was letting it build up. She took a backseat to her own life and she was ready to drive again.

There was a knock on the door and Dr. Benson stepped inside, sporting that gentle smile all doctors had. They must learn that during their 10-14 years of studying.

"Hey. Your dad is here to pick you up," she said. Piper got up from her seat and followed Dr. Benson out of the office and into the hallway, where her father was waiting for her. She was amazed at how quickly he got there from work. He definitely wasn't driving the speed limit.

They didn't say much to each other as they left the hospital. There was definitely a lot to say but Piper felt like it wasn't the time yet.

Though the school day wasn't over, he brought her home. That was the procedure when your child leaves school in an ambulance, she guessed. It wouldn't make much sense to put them right back where they were.

Neither of them said anything on the drive home. They didn't turn on the radio. Piper hardly noticed the sound of the engine. When they were inside, she expected the silence to continue. But the door shut, and he hugged her.

"Are you okay?" he asked.

"I'm fine."

"It sounded serious, but they said it was just a panic attack?"

"Yeah."

"What happened?"

"I don't know. A lot."

He pulled back and looked at her. She was still, giving him a moment. But she saw he was tearing up.

"You know you can come to me about anything, right?" he asked.

She nodded. "Yeah, of course."

"I know you've been having a rough time," he went on. "Don't feel pressured to deal with it alone. Or to pretend you're okay. Your feelings are important to me and I want you to know that, whatever it is, we can always work through it together. We're a team, you and I. I know things are changing, but that never will."

She managed to smile at him. She hugged him again, squeezing him close. She hoped he knew how much she loved him. How much she appreciated him. She didn't know how to tell him. He always supported her. He was always there for her. And, he always meant what he said.

Instead of saying all of that, she settled for, "I love you."

He kissed the top of her head. "I love you too, Kiddo."

CHAPTER THIRTY SIX

Piper took a few days off of school after her incident. She wanted to prepare for whatever her peers would throw at her when she got back. She tried not to let herself stress over it too much. Instead, she tried to focus on positives. Piper's doctor sent in a referral so she could get therapy. Hally finally had her cast off. She could see Autumn on her off days. She was trying to be more open with her dad.

Coincidentally, Hally got her cast off the same day Piper had her panic attack. Hally probably told her the date before, but to be fair, Piper had a lot occupying her mind. There wasn't much space for other information. When Hally found out what happened, she turned up at Piper's house unannounced.

"What the hell happened? Are you okay? I saw a bunch of people posting 'get well soon' shit," she said, grabbing Piper by the shoulders and looking her over for any visible ailment.

"I'm fine," Piper insisted. "I had a panic attack."

Hally looked Piper in the eyes. It seemed like she was trying to figure out if Piper was lying. The gears were going in her head, like *Is she really fine? Huh? Huh?* But she mustn't have found any doubt, because she released Piper.

"What happened?" she asked again.

"I just got overwhelmed, I guess," Piper answered. To be honest, she didn't understand it fully herself. That's why she was being set up with a therapist — she needed to understand herself to get better. "I couldn't handle it and I freaked out."

Hally let out a slow breath. "I'm sorry I wasn't there."

Piper waved the apology away with a wave of her hand. "It's not your fault. I think it would have happened either way."

"How do you feel now?"

"Honestly, I feel better. Maybe I just bottled stuff up too much or something. It feels like I needed a full-ass breakdown so I could come to terms with everything. You know?"

Hally shook her head. "Not really. But I'm glad you're a little better now."

"Me too. I mean, I definitely need to work on myself but doesn't everyone? We're all fucked up in our own ways."

"How profound," Hally teased.

Hally hadn't stayed for long that day. She was going to school the next day, so she had to do some homework. Piper spent the rest of the day relaxing and doing her best to manage her anxiety.

The next day, Autumn visited. They didn't say much to each other as they went up the stairs and into Piper's room. Piper was afraid Autumn was mad at her. But when she shut the door, Autumn kissed her.

"I was worried about you," Autumn admitted. "How are you doing?"

"Everyone keeps asking me that," Piper said. "I really am fine."

"You said that before…"

Piper put a hand on the other girl's cheek and smiled reassuringly. "I promise. This time I'm telling the truth."

Autumn nodded, showing no more doubt. She asked, "Do you want to talk about it?"

"Absolutely not," Piper replied with a chuckle. "I've talked and thought about it constantly since the moment it happened. I need to talk about literally anything else."

"Like what?"

"Anything at all!"

"What about fish?" Autumn suggested. "Do you want to talk about fish?"

"We can talk about fish," Piper agreed with a grin. She sat down on her bed and looked smugly at Autumn. "Did you know the ocean sunfish has teeth in its throat? It eats mostly jellyfish and algae and stuff and its mouth is shaped like a beak so it has pharyngeal teeth."

Autumn made a face. "That's as gross as it is cool."

"Right?" Piper agreed. Autumn sat beside her. Both of them turned so they were facing each other. Piper reached over and took one of Autumn's hands, playing with her fingers as she said, "As much as I love talking about fish, why don't we talk about you? I feel like we never talk about you."

"What do you want to know?"

Piper shrugged. "Anything. What school do you go to?"

Autumn hesitated, so Piper glanced up, making eye contact with her. If she didn't know better, she'd think Autumn looked embarrassed.

"I don't go to school," Autumn said.

"You graduated?"

"No. I dropped out."

Piper stopped fiddling with Autumn's hand and held it instead. "When?"

"Last year. I got expelled from the school I was going to and I was supposed to enroll in another one that was relatively nearby. But I never did."

Piper scanned her face curiously. Clearly, it was a hard topic for her. But she wasn't resisting. It seemed like she wanted to talk about it. Piper pressed on.

"Why not?" she asked.

Autumn was shaking her head to herself. She wasn't looking at Piper. "I was angry. I had a lot of hard times when I was younger and I wanted to take control of my future. So I made the decision myself, without anyone to tell me not to."

"Weren't your parents mad?"

"My dad kicked me out around the time I was expelled."

"Oh," Piper muttered stupidly. She sat closer to Autumn and wrapped her arms around her. "I'm sorry."

"It's okay," Autumn said. "I wouldn't want someone like him in my life anyways."

Piper nodded in understanding. "I think I feel the same way about my mom," she said. "For a long time, I did want her around. I was really upset that she wasn't. But after everything... I think I'm finally done with her."

"Look at us," Autumn teased, "Coming to terms with our shit parents."

Piper laughed. "I'm proud of us." She pulled back from their embrace. They were both smiling, which was reassuring. Being open felt good. Piper asked, "Do you miss school?"

"Sometimes. I mean, I think education is important. Learning is cool. But I definitely don't miss the academic part. I wasn't very good. Plus I went to a private Catholic school, so I definitely don't miss the uniform or how strict the rules were."

Piper looked at her incredulously. "You had to wear a uniform?"

"Pleated skirt and all."

"No fucking way!"

"Don't think about it too hard, I think your brain will explode," Autumn teased.

"Too late. The mental image is saved forever."

Autumn rolled her eyes and turned the conversation back to the original subject. "Anyway, I don't miss a lot of aspects of school. But I do miss some stuff. Being a reckless, rebellious teenager was fun while it lasted. And I had a partner in crime to live out all my vandalizing, breaking dress code, and hair-dying dreams with."

Piper smiled. "You had a girlfriend?"

Autumn shook her head. "No, me and Jo were best friends. We did everything together."

"Have you seen her since you left home?"

Autumn shook her head again, her smile turning sad. "We... lost contact. It's been a while since we talked."

Piper nodded. She couldn't imagine losing contact with Hally. It would tear her up inside. A best friend was like an extra limb. An extension of yourself. Being without her would leave Piper confused and disoriented. She would have to relearn everything she knew, without her extra limb that was always assisting her.

"I do have a reminder of her everywhere I go, though,"

Autumn went on. Piper raised a brow and Autumn point-ed to a scar on the right side of her bottom lip. It was tiny and unnoticeable until she pointed it out. It went around her lip, the way a lip ring would. "When I lived with my parents, we had all my birthday parties in the basement of our church. They invited a bunch of people from our church group including our pastor, who made his stance on gay people blatantly obvious. I was fifteen, and I genu-inely wanted to rip his eyes out every time he opened his mouth. So, Jo and I came up with a plan. In the middle of my fifteenth birthday party, I kissed her right in front of everyone I knew. I didn't expect my parents to get angry. I expected applause and crying—a change of heart—like in all those cheesy short films. But, when my dad saw, he yelled my name, and Jo flinched so hard she cut my lip with her lip ring. The next day at school, I was pretty bummed out and Jo told me that the scar was cool, be-cause it looked like we had matching rings."

Piper grinned at the story. She didn't know as much about Autumn as she wanted to. She was glad to have a peek into the girl's life, especially a part so innocent and reckless. She couldn't imagine what Autumn would look like in her Sunday best, her hair devoid of purple, prayer beads in hand. The thought made Piper giggle.

"You should talk to Jo," Piper said.

Autumn sighed. "I don't know, Piper. Before I left, we got into a huge fight. She wanted something different for me. Jo... she always had high hopes for my future. She thought I was going to do incredible things. But I wasn't looking ahead. I was thinking about the here and now and she thought I was just being stupid."

"Best friends fight," Piper said matter-of-factly. "But if you guys were really important to each other, shouldn't you fight to stay together?"

Autumn considered it for a moment. She was holding her breath. But then, she let it out slowly and nodded.

"You're right," she said. "I should try and reconnect with her."

Piper smiled, proud of herself for giving a useful bit of advice.

They both laid back on the bed. They were shoulder to shoulder, looking up at the ceiling. Piper loved moments like this. Moments when everything was so quiet and still in their little corner of the world, but she could hear birds chirping and cars passing by outside and her dad watching television downstairs. It made her feel whole. Present. It was a magical feeling, to know you exist in a world full of people that never stop moving and yet you remain still.

Their chests rose and fell in unison. Autumn linked their pinkies and Piper felt butterflies in her stomach, which was very normal whenever she was with Autumn. They did diminish a little as she got used to having her around. Not because she liked her less. In fact, every time Piper saw her, she liked her more than she did the time before. She was just able to function better. Her nerves died down.

"Hey, Piper?" Autumn whispered. Piper turned to look at her the same time Autumn turned as well. Their noses were almost touching. Piper could see every speck of colour in Autumn's eyes. "Can I ask you something?"

Piper tried not to be too captivated by Autumn's beauty so she could focus on what she was saying. "Of course. Anything."

"I really like you," she said. "And I'm not sure how formal I have to make this. I've never done this before. But would you like to be my girlfriend?"

Piper's face broke out into a grin. She bit her lip in a futile attempt to hide how overjoyed she was.

"You're such a geek," Piper teased. Autumn turned red and pouted, making Piper laugh. Piper put a hand on her cheek, her eyes soft and sincere as she said, "Yes, I would very much like to be your girlfriend."

Autumn was trying to hold her pout, but she gave up and smiled.

"Asshole," she said. She leaned forward and planted a kiss on Piper—her girlfriend's—lips.

CHAPTER THIRTY SEVEN

Autumn put on her helmet and hopped on her motorcycle with a heavy heart. She was going to her old best friend's house, her home away from home. Scratch that: her parent's house was never a home. Jo's house was Autumn's only home.

She started her bike and drove off down winding roads. When she stopped at a stop sign, she lifted her finger and traced the scar on her lip.

Jo was the first girl she'd ever loved. Nothing had happened between them beside that kiss, and it meant nothing to Jo. All it was was a trick, a way to rebel, but it was everything to Autumn when she was younger. She dreamed of a moment like that, and when she got it, it did not disappoint. She remembered how it felt to hold Jo close to her, to smell the smoke off of her clothes. It was a magical feeling, but not nearly as magical as the feeling of holding Piper.

It took Autumn no time to reach Jo's house. She'd remembered the route to the place off by heart when she was young, and getting there felt like she was on autopilot. She barely had to look. She knew exactly where she was going.

The neighbourhood Jo lived in was adjacent to where Autumn's parents lived, but the difference between them was like night and day. Autumn's parents lived in a gated community. The streets were lined with identical houses and expensive cars. They all had lush front yards that had to be well taken care of, or else they'd get complaints. During Christmas, the decorations had to be uniform and not overly extravagant and on the off-chance her parents let her go out after dark, she would be questioned endlessly by Neighbourhood Watch. She remembered it being so competitive all the time. Her mom was so focused on hiring the best maid or gardener, on buying the most expensive shoes and pantsuits, on having the most glamorous hair and nails. Money was a weapon to those people. They wielded it to shame and diminish others. That's why Autumn never asked them for a cent. It didn't matter how shit her apartment was or how many roommates she had to cram into it. She wouldn't take their bait.

Jo's neighbourhood was more like a collage. All the houses were different sizes and shapes and colours. Some of them strived to look like they belonged within the gate (choosing a cream coloured siding and having bright green lawns) but most of them stood alone. It was clear that most people on this side of town had the same amount of money, but vastly different priorities. Instead of wasting money on appearances, Jo's family took vacations. Autumn envied them to no end. Jo had been everywhere. She saw everything. Her house was more like a rest spot than a home, since they were only there while they planned the next getaway.

Autumn parked her bike in the long driveway and peered up at the small, red house. It was as suburban as a house could get. The siding was as pristine as the day it was first done. It had miss-matched shrubs lining the path and daisies in jagged lines on the lawn. The lawn was patchy in the areas the sprinklers didn't hit and there was a decaying jack o'lantern on the step. It wasn't perfect, but that's why she loved it. She took a deep breath, slipped off her helmet, and approached the door. Anxiously, she raised her fist and knocked.

The door swung open in a moment, and there stood Elena, Jo's mom. She gasped in surprise and delight, pulling Autumn into a hug.

"Autumn, darling! It's been so long!" she exclaimed.

Autumn felt warm in Elena's embrace. No one came closer to a Mother to Autumn than Elena did. She was the kindest, most supportive person Autumn had ever met. She always treated Autumn like her daughter.

As she pulled away, she tugged Autumn inside. "Come in, come in. What brings you to this part of town? Not that I'm complaining."

Elena's hair was salt and pepper, mixed with the slightest traces of black. The black hair suited her. It had never suited her daughter. Autumn wondered if Jo still dyed her hair red on a regular basis. She remembered the first time they'd done it, when they were both thirteen. They got a box kit from the local drugstore and dyed Jo's hair in her parents bathroom. They got red dye all over the white linoleum tiles. They scrubbed at it for an hour but it never faded. When Elena found out, she wasn't angry. She laughed and teased them for their carelessness. Then, she covered it up with a purple mat. Glen, Jo's father, never found out.

Autumn wondered if he knew by now. She also realized that, from spending so much time with Piper, she'd been wondering a lot more than she used to.

"I came to see Jo," she said, "And I feel so bad for not seeing you all in so long. How have you been, Elena?"

She decided that the best thing to do would be to steer the conversation away from herself. She wasn't sure how much Jo had told her mother about their argument.

Autumn remembered clearly the fight that had taken place between Jo and her the night she was kicked out. Jo was angry. She didn't understand why Autumn had to leave her behind. Autumn kept insisting that Jo deserved a future, one that she sure as hell wasn't going to get if she had to babysit her best friend every day. Jo disagreed. She said Autumn had so much life ahead of her. Said she was so smart. So talented. So charismatic.

"What? You're going to throw that all away? That and me?"

Autumn left without an extra word. They haven't spoken since.

Elena talked about herself, about Glen, about Taylor. Taylor piqued Autumn's interest the most.

"Oh my god, Taylor. He must be, what, seven years old now?" she asked wistfully.

"Yes, as of last spring. You should see him, he's growing like a weed."

"I bet he's a perfect replica of Glen, am I right?"

"Of course," her tone was mock teasing, and it made Autumn realize how much she'd missed this. "Though, he acts just like Jo."

"Oh, no. I'll have to stop by more, then. To help out with Taylor." she smiled. Elena smiled back wistfully.

"I'd love that." With a sniffle and an invisible tear wiped away, Elena asked the question that Autumn hoped she wouldn't. "So, what's kept you? Whenever I ask Jo, she goes rogue on me. Did something happen?"

Before she had to answer, she heard boyish squeals and the familiar song of laughter. Jo and Taylor entered the room, and Autumn's heart stopped.

Jo looked no different. Her red hair was slightly faded and due for a re-do, turning her hair orange in some areas. Her lip ring was now silver instead of gold, like it used to be. She wore a reddish-brown flannel and a pair of grey acid washed jeans. She stopped dead in her tracks when she saw Autumn.

Taylor, however, didn't take a moment of hesitation. He sprung to Autumn and hugged her legs, too short to reach up any further.

"Autumn! You're back!" he squealed. She ruffled his hair lovingly.

"You haven't forgotten me?" Autumn joked. "You were tiny the last time I saw you."

"I'm big now, look!" He stepped back and modelled the little growth spurt he'd gotten. Autumn swelled with pride.

"You are! And you're seven now?"

"Mhm," he hummed, grinning his boyish grin. His black hair was shorter now than it had been when he was younger. He liked his hair long then, liked twirling it around his fingers, but now his hair was so close to his head that ruffling it barely did anything at all.

Autumn was in the hospital when Taylor was born. She had slept over to Jo's house that night, and accompanied the family in the car to the hospital. Jo and her played Crazy Eights and Go Fish while thinking of baby names. She spent fourteen hours playing in the hospital waiting room with Jo. Autumn's dad called Gloria (Elena's Mom, who was babysitting the two girls) more than once to ask if Autumn needed to be taken home. Gloria insisted that the two were fine there every time.

Jo appreciated that. She wanted her and Autumn to see the baby before anyone else, besides her parents of course.

Anxiously, Autumn met Jo's eyes, and for a moment, there was a stressful silence. Then, Jo said something.

"Hi, Autumn."

"Hey, Jo."

Elena looked between the two girls, then took Taylor by the hand.

"Come on, Sweetie. Let's give the girls some privacy."

Taylor hollered about how it was unfair, and he wanted to play with Autumn too, and blah blah blah, but Elena escorted him from the room calmly. Jo and Autumn stood, watching each other, until Jo spoke up again.

"Um, do you want to go to my room and... talk? There's less of a chance of Mom eavesdropping on us there."

Autumn smiled sheepishly. "Yeah, sure."

They walked up the stairs and into the familiar doorway that still had a "No Boys Allowed" sign on the door, but it was poorly spray painted to say "Taylor and Joey ONLY." Autumn remembered putting up the sign when she was younger. They must have painted over it after she walked out of their lives. She felt a pang of hurt.

Jo closed the door behind them, and Autumn looked around in astonishment. Everything looked so... different.

"You changed your room," she said. Jo turned and looked around her own room, as if she was only noticing the change now. "It's black. I like it."

The once yellow walls were now pitch black with green stars stuck to them. They resembled the ones Autumn used to have on her ceiling as a night light. She noticed that the bed was still the same, but the blankets were checkered red and white now, and in place of an old doll house (that became a sketch table when she was fourteen) was a vanity mirror with makeup strewn across it. The same posters still littered the walls from Jo's fifteenth birthday party. Everything from Cage the Elephant to Paramore.

"It was the same for basically my whole life. I needed a bit of a change," Jo admitted.

"It looks cool."

Jo opened her mouth to say something, but closed it and changed her mind. After a few moments of awkward silence, she tried again. "What are you doing here?"

"Before we get into all that—" Autumn took a breath, avoiding the question at hand. "—did your dad ever find out about the red stains on the bathroom tiles? From dying your hair?"

The mood lightened quickly. Jo laughed. "No, actually he didn't. The other day, Mom told me that he showered in that bathroom, which is weird because he hates it for smelling like flowers—"

"Oh, yeah. Lilacs, right?"

She laughed again. "Yeah, lilacs. Anyway, he slipped on the purple mat and it moved, but he never saw the stain on the floor."

"He needs new glasses."

"He got new glasses. With hipster frames."

"No way!"

"Mhm. They make his head look so boxy."

"I wish I could pull off hipster frames."

"Don't we all?"

And suddenly, everything was back to normal. Autumn felt like it was coming together. She had Piper, which was all she would ever need, but now, she had her best friend back too.

Then, the question came up again.

"What are you doing here, Autumn?"

She sighed and tried to step around her words carefully. "You deserve an explanation for everything. And an apology. I'm so sorry for everything I said, and everything I did. It's all my fault. And, I missed you."

"I missed you, too. But, it's not all your fault. I mean, fuck, your parents kicked you out. That's... serious shit. We both said harsh things, and I could have made an effort—"

"It is not your fault! You didn't have my new address, how would you know where to go?"

"I still had your number, though. I should have called."

"Don't worry about it. Let me take the blame."

Jo rolled her eyes. "You're still stubborn, I see."

"That's fair. But, so are you. Can we be friends again?"

"No," Jo said firmly. Autumn felt her heart stop and crumble. Everything was coming together. Why was it falling apart? What had she done wrong?

Jo must have sensed the discomfort because she smirked broadly. "We can be best friends, though."

She sighed in relief. "Thank god. You scared the shit out of me, Asshole." She shoved Jo's shoulder, making the girl chuckle and pull her into a hug so tight, it was like both girls were falling apart, and only each other's arms could keep them together.

Jo was first to pull back from the hug. "Alright, well, now you have to stay over. How else will I figure out who this edgy, purple-haired girl is?" Jo insisted, using the word 'edgy' very ironically. Autumn rolled her eyes and ignored the comment.

Admittedly, Autumn's plan didn't go very far past making up with Jo. She didn't even know if that would work so she was fully prepared to be there for an hour, two at the most. She didn't expect to be invited to stay. Her original plan for the night was to go to Piper's. She was more worried about her girlfriend than she let on. Knowing Piper, if she knew how worried Autumn was, she'd probably try to hide her feelings. And Autumn certainly didn't want that. It didn't work out well the first time around.

Still, she just got her best friend back. She didn't want to jeopardize it again. So she said, "Yeah, I'll stay. But only out of pity for that awful, faded cheeto hair."

Jo punched Autumn in the arm.

"Bitch," she grumbled.

CHAPTER THIRTY EIGHT

Piper was home alone with Laura. She was home from school and her dad had to go to work. He didn't want to leave her by herself, so he asked Laura to stick around for the day. Piper could tell how worried he was about her, so she didn't argue when she found out he was having his teenage daughter babysat.

So far, Laura checked on her without actually checking on her. She would pass by Piper's room every so often, as if she forgot something in Samuel's room or the bathroom, and have a glance in. Piper pretended not to notice. She couldn't decide if she found it creepy or weirdly endearing. Either way, it said something that she was willing to take off work that day to watch her boyfriend's kid.

Fiancé, Piper corrected herself. It felt weird to think about. She hadn't said it out loud yet so it still didn't feel real to her.

She spent almost all day alone in her room, but eventually, when Laura was taking her rounds, she stopped and knocked on Piper's open door.

"Hey," Laura said with a perfectly pearly white smile. "Mind if I come in?"

Piper (who was reading *Huckleberry Finn* and wishing she hadn't loaned *The Outsiders* to Brent months ago) closed her book and nodded awkwardly. Laura looked comfortable but then again, Piper noticed her playing with her engagement ring. She stepped into Piper's room, her eyes scanning pictures of Piper and her dad, or her friends. She sat next to Piper on her bed, taking up as little space as possible. Piper did that sometimes, too. She thought it was polite to make yourself shrink, as not to inconvenience anyone.

Laura took a deep breath before she spoke. She looked at Piper with a serious look for once. Her Barbie-esque smile was nowhere to be seen. It was a bizarre picture, especially when Piper was so used to her being the image of politeness and cordiality all the time.

"You probably want to be left alone, so I'll cut to the chase." She took a deep breath, shook her pin straight black hair away from her face. "I should have spoken to you before I proposed to your father," she said. "I'm sorry. I realize that marrying your father is more than just marrying him. I get you, too."

"Lucky you," Piper muttered sarcastically. Laura disagreed adamantly and nudged her shoulder.

"I am lucky," she said. There was a lag in conversation, which wasn't a surprise. The two had never held a conversation past *"school's going okay."* Piper never had interest in talking to Laura. She always assumed the two had nothing in common. They were too different to connect in any way. Or maybe she just wanted to remain separated from her.

Out of nowhere, Laura asked, "Did your dad ever tell you how he and I met?"

Piper shook her head.

"We were in business school, down at the community

college. We were in the same class—he dropped out of that class later on, though. He had no interest in it—anyway, I was heartbroken over a fight I had with my girlfriend and he got the pleasure of sitting next to me. I was a mess. I was teary and whiney and an all around bag of sorrow. He was kind enough to give me his notes after class because I didn't take a single note the whole time. Anyway, we only talked in class and about class until he dropped out, and we had to find other ways to talk to each other. My girlfriend hated him, and he hated her, though he tried to pretend he didn't. One day, she told me that she didn't trust me because she thought I was cheating on her with him. She bought into all these gross stereotypes about bisexuality. But, he stood up for me. He told my girlfriend she was being ridiculous for accusing me of such a thing. She dumped me on the spot. That left me heartbroken again, and he was always there for me. After a while I got over her, though, and I understood what really mattered. He had been there for me. He had taken care of me. And not long after that realization, I fell in love with him."

Piper couldn't help but smile at the end of the story, but she forced the smile away as fast as it had come. She asked, "Why are you telling me all of this?"

"Because, I love your dad. And, I love you, and I want to be here for you. I know I haven't played a very big role in your life in the past. I know you're not my biggest fan. But I don't want to just be your dad's wife. The step-monster. I want you to know that you can count on me."

Piper paused, and surprised herself by inching closer to her father's girlfriend. Strangely, the story did make her feel more comfortable around Laura. Maybe it was because she wanted to make Laura feel better. Or maybe, more than likely, it was because of the way Laura said everything. Not like she wanted Piper to like her, or was trying to impress her, she was being genuine. It was radiating off of her.

"Can I ask you something?" Laura said. Piper blinked at her and nodded again.

Laura went on to say, "Piper our relationship up to this point has been... complicated. I don't want to pressure you into anything you don't want. And I'll understand completely if you say no. So I have to ask, could I be your stepmother? I would really love to."

Piper didn't want to think about it too long. She could see Laura's nervousness already. But she also didn't want to answer out of obligation. Or resentment. She wanted to understand the decision she was making before she made it.

It didn't take very long for her to understand, and to know what she had to do. For her father. For Laura. But mostly, for herself. She had to let go.

Piper managed a smile and nodded. "Yes."

"Are you sure?"

She nodded again. "Yeah, I am."

Laura looked relieved and very glad. Piper's smile only grew when she saw tears welling up in Laura's eyes, even though she was trying to keep it together. She exhaled heavily and said, "Thank you. So much." Laura stood to leave the room, but Piper stopped her.

"One more thing," Piper said urgently, "I need you to promise me something."

Laura looked mildly confused but nodded. "Of course. Anything."

"Promise you won't leave us," Piper said. Whether from the exhaustion of existing or from the vulnerability of her request, her voice sounded weak. "Both Dad and I can't take any more of that. We've been alone for a long time, and I'd like to be ready if you're planning on ducking out."

Laura looked sympathetic. She pulled Piper up to her feet and hugged her tightly. "I would never. Ever. I promise."

CHAPTER THIRTY NINE

"So, anything magical and life changing happen in your time without me?" Jo asked Autumn teasingly. They were sitting on the floor in her room, her laptop in front of them. They were watching a shitty chick flick, purely to make fun of it (or so they said), but at some point it became unbearable, so they turned it off.

Autumn initially laughed at the question, but she ended up with a wistful smile as she answered, "You could say that?"

Jo stared at her for a moment. "You're not on drugs for something, are you?"

Autumn scoffed at her. "Fuck no, I'm not on drugs. Why would you ask me that?"

"I don't know," Jo said, holding her hands up in surrender. "You're all starry-eyed and dreamy. And you keep smiling, it's fucking weird."

Autumn smiled and shrugged. "What, I can't be happy?"

"I never said that. I've just never seen you this happy."

"That's because you knew me when I was still in high school," Autumn said. Jo laughed and nodded in understanding.

"Makes sense," she said. "So, what happened that was magical and life changing? Other than leaving our shitty-ass school?"

Autumn always got this feeling when she thought of Piper. This warm feeling all over her. She never experienced anything like it before. Sure, she was in love with Jo for a while. But that was different. That kind of love was one-sided. Bitter. That kind of love stung when you thought about it and killed you to speak of. But in the short while that Autumn knew Piper, it was always great. It was so easy and yet so intricate and complicated.

"I met someone," she said simply. Jo was watching her closely, as if she was skeptical of that declaration. But when Autumn didn't elaborate, she had to ask for more information.

"And..? Who are they? What're they like?"

"Her name is Piper," Autumn went on. "She's incredible. She's funny and sweet and the smartest person I've ever met. She has all this random information stored in her brain. I don't even know how she does it. And she's thinking all the time. Like she literally never stops. It worries me sometimes. Like, how can someone's brain move so fast all the fucking time?"

"That only worries you because you've never used your brain."

"Gee, thanks."

"Sorry, go on."

"She's just... perfect. Like when you're a kid you hear all these stories about destiny and true love and shit and eventually, you stop believing in it. But I believe in it again because of her."

Jo made dramatic gagging noises like she was about to

vomit. "Ew, what did this girl do to you?"

Autumn rolled her eyes. "Can't you stop being an asshole for a second."

"Right, my bad," Jo chuckled. "I'm happy you found someone. Even if it means you're delusional and lovey dovey and whatever."

"I'm not delusional!"

"Come on, man. All this talk about destiny and true love? You sound pretty delusional to me."

Autumn simply smiled and shook her head. She didn't feel the need to defend her relationship. All that mattered was that her and Piper felt the same way. And clearly they did. They talked more than once about how the relationship felt. It was like fate. There was no other way to explain the feeling they both got. And even if it wasn't, who cares? The universe was massive and they were just two tiny specks. It didn't matter what they thought.

Wow, I sound like Piper, she thought.

"What about you?" Autumn asked. "What's new in your life?"

Jo had an obviously proud smile on her face, but she seemed hesitant to say whatever was on her mind.

"What is it?" Autumn pressed.

Jo sighed. "I'm graduating," Jo said slowly. "And I got into a pretty good university program. I mean, it's my second choice. I didn't get into my first but... I did it."

Honestly, Autumn did feel jealous. She was jealous that Jo was going to have the future they talked about having together before Autumn left. She was embarrassed that she didn't finish high school and didn't get the education everyone expected her to. She was embarrassed to live in a two-bedroom with four other people and work running odd-jobs for the locally owned grocery store down the street for cash.

But Autumn was also happy. She knew that future wasn't one she actually wanted. She wouldn't be the person she was now if she hadn't made the choices she did then. And university wasn't something she dreamed of the way Jo did. She never had a first and second choice. She just wanted to go to whatever school Jo was going to.

"That's fucking awesome, J," Autumn said. "I'm really proud of you. That's incredible."

Jo exhaled and looked away. She shrugged like it was no big deal, but Autumn knew her better than that.

"It's not a huge thing."

"It is a huge thing," Autumn insisted. "No one deserves it more than you. You've worked so hard. I know you want to look like you don't give a shit all the time but I also know you really buckle down when you have to and you can accomplish anything you want to."

Jo looked at Autumn, her smile a little sheepish but the pride was still there.

"You're such a sap," she said. When her voice wobbled, Autumn knew she got to her.

"Whatever you say. Come here." Autumn opened her arms to give Jo a hug. Jo rolled her eyes but gave in, both of them wrapping their arms around each other. They were never very touchy-feely people. It was uncommon for them to hug, even when they were kids. They play-fought all the time. Their biggest form of physical affection was fist bumps. But in Autumn's opinion, some things warranted hugs. Even if it was a little weird.

CHAPTER FORTY

On Saturday, Piper didn't have any plans. Autumn stayed over to Jo's house the day before and they must have stayed up late, because she wasn't texting Piper back. Then again, Piper texted her at nine o'clock a.m. She couldn't expect a reply for another few hours. That was just common sense.

Still, it was boring. She knew, realistically, Autumn wasn't the only person in her life. She could call someone else to keep her company. But part of her didn't want to. Part of her thought she should be by herself, for now.

She enjoyed her own company in simple ways. She liked turning her brain off to a good book, or making a giant snack and eating it greedily, or listening to her favourite music and dancing around the living room. Anything that gave her that refreshing sense of being wholly yourself without guilt.

Her father went out to pick up some groceries. He invited her to go with him, but she hung back. He'd be back soon, so it didn't matter whether she went or not.

The sky was clearer than it'd been in a while. It mustn't have been inhospitable outside, because the chill wasn't seeping through the walls like it did days before. For once, the day was warm. Warm and clear and safe.

When there was a knock on the door, Piper went through everyone she knew in her head in under a minute. Who would be knocking on her door on a Saturday morning? Her dad had a key. She assumed Laura did too. Autumn was with Jo. There was no way Hally was awake, etcetera, etcetera. She couldn't think of someone who would visit. But when they knocked a second time, she had to answer.

She opened the front door to the least likely visitors she could have dreamed of.

Brent and Drew stood on her step. Both of them were in jogging pants, sneakers and athletic jackets in the school colours. Brent had his gym bag on his back. They were clearly on their way to practice. So what prompted them to make a detour?

"Piper," Brent said, as if he was surprised to see her. "Hi. Um, h-how are you?"

He sounded about as awkward as she felt. Then again she was the one in her pajamas, so she had a leg up on him there.

"I'm fine, I guess," she muttered. How was she supposed to answer that? She was fine, but that sounded like a stupid reply, considering...

The three of them stood there for an uncomfortable amount of time, each of them expecting the other to speak up. Brent was fiddling with his pockets. Drew had his hand on Brent's shoulder, offering brotherly support.

"Uh... do you guys want to come in, or...?" Piper muttered. Brent shook his head quickly, but Drew was the one who responded.

"We can't stay long," he said. He nudged Brent gently. "*He* just had something he wanted to say."

Piper looked at Brent again. She couldn't help but remember how he looked, scared and shaking, balled up on the floor.

"I'm sorry," he said quietly. "I-I heard what happened. I had nothing to do with that stupid prank, of course, but I'm afraid my version of what happened after Christmas isn't the most accurate. I'm afraid it's my fault the story got so twisted."

He sounded genuine. She could hear it in his voice and see it in his mannerisms. He meant what he was saying. But Piper felt like his apology wasn't well deserved. Besides, after what she'd dealt with recently, Brent was the last person who owed her an apology.

"I appreciate you coming here and saying all of that," she said, "But really. It's okay. I don't blame you for anything. I know I said that before but it still stands." She extended a hand out to him. It took him a moment of consideration, but he reached out and accepted it. "Everything has been difficult and complicated lately and I'm sorry it's affecting you. I just want us to be friends."

Brent smiled and squeezed her hand. "Me too." Something seemed to dawn on him and he released her hand. He took off his backpack and rummaged through it, revealing her novel, *The Outsiders*, bent practically in half and crumbled pathetically. He held it out to her and she stifled a laugh at the state of it.

"I know, I totally wrecked it. I'm not the most careful person, I'm so sorry. But I got you this — hopefully it'll make up for it..." He continued to pull items out of his back until he pulled out a black hardcover novel and passed it to her. She was grinning ear to ear as she took it and tried to resist flipping through it. "It's special or something," he said with a shrug. He zipped up his bag and threw it on casually. "The lady at the bookshop said it was the anniversary edition. I thought, since you like it so much, you should have a cool copy."

She could have cried. Somehow—even though it was tossed in the bottom of his gym bag—it was pristine. There wasn't a fold or crumple in sight and it smelled new. She cleared her throat to attempt and contain herself.

"Thank you," she told him. "Really, this is awesome. You didn't have to do this."

He glanced at his shoes sheepishly as if he didn't give her the perfect present. "It's nothing."

Drew checked his watch and nudged Brent again. It was obvious that he didn't want to break up the exchange, but he said, "We're going to be late for practice if we don't go soon."

Brent nodded. He looked satisfied. Piper certainly was.

He looked up and held her gaze for a moment later. She was glad that he looked like himself now. He was glowing and though he looked a little puzzled, it was no more than normal. He often looked like he was mid-math test.

He went to step away but paused and announced, "Oh yeah, I did read it."

"You did?" Piper queried. "What did you think?"

"You were right. It was pretty fantastic. I really liked that one guy… his name was like candy or whatever."

She chuckled. "Sodapop?"

"Yeah! I liked him."

"Me too."

Drew cleared his throat and interrupted again, "Come on, Coach is going to lose it." Brent snapped out of whatever reverie he was in and stepped away from the house.

"Right. Uh, I'll see you in school, Piper," he said.

"See you in school," Piper repeated. She watched as Brent returned to Drew's truck, parked on the curb. Drew went to follow him, but Piper grabbed his sleeve. "Wait, just a second."

Drew looked behind him at Brent before turning back to Piper. "What's up?"

"Why did you bring him here?" she asked. "Don't get me wrong, I'm glad he came. But why did you?" She didn't want to sound rude, but he very well could have waited in the car. He was a very unexpected visitor, even if he was just accompanying his friend.

Drew shrugged nonchalantly. "He's like my brother," he said. "He's a nervous driver and he didn't want to come alone. I had to go with him."

Piper nodded in understanding. Without realizing it, she was flicking through her new book nervously. "I didn't think you'd want to see me after…"

Drew smiled and shook his head. "I probably should have been nicer to you that day," he admitted. "It wasn't your fault that he freaked out like that. He has panic attacks and most people don't know how to handle them. I do, so whenever I see it happen, all I want to do is protect him. Make him feel better. You can understand that, right?"

"Of course."

"I have nothing against you, Piper. I'm actually grateful for you. Anyone else wouldn't have given him the closure he needed. They probably would have blamed him as much as he blames himself."

Piper never thought of it that way. She never considered that someone else in the same situation as her might have penalized Brent. Made him feel worse. She just wanted everyone to move on, starting with herself and extending to those around her. She wanted to fix things.

"What about Hally?" Piper asked, crossing her arms and cocking her eyebrow like a disappointed mother. Drew sighed.

"What about Hally?" he repeated.

"You can admit you were wrong to me, but have you done the same for her?"

"It was all a misunderstanding—"

"It seemed pretty straight forward."

"You don't know the full story," Drew insisted.

"I don't have to," Piper retorted. "She does."

He opened his mouth as if he was ready to argue, but he decided against it. He closed it without a word and while anyone else's face would be coated in annoyance or frustration, his was only acceptance. He didn't speak as he walked away from her step and got into his truck, but he honked rhythmically as they pulled away.

CHAPTER FORTY ONE

When Autumn finally woke up, it was past noon. That wasn't abnormal. Since she left highschool, she saw no real point in getting up at the break of dawn. When she was a teenager living home, getting up extra early meant a few hours by herself when the house was quiet. While she didn't share Piper's love for peaceful silence, she did appreciate it. It was a rare and pleasant experience, in a loud, fast paced world.

Jo's house wasn't quiet. Then again, in all of Autumn's years of knowing her, her house was never quiet. Not unless it was entirely empty. Or at least, that was what Autumn assumed.

They fell asleep on Jo's bed. Autumn couldn't remember the exact time, but the sun was coming up. They always did stay up past bedtime. Even when they were little.

Jo was still asleep beside her. Unlike Piper, Jo was no sleeping beauty. She slept with her mouth open and she snored and she moved so much, it was like she was fighting an imaginary monster. Autumn almost forgot how chaotic sleepovers used to be. It was a good thing Autumn was such a heavy sleeper.

She saw the good morning text from Piper and smiled.

She loved that, even if it made her head swell to know she was the first thing Piper thought of in the morning. At least the feeling was mutual.

She grabbed one of Jo's pillows and whacked the sleeping lump with it. Jo groaned and—with impressive accuracy—punched Autumn in the stomach.

"Ow!" Autumn exclaimed. "If I had to know you were gonna do that, I would've left without telling you."

Groggily, Jo sat up, her hair wild and her eyes barely open. "Wouldn't be the first time," she grumbled. Autumn leaned back and sighed, a mixture of guilt and frustration. Jo waved a hand.

"I'm just fucking with you," she said. "Always so sensitive." She stretched and yawned. Autumn could hear her back and wrists crack as she spread out.

"Jesus, are you falling apart or something?"

Jo smiled tiredly. "You're just mad that I have sick sound effects." When Jo finally relaxed again, she looked at Autumn as if for the first time that day. "Wait, you're leaving?"

"Look who just landed," Autumn quipped sarcastically. "Yes, I'm leaving."

"Why?"

Autumn shrugged. Jo raised a brow.

"Going to see the wife?" she teased. Autumn rolled her eyes, even though she turned noticeably red.

"Something like that."

Jo smirked and nodded. "Do you want food or something before you go?"

"Nah, I think I'll live. Thanks."

They both left Jo's room and walked down the stairs, their footsteps combined sounding like rhythmic drums. There were sounds coming from every corner of the house.

It sounded like there was a television on in every room, though Autumn highly doubted that. Elena hated when they weren't in the *"present moment as a family."* Autumn silently wished her luck. She'd need it to make that insane dream come true.

Jo leaned against the doorway as Autumn put on her boots and laced them up. They didn't say anything to each other, presumably because they were both still fatigued. Sleep lingered like nothing else. Except, maybe booze.

Autumn stood up straight again once her shoes were fastened to her feet and looked at Jo.

"You'll thank your parents for me?" she said. Jo chuckled.

"You've been coming over since we were infants," she replied. "I think we're past *thank-you's*."

Autumn smiled. "That's the difference between me and you. I'm never past *thank-you's*."

Jo stared at her for a second in a similar way to how she did the last time they saw each other; as if she was trying to commit every inch of her best friend to memory. Scanning her to make an artificial Autumn in her mind to keep her company. Autumn ignored the feeling that she should bark *"Later!"* and walk out, same as any other day. Because it wasn't the same. Nothing ever would be. So, she grabbed Jo by the arm and pulled her into a hug.

"I'll call you tomorrow," she said. She felt Jo hesitantly wrap her arms around her waist.

"You better."

Autumn pulled back. She wasn't the best at reading expressions (well, other than her girlfriend's) but she hoped she eased Jo's mind some.

She left the familiar porchway, into the awkward middle ground between cold and mild. It was coming up on

February, the month the sun might finally return.

Piper and her dad were putting away groceries in the kitchen. Piper could feel that he was doing all the heavy lifting. And he was moving faster than he normally would. He was giving her less work. She felt delicate, in a weirdly satisfying way. Like a porcelain doll, newly glued back together.

She was on her tiptoes, trying to put away a box of pasta in the top shelf, when there was a knock on the door. She didn't stop what she was doing, since her dad called out that he would get it and left the kitchen. She heard faint greetings from the foyer and two sets of footsteps approaching. Then, someone reached from behind her, took the box right out of her hand and placed it gently on the top shelf. She smiled, as she knew exactly who it was.

She turned to see Autumn, smiling cheekily at her.

"Hey, Short Stuff," she teased. "I got something for you."

Piper smiled, ready to say something witty and cute in response, but she didn't get a word out before Autumn revealed her present. It was a mini cactus in the most beautiful pot she'd ever seen. It was a woodland scene, with birds and squirrels and an elegant, fully grown doe in the centre. The pot had little scratches on it, like tiny, shallow cracks. It almost looked on purpose. Like every crack was a rain droplet plummeting toward the grass below.

"Autumn," Piper breathed as she reached out and let her girlfriend place it in her hands. "It's beautiful. Thank you."

"I was going to get roses but you don't seem like a traditional flower type. You really like it?"

"I love it. God, I hope I don't kill it," she chuckled.

Autumn smirked and shook her head.

"I doubt you can kill this one," she said. "Cactuses are tough. Plus, it looks like it's had some wear and tear already. And look: it's still beautiful."

Piper looked up at her through her eyelashes with a lopsided grin. "Is this cactus a metaphor for my misfortune?"

Autumn shook her head again. "No, that cactus is a reminder. Yes, that you're beautiful and strong. But mostly that your girlfriend is awesome and will stab someone for fucking with you."

Piper laughed. "Thank you, you're the best." She enveloped Autumn in a hug. She met her dad's eyes over her shoulder. He was smiling at them, holding a jar of pizza sauce like it was a prestigious award. She loved that she could see pride in his eyes and nothing more. That was all he offered; pride and care. He laid down the jar quietly and snuck out of the room to give them some privacy.

"Did you have an okay night?" Autumn asked, not releasing the hug. "Didn't miss me too much, did you?"

"Was my text too obvious?"

"Just obvious enough," Autumn replied. "I love you, Piper."

Piper held on tighter, her smile almost splitting her face in half. She tried to reply as if her heart wasn't exploding out of her chest. "I love you, too."

CHAPTER FORTY TWO

Piper couldn't hide from school forever. Honestly, she didn't want to. She wanted to enjoy what was left of high school. Everyone always said it was the best years of her life. She was starting to believe them.

She'd be lying if she said she wasn't nervous about it, though. After making such a scene, returning felt like a final boss; terrible and scary and worse than everything leading up to it. But unlike every video game she ever attempted, she was ready for this final boss. She was prepared for whatever it would throw at her, may it be petty bullying or fire balls.

Autumn drove her to school that morning, which was very noble of her. Even if she was a little grumpy in the morning and not very talkative before noon, she still attempted some words of wisdom when they stopped at a red light and gave her a supportive kiss when they arrived in the school parking lot.

If Piper thought she had eyes on her before, she couldn't imagine the stares when she arrived on a motorcycle after she'd apparently had a *"heart attack"* in the middle of the hallway. Luckily, her friends were waiting outside for her.

They were the weirdest group when you looked at them from afar. They didn't look like they belonged together. A beauty queen, a nerd, an artist, two jocks and a friendly giant. They all banded together for her. Even though all they had in common was her.

Maya was talking Brent's ear off, the same way she did Piper when they first met. Hally and Locke seemed to be exchanging fashion tips, even though they were on opposite ends of the style spectrum. Hally was admiring their eyeliner while they compared shoe heights. The least likely pair were Joseph and Drew, standing slightly apart from the group, deep in conversation. Lost in their own world, in a way that was very familiar to Piper.

As she approached, all conversations halted for her. Their eyes all fell on her. Even though no one said anything for a moment, she could feel a warmth coming over her.

"I'm not a hologram, you can hug me," she said jokingly and they all whirled to life again. She was tackled in more than one hug at once. Hally was first, of course, but Maya and Joseph latched on as well. The boys and Locke held back, which was to be expected.

"Oh my god, it felt like you were gone for literal years. I have so much to tell you," Maya began. "I got an A in my art project and we start the set for the spring concert this week and I failed my math test but I'm doing a retest today and—"

"Maybe fill her in later," Locke suggested, a smile on their face.

"Right. We can talk about it later," Maya said.

"Can't wait," Piper replied.

"I missed you so much," Hally whined. "Maya's right. It felt like forever."

"Yeah, without you, there was no one to do a really good job pretending to listen to me," Joseph teased. Piper pouted.

"Is it that obvious when I'm not paying attention?"

Everyone around her nodded and she shook her friends off of her, pretending to be upset.

"Don't sweat it," Brent said. "I'm always pretending to listen to people."

"That's probably why you cheat off all my tests," Drew retorted.

"No, I do that because you said I could."

"You got me there."

"Seriously," Joseph interrupted the exchange, drawing Piper's full attention. He looked different since she last saw him. Everyone did, but him especially. He looked brighter. Less fidgety. His shoulders were relaxed for the first time since Piper met him. Possibly before then. "It sucked not having you around."

She smiled at him. "I'm back now and I'm not going anywhere. Unless I do have a heart attack."

"Wouldn't that be ironic," Hally muttered.

"I'm not sure if ironic is the right word," Drew corrected. Piper expected Hally to give him a death glare and roll her eyes but she just laughed. Something definitely changed since she left.

The first bell rang and they all began piling into the building, Piper grabbed Hally's arm and pulled her back so they were walking in together, behind everyone else. It still felt weird to her to see Hally without a cast. That felt like a lifetime ago, and yet, like yesterday.

"What happened?" she asked.

"What do you mean?" Hally responded.

"With you and Drew? I thought you hated him."

"I did, but…" Hally exhaled and shrugged. "He came to my house and we talked. For hours, actually. He told me he was pretending to be someone he wasn't and he shouldn't have brought me into it but he wanted to push the narrative even harder. At first, I was pissed. I mean, he was using me. But… I guess I was using him, too. I hardly had feelings for him, I just thought he was pretty. Besides, you guys were in a very similar situation. Only, he knew before he started dating me."

Piper screwed up her face in confusion for a moment before it dawned on her. She stared ahead at Drew. he was walking with Brent like he always did, but she couldn't help but follow his eyes, which were focused on Joseph walking ahead of him.

She smiled as she understood. The picture was putting itself together nicely in her head. She wanted to ask Joseph about it, but she wouldn't want to invade his privacy. She turned back to Hally.

"What does that have to do with him cheating on you? I thought you said he was flirting with some college girl," Piper asked. Hally shook her head.

"He said it wasn't mutual. He said he was getting a beer and she approached him and wouldn't leave him alone. For all I know, this is all a load of bull, but I trust him. I mean, he was a good kisser, but he didn't show a lot of interest, so I can't see him seeking some cheap thrills from someone else anyway. Well, another girl, at least."

Piper nodded in understanding. "So, you guys are all good?"

"Yeah. And you and Brent..?"

Piper smiled. "Yeah," she said. "We're good."

CHAPTER FORTY THREE

School wasn't unbearable. In fact, it was great. Having all her friends united felt amazing. They could all look out for each other, no matter how different they were. That was a powerful feeling.

She expected to be picked on a lot more than she actually was. The most pestering she got was genuine concern and not mean spirited. It didn't take long for her to get acclimated with her new school dynamic. Good things were always easy to get used to. Like a warm bath, or a sweet flavour.

She was getting used to Laura, too. And she was getting to like her. Maybe like wasn't a strong enough word for a woman she was starting to think of as a mother. Love was a scary word to throw around, though. Even if she trusted Laura not to leave.

Her and Samuel decided on a summer wedding and their house was slowly but surely getting enveloped in wedding dress catalogues and venue brochures. Not to mention sample flower arrangements. The smell of roses could be made out from a block away.

Piper never cared much about giant, white weddings. But she had to admit, helping Laura arrange hers was pretty exciting. Especially for Hally, who visited almost every day just to flip through the magazines with them.

Maya loved weddings. She was thrilled when Samuel said Piper could invite all her friends. But she didn't get to help out much with the early preparations, like the ordering and booking months in advance. She was busy preparing for an art gallery happening at the school, two weeks before Spring break.

She wouldn't let anyone view her collection of paintings. She wanted it to be a surprise. Locke didn't even get the privilege, which was a major surprise to Piper. They were more excited to see it than everyone else was. They were used to being a part of the creating process. Piper was sure sitting on the sidelines was killing them.

When the night finally came, they all dressed up. They definitely overdressed, but that was what Maya asked everyone to do, and who were they to disobey her wishes on her special day.

Maya had to be there early to set everything up, so Hally was the one who picked up Piper, Autumn and Locke. Even though it was a school event, Piper invited Autumn. It wouldn't be a night out without her.

Brent, Joseph and Drew drove together and the seven of them met in the foyer of the school. The gallery was set up in the gym, as all big events were in a small high school. They walked in together and followed the same line everyone else was, looking at all the art and pretending they weren't just there for one person.

Piper and Autumn were walking a little behind the rest of the group. Autumn had her arm around Piper's waist, the two of them attached to each other as if they were one person.

"When do you get out for Spring break?" Autumn

asked out of the blue. Piper looked at her skeptically.

"We get out April 2nd," Piper replied. "Why?"

"Do you remember when you asked me if we could run away together?"

Piper thought back with a fond smile. It was a sad, desperate attempt to move away and somehow forget her troubles. Even if it was unrealistic and she knew they couldn't. At the time, it was tempting.

"I told you we would, one day," Autumn went on. "So, are you still up for it?"

Piper rolled her eyes incredulously. "To run away?"

"Just for a week," Autumn said. "I have a guy lined up who's willing to rent us a camper. We can go on a road trip. See if there's anything outside of this Mega-Block town. I already asked your dad and he said he's cool with it if you are."

Piper stopped walking, which successfully stopped Autumn as well and held up the line behind them.

"You're serious," she declared, as if Autumn didn't know. Autumn chuckled and nodded.

"I'm serious," she confirmed. "But, don't feel pressured to go if you don't want to. I know it's big and nothing is set in stone so we can back out at any point—"

"Shut up, of course I want to go!" Piper said with a grin.

"Really?"

"Yeah, really! That sounds awesome! Let's do it!"

Autumn pulled Piper closer to her and kissed her cheek. "Let's do it."

"Hey, lovebirds!" Hally shouted from way ahead of them. "Maya's gallery is right here. Hurry your asses up!"

They exchanged a look before they rushed toward the

gallery. Their shoes clicked and echoed against the gym walls as they skidded to a stop with all their friends. She could hear everyone complimenting Maya, but from behind them, she couldn't see what they were looking at. Then, she felt a pair of hands on her shoulders, steering her away from Autumn.

"Out of the way!" Hally said from behind her as she made their friends part like the red sea for Piper. "Let the little one see!"

"Hey!" Piper grumbled, but she didn't correct her. When Hally released her, she was standing in front of everyone, facing a wall of paintings. Her jaw dropped.

The main piece was her art project she made Locke and Piper model for. It was a painting of the three of them together, sitting below the stage. They were all smiling, paint on their hands and glitter haphazardly decorating their faces. It was acrylic paint and it was packed on heavy. Piper could tell, because their skin had so much texture and layers and the glitter bent around their skin elegantly. Around their painting, there were small paintings of the others. One for Hally, one for Drew, one for Brent and one for Joseph. They didn't have as much depth to them, but they were equally as beautiful.

"Maya, this is insane," Piper managed to say in her astonishment. "I mean, I knew you were an artist, but this..."

Maya was chewing on the nail on her index finger. "Do they look okay? I was worried I screwed up your nose. I only noticed yesterday that the bridge of your nose is a little crooked but I made it perfectly straight. Does it still look like you?"

Locke, who had their arm around her, said, "It's perfect. They're all perfect."

"They're right," Piper agreed. She was shaking her head in disbelief as she took a step closer to see every detail of every painting. "Each and every one is perfect. You did an amazing job."

Maya nodded and Piper could see her nervousness washing away into excitement. She put her hands in her pockets and broke out into a full grin.

"Thank God they don't suck. I spent so long on each of you," Maya said. "Especially you, Piper. You're really hard to paint. I'm not sure what it is, but there's something about you that's really hard to capture on a canvas."

As Piper stood there, staring into her own eyes, she could see it. That something she had that no one could capture, no matter how hard they tried. And this year really tried, in more ways than one.

The rain.

It had always been there, waiting patiently. Even in the surest droughts or the biggest wind storms. Even as the sun began to rise on her, after years of waiting for it. It stayed. As she came back into reality and listened to her friends chatter about art and felt her girlfriend's hand take hers, she was overwhelmed with euphoria.

She could smell the rain, even on the sunniest day.

FROM THE AUTHOR

Big thank you to Matthew LeDrew and Engen Books for giving me the opportunity, and the unwavering support, to write this novel. And to AJ Ryan, for editing and for understanding it better than I could've imagined.

Thank you to my mom, superwoman, for everything she's done for me to get me to this point. Thank you to my brothers, for being my best friends and cheerleaders. Thank you to my wonderfully supportive friends, who had to listen to me talk about this novel every day. You have incredible patience. Thank you to my pop and nan, who asked about this book constantly since I said it was being published. I hope it was worth the wait.

Thank you to my teachers, the fantastic, enthusiastic weirdos who told me I could do anything and meant it.

ON SALE NOW FROM ENGEN BOOKS

Enjoy more from Engen's Romance line!

ABOUT THE AUTHOR

Lily McCarthy is an author originally from Tor's Cove, Newfoundland.

They enjoy reading, writing, and spending time with their brothers.

*Quick Bright Thing*s is their first novel.

www.ingramcontent.com/pod-product-compliance
Lightning Source LLC
Chambersburg PA
CBHW011424010726
47494CB00011B/2483